Josiah didn't want to think about Annabeth's going home.

He didn't want to think about the mill being empty once more, about his life being even emptier than before.

"Annabeth—"

She interrupted him with a searching glance. "At the mill you called me Annie. Why?"

He hadn't realized it, but she was right. *Oh, hell, Annie.* It had just slipped out, born of frustration and need and guilt. "I don't know. Annabeth is a nice name, but it's a mouthful. Annie is sweet. It fits you."

After another short silence, in a voice so soft he strained to hear it, she solemnly remarked, "I like it."

So did he, Josiah thought just as solemnly. God help him, so did he.

Dear Reader,

It's another great month for Silhouette Intimate Moments! If you don't believe me, just take a look at our American Hero title, *Dragonslayer,* by Emilie Richards. This compelling and emotionally riveting tale could have been torn from today's headlines, with a minister hero whose church is in one of the inner city's worst neighborhoods and whose chosen flock includes the down and out of the world. In this place, where gang violence touches everyone's lives—and will continue to touch them throughout the book in ways you won't be able to predict—our hero meets a woman whose paradoxical innocence will force him to confront his own demons, his own inner emptiness, and once more embrace life—and love. *Dragonslayer* is a *tour de force,* not to be missed by any reader.

The rest of the month is terrific, too. Marilyn Pappano, Doreen Roberts, Marion Smith Collins, Beverly Barton and new author Leann Harris offer stories that range from "down-home" emotional to suspenseful and dramatic. You'll want to read them all.

And in months to come look for more irresistible reading from such favorite authors as Justine Davis, Linda Turner, Paula Detmer Riggs, *New York Times* bestsellers Heather Graham Pozzessere and Nora Roberts, and more—all coming your way from Silhouette Intimate Moments, where romantic excitement is always the rule.

Yours,

Leslie J. Wainger
Senior Editor and Editorial Coordinator

SWEET ANNIE'S PASS

Marilyn Pappano

Silhouette®
INTIMATE MOMENTS®

Published by Silhouette Books New York

America's Publisher of Contemporary Romance

SILHOUETTE BOOKS
300 East 42nd St., New York, N.Y. 10017

SWEET ANNIE'S PASS

Copyright © 1993 by Marilyn Pappano

ISBN: 0-373-07512-X

First Silhouette Books printing August 1993

All the characters in this book have no existence outside the
imagination of the author and have no relation whatsoever to
anyone bearing the same name or names. They are not even
distantly inspired by any individual known or unknown to the
author, and all incidents are pure invention.

®: Trademark used under license and registered in the United States
Patent and Trademark Office and in other countries.

Printed in the U.S.A.

Books by Marilyn Pappano

Silhouette Intimate Moments

Within Reach #182
The Lights of Home #214
Guilt by Association #233
Cody Daniels' Return #258
Room at the Inn #268
Something of Heaven #294
Somebody's Baby #310
Not Without Honor #338
Safe Haven #363
A Dangerous Man #381
Probable Cause #405
Operation Homefront #424
Somebody's Lady #437
No Retreat #469
Memories of Laura #486
Sweet Annie's Pass #512

Silhouette Books

Silhouette Christmas Stories 1989
"The Greatest Gift"
Silhouette Summer Sizzlers 1991
"Loving Abby"

MARILYN PAPPANO

has been writing as long as she can remember, just for the fun of it, but a few years ago she decided to take her lifelong hobby seriously. She was encouraging a friend to write a romance novel and ended up writing one herself. It was accepted, and she plans to continue as an author for a long time. When she's not involved in writing, she enjoys camping, quilting, sewing and, most of all, reading. Not surprisingly, her favorite books are romance novels.

Her husband is in the navy, and in the course of her marriage she has lived all over the U.S. Currently, she lives in North Carolina with her husband and son.

Prologue

Josiah Miller sat at the kitchen table in the darkened farmhouse, his hands clasped together loosely in front of him. The sun had set hours ago, but he hadn't bothered to turn on any lights. He could see. There was enough moonlight to illuminate the items spread out in front of him.

A bottle of pain pills, given to him six months ago when he'd broken his hand while working on the tractor.

A bottle of whiskey, cheap and strong, the kind that could burn a hole right through you.

The notice from the bank about last month's auction, when he'd lost two hundred acres of the best farmland he'd owned.

And a photograph, protected behind glass, of the sweetest, prettiest little girl he'd ever seen. She was eight months old in that picture. A month later her mother had taken her away, and he hadn't seen her since.

Today—this long, silent, lonely Tuesday—was her birthday. Today she was four.

Staring at the photograph, he listened to the house. It wasn't silent. Nothing ever was. The grandfather clock in

the front hall was ticking. A weathered old board creaked.
The refrigerator motor switched on, then off again. A fau-
cet somewhere leaked.

No, it wasn't silent, but it was dead. No one lived here but
him. No one laughed, no one cried, no one spoke. The heart
of the house had left when Caroline had taken Kylie away,
and the soul had died soon after. *He* had died then, too, but
his body just wouldn't give up. No matter how hard he
worked it, no matter how many risks he took, no matter
how fervently he prayed to end this pain, he was still here.
Still alive.

But dead in the ways that counted.

He had never before considered suicide. Soon Caroline
would feel guilty, he had told himself, and would let him see
Kylie again. Someday she would grow as tired of their baby
as she had of *him,* and she would bring her back to Dutchman's Valley. One day, when Kylie was old enough, she
would see his name on her birth certificate, and she would
come home to the farm to satisfy her curiosity.

But deep in his heart he knew that Caroline was never
going to feel guilty. She was never going to let him see his
daughter again. And by the time Kylie was old enough to
come looking for her father, it would be too late. She
wouldn't care.

He was never going to see his little girl again. Never going to hold her or kiss her or sing her bedtime lullabies.
Never going to see her grow up or watch her marry or know
her children. He was never going to share even one of her
birthdays.

He was never going to be a part of her life.

So what use was there in holding on to his own life?

Picking up the pill bottle, he wrapped his fingers around
it, completely enfolding it, hiding it from sight. He had
played up the pain of his smashed hand to the doctor, had
gotten double the number of pills the doctor had intended
to give him and then had never taken even one. He had told
himself once he'd gotten home that he didn't need the pills,
that the physical pain wasn't so bad, that it was a nice

change from the spiritual pain he'd endured so long. Had he subconsciously been saving them for tonight?

Twisting off the lid, he emptied the contents into his palm, into the same hand that had been encased in plaster, that had been responsible for the prescribing of the medication. Twenty pills, small and round and white. They were tiny to be so potent. The doctor had gravely warned him about their use, about how often he could take one, and all the things he couldn't do while using them. They would be so easy to swallow, so easy to use for the one purpose the doctor hadn't imagined. Josiah found it rather appropriate himself. They were painkillers, and, God help him, he had a lot of pain to kill.

He poured the tablets onto the table, scooping them into a neat little pile, then picked up the liquor bottle and uncapped it. He had bought the bottle a long time ago, before Caroline had left, when he'd been working impossibly long hours in the fields and coming in late to find Kylie already asleep and Caroline ready to fight. And, Lord, they had fought. They had screamed and yelled until finally he'd quit caring. He had stopped listening to her, had stopped talking to her, had stopped paying any attention at all to her. She had ranted and raved, had whined and argued and pleaded, and he had ignored her.

She had gotten his attention, all right, the day she had driven away from the house with everything worth taking. The day she had taken Kylie from him.

Lifting the bottle, he took a drink and shuddered before he had even swallowed. He had developed a taste for beer back when he was in college, when he and Caroline were first together and falling in love, but he hadn't had a drink since then. Drinking was too dangerous on a farm; if the booze itself didn't get you, the hangover would.

He took another drink, then picked up the photograph. All the moonlight showed was a shadowy figure inside the frame, but he knew the details well. They were etched on his heart: silky hair of a shade halfway between Caroline's blond and his own brown, dark brown eyes with a mischievous light, a crooked smile and dimples that came from neither her mother nor her father. Her dress was summery, sleeveless with a big white collar and lavished with lace and ribbons. She had been a beautiful baby, and she must be a beautiful child.

Thanks to Caroline, he would never know.

He stared at the photograph a long time, as if he could actually see it in the moonlit room. As if he could actually see *her*.

Then he screwed the lid back onto the whiskey and scraped the pills back into the bottle. He was already dead inside. What did it matter if his body caught up with his soul tonight or tomorrow, next week or next year?

Leaving everything on the table except the photograph, he went down the hall and into his bedroom. He set the frame on the nightstand, then stripped off his clothes and stretched out across the bed. For the first time in nearly twenty hours, the tension seeped from his body. For the first time in longer than he could recall, he drifted off to sleep easily, naturally, murmuring softly just before he dozed.

"I love you, Kylie."

Chapter 1

Wednesday was a bright, mild day, warm enough to be comfortable in shirtsleeves and cool enough to remind you that fall was here and winter was on its way. Josiah sat in his grandfather's rocker on the front porch, finishing his lunch of ham sandwiches and thinking about the work that awaited him. All things considered, late fall and winter were easy times on the farm, nature's reward for lasting through one more harvest. The last of his crops was in. The fields would rest now, and so would he. He still had stock to tend and repairs to make and next season to plan for, but for these next few months he would take it easy.

He might even get some work done on the house. He had been born here nearly thirty-five years ago, delivered by a midwife from up in the mountains in the same bedroom that he claimed for his own now. Once this had been a pretty place—nothing fancy, but nice for these Arkansas hills. Now it was badly in need of a paint job, some not-so-minor repairs and a thorough cleaning. The driveway was so rutted that his truck scraped badly and there was no way a car could get through, and the mailbox leaned precariously to one side. The yellowed grass was sparse, and there were great patches where it was gone completely, and the flower beds, his mother's pride and joy, were filled with weeds and the brown stalks of last summer's blooms. Maybe this year he would get around to fixing it up again.

After he reshingled the barn roof and rebuilt the sheds out there. And repaired the fence and worked on the tractors and overhauled the truck. After he paid taxes and made his next loan payment and bought supplies and seed and fertilizer and pesticides.

After all that was done. If he had any energy. If he had any money. If he could find a way to care.

Finishing the last sandwich, he set the plate on the floor, then propped his feet on the railing and leaned back in the rocker. All morning he had refused to think about last night, about how close he had come to ending it all. Now he wondered grimly whether the fact that he hadn't was a success or just one more failure. He was well acquainted with failure. He hadn't been able to finish college the way his father had wanted. He hadn't been the kind of husband Caroline had wanted, hadn't given her the kind of life she'd expected. He couldn't make a go of this farm, even though it was the best land in the valley. The only thing he'd been really good at was loving his little girl, and he couldn't even find her to do that. He had disappointed everyone else; was he destined to disappoint himself, too?

But maybe, in spite of the pain, he just wasn't ready to give up yet. Maybe someday Kylie really would come home, and how would she feel if he weren't here waiting? As long as there was a chance of seeing her again, he had to grab it and hold on. He could endure anything if it meant seeing his daughter again someday.

Someday.

The sorrow that thinking of Kylie always brought was pressing down on him when a puff of dust down the dirt road caught his attention. No one ever came out this far except the mailman—the farm was the last place along the road before it dead-ended a mile away—and it was too early for him. Josiah never looked forward to the mail. All it brought was bills that he could barely manage to pay and twice-a-month letters from his mother over in Fort Smith.

It never brought news of Kylie.

Finally the car appeared out of the trees and slowed to a stop in front of his house. At least the driver had the sense not to try to pull the ancient, beat-up Volkswagen into his driveway. Being so small and low to the ground, it would probably fall right to the bottom of one of the ruts, and he would feel obligated to spend a good part of his afternoon getting it out again.

The Beetle was a convertible, the top up, and was loaded with what surely must be every possession its owner could cram inside. He couldn't see the driver herself until she climbed out, closed the door, which didn't catch, and closed it again with a slam. Then she started toward him.

She was blond, tall and slender, wearing jeans and a T-shirt, like most women in the valley—although she wore them better than most women. Her jeans were faded and tight, her T-shirt thin and tight. Both garments clung in all the right places, emphasizing the roundness of her breasts, the curve of her hips, the length of her legs. Emphasizing her womanliness.

Josiah found a bitter amusement in the fact that, after so many years, he could even recognize womanliness. It had been so long since he had looked at a woman, since he had noticed breasts and hips and legs. So long since he had thought of a woman as anything other than just one more person he didn't want bothering him.

This woman removed her sunglasses as she approached, tossed her hair over her shoulder and came to a stop at the foot of the steps. "Josiah Miller?"

Her voice was husky, the sounds gently rounded. Southern and undeniably feminine.

Another first, he thought. Generally he found voices annoying things, grating irritants that asked too many questions, gave too much advice, offered too many worthless platitudes.

Go after her, Josiah. That's all she wants. Sweet-talk her back home.

Of course she'll let you see the girl. You're her father.

It'll be all right. Just give it time. You'll get over losing them.

And the worst ones of all: *It's probably best for Kylie. She's better off with her mother. And someday you'll meet someone else. You'll have more kids.*

Grimly he focused his attention on the woman again. He didn't swing his feet to the floor or stand up or offer his hand. He'd spent a solid year after Caroline left discouraging people from dropping in on him, convincing them that he really meant it when he said he wanted to be left alone. He had been so mean and rude that year that everyone, with the exception of his mother, his aunt and his uncle, had given in—and even those three knew better than to come visiting without a good reason. And so he didn't speak or offer any sort of greeting at all. He simply nodded.

"I'm Annabeth Gibbs. I understand you own the mill across the road."

His gaze shifted from her to the sawmill. It had been built more than a hundred and fifty years ago by the great-great-great-grandfather he had been named for, the first Miller to come to the Ozark Mountains, who had appropriately been a miller. He had sawed wood and ground meal and farmed to support a family of six sons and three daughters. The mill had closed down in the 1940s—the highway the state had built had brought new business to town and made the miller's service unnecessary—but Millers had farmed in Dutchman's Valley ever since.

But Josiah would be the last.

"What about it?" he asked flatly.

She moved onto the first step and leaned one hip against the rail. When it wobbled against her slight weight, she straightened again and glanced around. Seeing all the repairs that needed making, all the work that needed doing? he wondered.

"I'd like to make you an offer."

"It's not for sale."

"I don't want to buy it. I'd like to rent it."

He gave her a long look. "Rent it," he repeated skeptically. "For what?"

"To live in."

For the first time in longer than he could remember, Josiah was tempted to smile. Only a city woman could possibly think that was a reasonable suggestion. Only a city woman could even consider living in a place that had stood more or less empty for the past fifty years, in a place that had never been intended for living.

She knew he thought the idea foolish—he could see it in the way she straightened her shoulders and raised her chin an inch or two. "It has electricity," she pointed out.

That was easy enough to see, he conceded. The lines ran across the road and hooked up to the farm's supply.

"And it has water."

That was also true. His grandfather, the last miller, had insisted on both power and plumbing, more to show off his prosperity than out of necessity. Still, electric lights and a tiny half bath didn't make for the comforts of home. There was no bathtub, no air-conditioning, no kitchen facilities, and the only heat came from an antique wood-burning stove.

He pointed all that out to her, and she simply shrugged. "I'll manage."

He glanced across the road at the mill again. As a kid he had watched his grandfather occasionally get the old place going for a special demonstration for some group or another. When his mother's quilting bee had met there every winter week, weather permitting, he had tended the old Franklin stove to keep the place warm. He had swam in the pool and played with his cousins inside the mill, had eaten countless picnic lunches underneath the trees, had necked with his high school sweetheart in a rainstorm under the shelter of the mill's porch. He had spent hours there with Caroline, had made love to her in the grass alongside the pond, had taken Kylie there for the pure pleasure of witnessing her delight in the waterwheel and its splashing, dancing music.

He hadn't been there in more than three years. Even on the rare occasions when he sat out here on the porch or when he drove out on his way into town, he never looked at it—never *really* looked. The place had practically quit existing for him.

And this woman, this stranger from the city, wanted to live there.

"Who are you?"

Her smile was tentative, as if she didn't expect to see it returned. "As I told you, my name is Annabeth Gibbs. I'm from South Carolina. I've come here on a grant from the state to document the history of Dutchman's Valley."

Ah, the historian. He had heard talk about her the last time he was in town—gossip that he hadn't bothered listening to. The state's project didn't concern him—he wouldn't let it—and so he had refused to concern himself with it.

But that was before he'd known that the state's historian was young, blond and pretty—like Caroline. That she was a foolish woman from the city who couldn't possibly relate to the people in these mountains—again, like Caroline. Or that she wanted to live across the road from him.

"The mill isn't suitable for living."

"Could I be the judge of that?" she asked politely. "I'm willing to pay you a fair price, Mr. Miller." She named a sum, then continued. "I can pay it on a monthly basis or give you the entire amount up front, whichever you would prefer. In return, I'd like a one year's lease on the place."

He stared past her, considering her offer. On a monthly basis, it would be a nice bit of extra cash to help him get by. In a lump sum, it would make his last two loan payments and still leave some over for a few luxuries, such as fixing up the house.

The muscles in his stomach tightened. He didn't want a neighbor out here, didn't want a stranger out here. He didn't want his attention drawn every day to the mill because he knew someone was living there. He didn't want the intrusions she would bring to his life.

But he needed her money.

Taking his silence as consideration, if not actual acceptance, she went on. "I came by yesterday, but you weren't here. I looked in the windows, but I'd like to go inside if I can. Do you have the key?"

"I'll have to find it."

"I'll wait." She smiled that strange little smile again, as if she expected to be rejected. Did she know, he wondered, that when she started trying to talk to the people in the valley, trying to *document their history,* that she would be rejected? As a rule, folks up here didn't welcome outsiders. If he was lucky, she would get so frustrated that she would leave long before her year was up.

But when was the last time he'd been lucky?

He lowered his feet to the floor and stood up, setting the rocker in motion. Leaving the woman on the steps, he went inside and straight to the shelf in the kitchen where the mill key hung on a hook. For a moment he held it, his fingers wrapped tight about it so that the jagged edges bit into his palm. Maybe he should just hand it over and let her go by herself. He had no need to go inside again.

But he wasn't sending a stranger over there alone.

When he finally returned to the porch, he found her standing exactly where he had left her. She brushed a strand of hair back and set off toward the mill, leaving him to follow. At her car, she stopped to get her purse. To avoid looking at her as she bent at the waist to reach into the passenger floorboard, he studied the car instead.

It looked about as old as she did, but battered and badly in need of a new paint job. There were dents and dings in every piece of metal, and the convertible top looked so rickety that if she put it down, he suspected, it wouldn't go back up. It was one of those cars that, if the owner ever decided to get rid of it, she would have to pay someone to take it off her hands.

But apparently it ran all right. It had gotten her from South Carolina to Dutchman's Valley. And considering the shape of his truck out back, he wasn't in any position to criticize.

She slammed the door hard enough to catch on the first try, then they continued across the road and a small clearing to the mill. Josiah half hoped that the key wouldn't work, but the lock turned and the door swung open with barely a squeak. He stepped back so she could enter first, not because he was feeling gentlemanly—he'd lost all the good manners his mother had taught him about the same time he lost Kylie—but because he wanted to delay the moment when he would have to face all those old memories.

Annabeth stepped inside, her lungs immediately protesting the dust-laden air and the old, moldy smell. Everything needed a good cleaning, from the black wood-burning stove to the floor to the windows to the ceiling. Grime covered every ancient windowpane, and her shoes left a ghostly trail of prints in the thick dust on the floor. Huge, intricate spiderwebs filled every corner, and years-old ash spilled out of the stove.

Hilda Franks, the librarian in town who was helping on this project, had warned her that the mill was uninhabitable, and Josiah Miller obviously shared that opinion. He thought he had some ignorant city girl here with more money than common sense. He also thought, she would bet, that she might stay a few weeks, maybe even a month, before the lack of conveniences sent her racing back into town.

But he would be surprised. She had lived in places more primitive than this. She had spent two harsh winters in the Allegheny Mountains of West Virginia and another in the Blue Ridge of Virginia and North Carolina. She knew what it was like to get up in the middle of the night when it was twenty degrees or colder outside with a foot of snow on the ground just to visit the outhouse fifty feet out back. She had cooked over an open fire, had hauled water a hundred yards uphill from the nearest stream for bathing and cooking and had done her work by the light of a kerosene lamp. She wasn't as fragile, helpless or ignorant as she seemed.

The mill consisted primarily of one large room, with a loft about one-third its size centered overhead. One corner held a long wooden table, built directly into the wall. That would serve as her kitchen, she decided. She had a hot plate and a toaster oven in the car, Miss Hilda had offered her a refrigerator whenever she found a place to live, and in a pinch the Franklin could be used for some cooking. At the same end but in the opposite corner, a crooked door led to the bathroom. Spiders had taken up residence in the small sink, and the toilet bowl was rusted and dry. She jiggled the handle, but no water came out.

"The water is brought by pump from the stream," Josiah said from somewhere behind her. "I doubt there's even a pump out there now. It'll have to be replaced."

Leaving the bathroom again, she nodded her understanding when she saw him. She didn't bother asking if he would do it. If he offered, fine. If he didn't, she could take care of it herself. She had never installed a pump all by herself before, but she had helped, and she had some good howto books in the car.

The stairs leading to the loft were smack in the center of the room. The railings and spindles were rough and splintery. There was an unfinished feel to them. Of course, this had been built strictly for business, she reminded herself. Back then, fine finish work was saved for where it mattered, and in a sawmill, it didn't matter.

The loft was big and empty. It was built against the front and back walls and was enclosed on both sides by three-foothigh rails. Like the rest of the mill, it was dusty and smelled of years gone by. There were four windows up here to let in light and a high-beamed ceiling overhead. It would be a cozy place to snuggle on a cold night and watch the flames in the stove below, a peaceful place on a summer night with the windows open to the night air, to the songs of the birds and the crickets and the water.

Wondering where Josiah was, why he was so quiet, why he hadn't followed her, she went to one side rail and looked down. He was standing in front of the stove, opening and closing one of the rusty doors. After seeing the mill two days ago, she had asked Miss Hilda who owned it. The librarian had told her his name and where he lived. She had said he was a farmer and that he lived alone, that his family was one of the oldest in the valley, and that farming was a tough prospect in the Ozarks and had been particularly rough for him.

She had told Annabeth quite a bit without getting too personal, but she hadn't told her that he was young—somewhere between thirty and thirty-five, she guessed. She hadn't said, either, that he was handsome. She had warned that he wouldn't want a neighbor out here, but she hadn't warned that he was over six feet tall, broad-shouldered and muscular. She hadn't warned that he had hair a gorgeous shade of dark brown, plain and thick, long enough to cover his collar in back, or that he had eyes of a similar color. She hadn't warned that he had strong hands, capable enough to earn a living from the land, powerful enough to make a woman feel safe, maybe even gentle enough to make her feel loved.

Miss Hilda hadn't warned her at all that he carried about him an immeasurable air of sadness.

He turned then, as if remembering that he wasn't alone, and his gaze slowly lifted to meet hers. Very handsome, she thought.

And very sad.

"I told you it wasn't suitable to live in."

She rested her hands on the rail, feeling the rough wood prickle. "You want more money," she said, her tone resigned. "Well, I can't offer more in rent—the grant has to support me until the project is finished—but maybe we can work something out. Maybe I can give you something else."

His gaze narrowed and turned hard as he subjected her to a thorough inspection. "Another Sweet Annie, huh?" he asked with a scowl. "Is that how you do business in South Carolina?"

"Sweet Annie?" she echoed. Her mother called her sweetheart, and her stepfather, when she was little, had called her Annie—at least, until her mother had put a stop to it—but no one had ever combined the two. She rather liked the sound of it . . . but it was clear from his expression that he hadn't meant for her to like it.

Ignoring her bewilderment, he turned toward the door. "No, thanks. I'm not interested."

"In what?" Annabeth asked as she hurried down the stairs to catch up with him. "Renting the mill to me? Earning a little extra income for nothing but tolerating a new neighbor?" She rushed through the door and skidded to a stop when she saw him leaning against the hitching rail that had tethered the horses of the mill's long-ago customers. "A little free help around the place?"

He scowled again. "Exactly what kind of help are you offering?"

"I've shingled a roof before, and I'm not bad with a paintbrush. I'm a tolerable farmhand, a good housekeeper and a great cook." She leaned against the opposite end of the rail, hooking her arms over it. "I'm not much of a baker—my bread doesn't rise and my cakes always fall—or a very good seamstress, but—"

"But you're damned good in bed. Right?"

Slowly she turned to stare at him, then backed away from the rail, away from him. "I don't think that's any of your business," she said, her voice unsteady with dismay. "If you think I want this place so badly that I'm willing to—to . . ." Embarrassed, she let the sentence trail off.

"You're offering to fulfill all the other wifely duties," he dryly pointed out.

"Haven't you ever heard of a housekeeper? Or a hired hand? Would you sleep with them if you had them?"

"Honey, I wouldn't sleep with a wife if I had one," he retorted, his tone sharp and mean. He started across the clearing toward the road, leaving Annabeth standing there and the door behind her wide open, the key in the lock.

"What about the mill?" she called.

For a moment she thought he was going to ignore her, but finally he stopped and turned. "You get a lease, and I'll sign it. The rent's due on the first of the month. I'll install a pump when I have time. And don't run up my electric bill, or you just might find yourself reshingling my barn."

She watched until he was out of sight behind his house; then she leaned heavily on the rail, pressing her palms to her warm cheeks. Had he thought, when she'd said she could give him something else, that she was offering him sex? she wondered, replaying the scene in her mind. She decided that, yes, if a man had received such an offer before, he could have mistaken her innocent suggestion for something far less so. And she imagined that, as handsome as he was—and single, too—he probably got his share of offers.

But he shouldn't have jumped to conclusions. Anyone who knew her well could attest to the fact that *she* never made such offers. Her reticence in that area had, in fact, been a major sore point with the last man she'd gotten involved with—that, along with her habit of working hundreds of miles away from home. He had refused invitations to visit her in whatever remote community she was living in, had pouted over her absences when she was home and had comforted himself with other women when she was gone.

And Josiah Miller had the conceit to think—

A lonesome howl interrupted her thoughts. Across the road, her dog was standing on the front seat of the Bug, his paws resting on the door, his long ears flopping down and making him look even more pathetic than usual. She hadn't asked her new landlord if he objected to her having a pet, but surely he didn't. Surely he had animals of his own on the farm. And it wasn't as if Emerson were a pet, exactly. He was a lazy creature who did her the courtesy of chasing away the emptiness of living alone in exchange for food to eat and a warm, dry place to sleep. She didn't own him, and he didn't own her.

"All right, all right," she grumbled, pulling her keys from her purse and heading toward the car. "I'm coming."

At the sound of the howl, Josiah paused in the act of rinsing his lunch dishes to listen. He hadn't noticed a dog in the car, but considering all the boxes and bags she'd had packed inside, he wasn't surprised. He didn't mind. He would enjoy having a dog around a lot more than that woman.

That woman with light-brown eyes and sun-touched golden hair and legs that were far too long.

That woman who was going to be his neighbor until the cold weather set in and chased her into town, or until frustration set in and chased her back to South Carolina.

That woman he had just insulted.

But you're damned good in bed. Right?

What in the world had made him think she was offering that sort of service? Because she had offered to perform every other duty a farm wife took on? Because her voice was husky and promising and softer than any he'd heard in a long time? Because she was pretty and blond and reminded him in ways of Caroline, who had thought that being damned good in bed was deserving of more than he'd had to give her?

He stacked the dishes in the sink, then went to the table. He had skipped breakfast this morning, preferring to eat an apple in the barn over sitting at the table where he'd spent such a long time last night. That was also why he'd eaten his lunch outside. Now he put the bottle of whiskey at the back of the highest cabinet shelf, and he tucked the pain pills into a distant corner of the junk drawer, behind two padlocks that had no keys and three keys that had no locks. The notice from the bank went into the dining room, on the dusty table that served as his desk now that there was no family to eat meals there.

A tolerable farmhand, a good housekeeper and a great cook. He didn't need a farmhand until spring—although he doubted, slender as she was, that she would be of much use in the fields—but he sure could use a housekeeper *and* a cook. He had let the cleaning slide for far too long. After an entire season of eighteen-hour workdays, seven-day work-weeks, dusting and vacuuming hadn't ranked high on his list of priorities. As for cooking, he had learned to get by on soup and sandwiches, bacon and eggs and canned biscuits. That was probably what he missed most about Caroline— her cooking.

It certainly wasn't the sex, he thought with a scowl. For months before she left, there hadn't been much of that—at least, not between them. He just hadn't been able to muster much desire for the woman who screamed and nagged and picked at him all the time. She had never been satisfied with anything he'd done. She had resented every penny he had paid his hired hand, and when he'd been forced to let the kid go, she had resented the extra hours he had to put in to make up for it. She had been jealous of the time and attention he'd given Kylie, yet when he had tried to give her attention, too, she hadn't wanted it. He had been stupid at the time, but later he had realized that she'd been getting it elsewhere. Attention, and who knew what else?

From him, all she had wanted was *out*—out of the val-ley, out of the mountains. She had been raised in Little Rock, and she had wanted to go back. At first she had wanted them all to leave. He could find a job in the city, she had told Josiah—construction, maybe, or factory work. She hadn't cared that either one would have made him crazy, that leaving the farm would have made him crazy.

But after a time, she hadn't cared one way or the other whether he accompanied her, and it wasn't long after Ky-lie's birth that getting out had included getting out of their marriage. Getting *him* out of *her* life.

Tired of thoughts of Caroline, he left the house and headed for the barn. A chicken, scratching in the dirt, scur-ried out of his way, then berated him with an annoyed squawk. In the corral, his last remaining horse trotted over for a pat and a scratch. At one time, the farm had been home to some good stock—two dozen head of cattle, three dozen chickens, a small herd of goats, six horses and varying numbers of cats and dogs. He'd sold off all but three of the cows, this one old mare and a dozen of the chickens. The cats had died of old age, and Caroline had taken the shepherd dog with her. It was just about the only thing in Dutchman's Valley she'd taken a fancy to.

Like the house, the outbuildings needed some serious work. They leaked when the rain fell and shuddered when the wind blew. Though the barn was still sturdy after a hundred and fifty years, the shed, a small structure built onto one side, leaned over dangerously. One good shove—or one strong wind—would topple it to the ground, and the workshop in back wasn't in much better shape. He had gotten by the last couple of years with patching and shoring up, but there was no denying that this winter the two buildings had to be replaced.

He loved farming, he really did, and he was good at it. But this was one business where being knowledgeable and experienced and doing everything right didn't count for much. He could know everything there was to know about preparing the soil, about planting and cultivating and harvesting, about fertilizers, insecticides and pesticides. He could learn the strengths and weaknesses of every variety of seed put out by every company in the U.S. for every crop he grew. He could take every piece of equipment apart and put it back together in better shape than before. Tractors, combines, balers, pickers—he knew them all. He could learn the financial side, too—interest rates, market prices, land prices, seed and chemical and machinery costs.

But he still couldn't succeed.

He couldn't control the sun. He couldn't predict the rain. He couldn't make the warm spring weather come when it was supposed to come, couldn't convince the clouds to share their precious water. All he could do was his best—till the ground, plant his crops and work and wait. Hope they didn't wash away in heavy spring rains. Pray a late frost didn't kill tender new plants. Stand by and watch as relentless summer droughts withered the crops in the fields.

All he could do was his best.

And all too often, in farming, his best wasn't good enough.

He rummaged through the workshop and the storage shed before finding what he wanted in a dusty corner of the barn. The pump came from the farm's own system—when it had broken a few years ago, he had taken it off, intending to fix and then reinstall it. But something had interfered—he didn't remember what now—and he'd had the money to buy a new pump, and so he had. It had been easier for him, and keeping the interruption in the water supply brief had made Caroline happy. But he had kept this one, and when he'd finally found the time, he had fixed it. It always helped to have a spare around.

He gathered the tools he needed from the shop, then headed across the road. Annabeth had moved her car into the clearing in front of the mill, and the mill door and downstairs windows stood open. There was no sign of her— not that he was looking too hard, of course—but the dog he'd heard howl earlier was lying in a patch of sun-warmed dirt near the end of the mill.

When he became aware of Josiah, the dog roused himself and slowly stretched before approaching him. He was the sorriest-looking animal Josiah had ever seen. With floppy ears, a fat belly and a scruffy brown-and-black coat, he looked older than the hills, and ugly, too. A few feet away, he came to a stop, seeming to just sort of settle onto the ground, and gave Josiah a long, soulful look.

He ignored the dog and continued walking around the mill and along the banks of the stream until he reached the old pump house. His grandfather had been an orderly man. He had built everything as if it had to last at least a hundred years. This pump house was a good example. However, if the pipes weren't in good shape, Annabeth Gibbs would have to find another place. He wasn't spending the time or the money to make the mill livable, not when there had to be something available elsewhere.

A rustle in the leaves quieted as the dog sank down beside Josiah. Another rustle a moment later announced his owner's arrival. Crouched as he was, all he could see of her were her feet in scuffed leather tennis shoes that bore a well-known and ridiculously expensive brand name.

For a moment she remained silent. Not speaking to him after his earlier insult? he wondered. Then her feet shifted and suddenly she was crouched, too, sitting back on her heels with her arms around her knees. "Need any help?"

He didn't glance at her. He could see enough—golden hair, white shirt, faded jeans—from the corner of his eye. "What do you know about pumps?"

She moved again, and he saw a soft blur, an impression of hair swaying, a tanned arm. "I know you need one to get water from a well or a spring. Since there's only the one bathroom and no tub in the mill, you could probably get by with a one-third horsepower, one-stage pump, although this one is probably more powerful. But if you wanted, you could probably do away with the pump completely since the stream does come downhill here. You could just set up a gravity-line system, although I'm not sure—"

"No, thanks," he interrupted, bending forward to tighten a fitting. "I don't need any help."

She became silent again, and when he finally looked at her, he saw that she was smiling smugly. All right. So she did know something about water systems. For a woman from the city, she wasn't *totally* uninformed.

"Has this water been tested lately?"

"It's safe to drink."

"No pesticides?"

He gave her another look. "No."

"How do you farm without pesticides?"

"I use them occasionally."

"Then how do you know they're not in the water?"

His look grew strained. He wasn't used to even carrying on a conversation, much less being questioned like this. "I get my water from the stream, too. I'm not going to poison my own water." Sitting back, he gestured around them with one hand. "Do you see any fields around here?" Like more than half of the land he owned, this section was too hilly and the dirt too poor to grow anything but trees that could sink their roots into rocks and weeds.

But she wasn't looking around. Her attention was on his hand. He knew without looking what she saw. The scars—one long one that cut across the back of his hand, the others oddly shaped—were pale against the brown of his skin, and two fingers were just the slightest bit crooked. With a grimace, he returned to work on the pump.

"What happened?"

"You're nosy," he muttered, leaning forward to secure the last fitting. He reached back to drop the wrench in the toolbox and caught her smile—not the hesitant gesture he'd seen earlier at his house or the smug one a few minutes ago, but a real, genuine, happy smile. It made her look even prettier, younger and entirely too cheerful for anyone living in his world.

"I know," she said unapologetically. "I want to know everything about everything."

"And that's why you go poking your nose into other people's business."

"You don't like the idea of a history of Dutchman's Valley?"

He flipped open the cover to the wiring box, then brushed away a few cobwebs. "I don't see any need for it. You really think anyone who doesn't live here is going to care?"

"Sure." She stood up, glanced around, then settled on a nearby fallen log. "A lot of people are curious about the old ways. As we get older, we get more interested in the past. As life gets tougher and society gets more fractured, we're drawn to the good old days, when life was simpler."

"Simpler doesn't mean easier. 'The good old days' are a myth. People worked harder then than they ever do now, and they were rewarded for it by *maybe* having enough food to feed their kids one more meal."

"You're a pessimist."

She made the announcement in a pleasant, even tone, as if she were merely stating a fact—such as *you're big* or *you have brown hair*—and not something of an insult. But in a very real sense, she was right. As far as his personal life was concerned, he *was* a pessimist. He'd lost hope a long time ago, and he doubted he would ever get it back again.

At the same time, though, he was as optimistic as any fool could be. He was a farmer, wasn't he? Every spring he was out in the fields, planting seeds by the ton, knowing that too much or too little rain and too much or too little sun might very well destroy his crops and hoping for success, anyway. Praying for it. Counting on it. And every spring, even when his last harvest had been bleak, even when his best year ever hadn't been good enough, even when he'd sworn that he would quit working himself to death, would quit gambling his life and his land and his future on the capricious whims of nature ... every spring he was out there again. Trying again.

"So what does this history of the valley involve?" he asked, reaching for an ancient bucket his grandfather had stored inside the pump house and going to the stream to fill it.

"Reading a lot of books and papers. Combing through public records—birth, marriage, death, divorce, tax. Talking to whoever will talk to me."

"You know, most of the folks up here aren't going to be too enthusiastic about telling their life stories to some stranger from South Carolina." He emptied the water into the pump, then returned to the creek for another bucketful.

"I know. That's why I plan to stay here at least a year. Eventually people will get used to me, and I'll no longer be some stranger from South Carolina."

"No, you'll be that strange city woman trying to make a home in the sawmill."

Smiling, Annabeth stood up and held her hand out for the bucket. Priming the pump was one thing she could do herself, even if he didn't want her help. He looked at her for a moment, his eyes dark and measuring, then handed it over.

Her smile didn't slip as she took the full weight of the bucket—easily ten pounds or more—but her fingers did. She had to clutch the handle tightly to stop from dropping it, and even then she spilled about a third of it.

On the next trip, though, she didn't spill a drop, or on the ones that followed. When the water started bubbling back out of the pump, she stepped back and, while Josiah replaced and tightened the plug, she examined the bucket. "Did one of your relatives make this?"

He flipped on the power, and the pump came on. She only hoped there were no problems in the piping. She really did want to stay at the mill, but somehow she didn't think her landlord would be willing to repair or replace the pipes, not for the rent she was paying and not when she would be here only a year.

"I imagine my grandfather made it," he replied at last as he stood up. "Or maybe his father."

"Nice work." It was made of wood, even the narrow hoops that held it together, and waterproofed inside with some type of pitch. The handle was no more than a length of rope, threaded through holes on each side of the bucket and knotted. It was strictly utilitarian—not fancy, not pretty, but durable.

She gave it back to him, and he put it in its place in the pump house. He closed the wide door and secured the lock—a thick wooden shim that fitted into a groove on the doorframe—then picked up his tools.

"I take it you're one of those who isn't enthusiastic about telling your life story."

He didn't even glance at her, but started off toward the mill again. "You wouldn't be interested."

"Of course I would. I'm interested in everyone." She followed him, and after a moment or two, lazy old Emerson waddled along, too.

Josiah came to a sudden stop at the back of the mill, so that she had to draw up quickly to keep from running into him. "Well, I'm not interested in telling it. Now, I don't need any more help here. You can go on and do whatever it was you were doing when I came."

She wanted to ignore his all-too-clear invitation and stick around anyway, but she knew better. Making new friends, especially with people who lived in places like this isolated valley, rarely came easy, but the results, when it eventually happened, were worthwhile. Josiah Miller might not think much of her or her reason for coming here, but when he got to know her, he would like her. Most people did.

And then he could provide valuable help. If he accepted her, then others would. They would assume that if Josiah found her trustworthy, they would, too. They, in turn, would introduce her to still others, and before long, just as she'd told Josiah, she would no longer be some stranger to be regarded with suspicion and distrust. She wouldn't be poking her nose into other people's business, as he'd put it, but a friend asking questions to satisfy genuine curiosity.

"All right," she agreed, taking no offense at his bluntness. "Thanks for installing the pump. If you'll stop by the mill before you leave, I'll give you a check for this month's rent. And as soon as I get unpacked, we can draw up some sort of lease for both of us to sign, all right?"

Giving her a look in which the trust she was so blithely counting on was woefully absent, he simply nodded, then waited for her to leave. Returning his flat, vaguely wary look with a smile, she did just that, scuffing through the fallen leaves to the clearing and then inside the mill.

Inside, her smile slowly faded. She was being awfully optimistic, talking about unpacking, when she had to clean this place first. Cobwebs and ashes, she didn't mind dealing with. They were a cinch compared to the dust that covered everything. But she didn't dwell on the task. In town this morning she had bought the necessary supplies: broom, mop, bucket, cleanser and pine cleaner. Now it was just a matter of putting them to work.

As she worked, she wondered about her landlord and why he wasn't married and raising a handful of kids. About why he sometimes had such a hopelessly sad look in his eyes.

About what had happened in his thirty-some years of living that he was convinced wouldn't interest anyone.

She *didn't* wonder why he lived up here in the back of beyond, working at such an impossibly hard job. She had met enough farmers in the last five years to know that men didn't choose to farm—the farming chose them. Most likely there had never been a doubt in Josiah's mind, from the time he was a small child, about how he wanted to earn his living. Working the land got into a man's blood, into his heart. Giving up the job and the land would be like giving up himself.

Still, why was he doing it alone? Why had he never married—or if he had, where was his wife and what had gone wrong with the marriage? Was that why he was sad—because he'd had an unhappy love affair?

Given free rein, her imagination would give him a dozen different stories, a dozen heart-tugging tragedies to explain the look in his eyes. Stories were part of her job—telling them, listening to them, writing them down, passing them on. Oral histories, she called them officially, but really they were simple stories of birth and death and of the living in between.

No doubt, Josiah Miller had seen some of that "living in between," but she hadn't. Nothing very special had happened in her life. She was thirty years old and had never been married, hadn't even come close. She had been in love a few times, although not the kind of love she was looking for, not the enduring, break-your-heart-if-it-ends sort of love. She had held a variety of jobs, but history, especially with a personal touch, had always been her passion—a gift from her stepfather, a professor of history at the College of Charleston in South Carolina. He had helped her get the first grant that had sent her off into the farthest reaches of the Blue Ridge Mountains, conducting hundreds of hours of interviews, filling tape after tape, notebook after notebook, with the lives of the people she'd met.

It had also been her stepfather's suggestion that she turn those notes and the resulting papers into a book, a modest volume that had been published three years ago by a university press. Neither the distribution nor the money had been great, but the satisfaction Annabeth had found in the whole process had been tremendous. And so she had gone out again, this time into the mountains of West Virginia. Now, with her parents' approval, here she was in the Arkansas Ozarks.

Their approval had been important to her on this one. Her selection of the Ozarks in general and of Dutchman's Valley in particular hadn't been entirely innocent. She hadn't made that decision based on the valley's remote location or its beauty or its more than one-hundred-fifty-year history. She had chosen it because the valley's history was, in part, her own. Because she had family—a father, maybe aunts and uncles, maybe grandparents—here, even though she'd never met them. Even though it was doubtful they would want to meet her. This time the interviews would be personal.

Her mother had been reluctant, her stepfather encouraging. Annabeth had overheard them talking late one night, had heard the only father she'd ever known reminding her mother that they had known it would come to this. Someday, they had realized, documenting other people's history wouldn't be enough for her. Someday she would want to know her own.

Her mother hadn't been easily swayed. Although she hadn't said so, Annabeth knew her mother was afraid for her—afraid that she would be rejected by her father, the same way he had rejected Lynette more than thirty years ago. Afraid that she would be hurt by these strangers who shared blood and history with her. But Lynette needn't have worried. Annabeth wasn't looking for acceptance. Her stepfather and his family had long ago given her that. She had enough love, enough relatives, enough family ties, that she didn't need any more.

What she wanted was knowledge. Answers. A more thorough understanding of the people she'd come from. When had they come to Dutchman's Valley, and where had they lived before? Had they farmed the land or earned their living at one of the few businesses in town? What had they accomplished in the years they'd lived here? Had they been respected by their neighbors? Had their deaths brought mourning or celebration? How had they accumulated the small wealth that, thirty years ago, had made them the most powerful family in the valley?

She wanted to know if she looked like any of them, because she certainly didn't resemble her mother's side of the family. She wondered if her strength, so different from her mother's fragile nature, was inherited from her father or learned from her stepfather. She wanted to find out if she had any brothers or sisters here to complement the one brother and two sisters at home.

Half brother and sisters, she corrected. Because her mother's relationship with her father had lasted less than three months, because he had denied ever being intimate with her and had sent her away in a fit of anger, Annabeth would never have a real, one-hundred-percent, same-mother, same-father brother or sister. She would never find anyone to make her whole.

Usually that knowledge didn't bother her.

Now, once again in a new place, this time in a special place, in the place where her life began, it did.

It made her feel alone.

Chapter 2

By the time he stopped working for lunch Thursday morning, Josiah knew more about his new neighbor than he'd ever wanted to know about anyone.

He knew she was a hard worker. When he'd finished cleaning and checking the pressure tank and making certain the water system was working all right, she had already swept the loft and the stairs clean and had scrubbed the bathroom with water carried from the stream in a blue plastic bucket.

He knew she was stubborn, too, and more than a little hardheaded. "Where are you staying tonight?" he had asked as she'd written him a check for the rent, and with a self-satisfied grin, she had pointed to the loft overhead. And she had stayed, even though the place was far from clean. Even though she'd still had fifty years of dust to sweep away, fifty years of mustiness to air out.

He knew she was an early riser. He had seen her, a blanket wrapped around her shoulders, a coffee mug cradled in her hands, sitting on the rocks beside the millpond when he'd left the house this morning. He didn't know exactly what she was doing there, because that one quick glance was all he had allowed himself. He wasn't going to get in the habit of looking for a mane of golden blond hair or a flash of too-long legs every morning.

He knew she had to be crazy to try living over there. That old Franklin was going to require a lot of wood to get through the winter, and there was nothing so sophisticated as a thermostat on it. Sometimes it would be too hot, and sometimes it wouldn't be warm enough. The end of the room where the stove sat would be significantly warmer than the other end, and the loft was always going to be the warmest of all. The water system he had worked on yesterday would provide her with plenty of water—with plenty of fifty-eight-degrees-year-round water. That was fine for cooking and drinking, but there was no way she was going to be able to bathe or wash that long blond hair in it.

And how was she going to cook? How was she going to keep food? How would she amuse herself? The mountains surrounding the valley didn't make for good radio or television reception; without an expensive satellite dish, snow was the best she could hope for on every channel. As for a telephone, the lines stopped at the Hilton place, three miles closer to town. And when winter came, there would be snow and ice and days on end when stepping outside your door meant risking a broken neck.

There was no doubt about it. She was crazy.

She wouldn't last long here.

And he would be glad to see her go.

He was halfway to the house, taking a break for lunch, when he saw her, already on his mind, now on his porch. She was sitting on the porch swing, her mutt at her feet, a notebook open in her lap. The dog noticed him first. He raised his head, fixed his gaze on Josiah and gave a low whimper. Then he dropped his head to his paws again, his ears dragging on the floor, and made a soft, snuffling sound.

Annabeth was smiling that damned bright smile when he reached them. "Hey," she greeted him, somehow giving

that simple little word a long and decidedly Southern twist.
"Since you went to so much trouble on the pump yesterday, I thought I'd repay you with lunch. I hope you don't
mind."

His gaze shifted from her to the foil-covered dishes beside her on the swing, then back again. She was wearing
yellow today, a pale yellow shirt and indecently short shorts
the color of the brightest, lemoniest daffodil. But, no, they
were perfectly modest shorts, he saw when she put down her
notebook and stood up. They just seemed indecent because
her legs were so long.

She offered him the first dish, and he lifted the edge of the
foil. It was a casserole, still warm, of brown rice and broc-
coli, cheese and mushrooms that smelled better than anything he'd ever fixed for himself. The second plate held pork
chops and wedges of sweet, buttery corn bread, and the
third, a saucer, contained two pieces of peach pie.

She stood there, her expression open and somewhat expectant, waiting for him to say something—*thank you, I
appreciate this, I don't want your food, leave me alone.*
When he didn't, shadowy disappointment crept into her
eyes, and she awkwardly turned to pick up her notebook.

"I—" That one little sound made her stop. He finished
with a shrug. "I'll get some dishes."

She smiled again, relieved, and he quickly turned away,
going around the porch to the back door. In the kitchen he
washed up, then took the dishes from the cabinets and the
drawers: two plates, two glasses, two each of knives, forks
and spoons. God, how long had it been since he had shared
a meal with someone? Christmas. Nearly eleven months. He
could at least have had the manners to invite her inside, instead of leaving her out there on the porch.

But the house needed cleaning, and there were things
around that he would prefer not to have noticed—a few of
Kylie's toys that Caroline had left behind, a teddy bear that
he'd found stuffed behind a door, the torn halves of his and
Caroline's wedding picture, photographs of Kylie and, on

the table where she'd left it, undisturbed in more than three years, Caroline's wedding ring.

He filled the two glasses, one with orange juice, one with fresh milk. He never had anything else in the house to drink. He had never cared for soda, hadn't learned to make decent coffee and had never mastered the proper proportions for tea.

Balancing the glasses on the plates, he carried the dishes out front. While he was inside, Annabeth had pulled a small, rickety table over to the swing and had removed the foil from everything but the pie. He wordlessly offered her a choice between the glasses, and she accepted the orange juice, then the dishes.

"Have you always lived here?" she asked as she began dishing out the meal.

"Pretty much." He pulled his grandfather's rocker closer and sat down to watch her. She put a small serving of rice on her plate, one twice as large on his, the littler pork chop on hers, the big one on his. After adding a large chunk of corn bread, she handed his plate to him, then took barely a crust for herself.

His look must have been disapproving, because she glanced at the bread. "I only like the crust," she explained. "I also only eat the outsides of biscuits and the edges of pizza crust." Changing the subject without pause, she asked, "What does 'pretty much' mean?"

"I went to school in Fayetteville for three years."

"What's there?"

"The University of Arkansas."

"Were you studying for some sort of agriculture degree?"

He nodded.

"Why? You'd lived all your life on a farm. What could you possibly learn in school?"

"You don't even hear the word agriculture much anymore. It's agri*business* now. Everything's a lot more complicated now than when my father or my grandfather was farming."

"Why didn't you finish?"

He gazed off over her shoulder. He had dropped out after his junior year because he had been young, foolish and in love. Because sleeping with Caroline on the odd nights when her roommates or his were gone had no longer been enough. Because it hadn't seemed right, going home and leaving her every night. Because he had been eager to marry and start a family and so, he had thought, had she.

Finally he met her gaze again. "I had my reasons." She could think it had been money, or that he had flunked out. She could think whatever she wanted as long as she didn't ask him about his marriage.

"Are those three years the only time you've lived away from here?"

He nodded.

"And farming is the only career you've ever worked at."

Her choice of words almost amused him. "Career? Honey, this isn't a career. It's a losing proposition."

She regarded him seriously. "Times are hard for small farmers. Anyone who's managed to stay in business the last ten years has truly accomplished something."

"Right. They've got a load of debt they'll never get out from under and a future that doesn't look much, if any, brighter." He heard his sarcasm and was immediately shamed by it. He knew better than to talk about hard times, especially with a stranger. Caroline had never cared, even though his hard times had directly affected her. This stranger, this city woman, certainly wouldn't care.

"I understand this valley is the best farmland in the region. You could sell it."

"No," he said flatly. "I can't." Again, he didn't care what she thought he meant—that he was so heavily in debt that he couldn't afford to sell, that he couldn't find a buyer or whatever. The simple fact was he couldn't leave here. He couldn't sell the land and get a regular job. He couldn't live in a city.

She fell silent for a while, and he took advantage of it to finish his meal. When he set the plate aside, she handed him the saucer with the pie, shaking her head when he offered her a piece.

"There's not much farming done in the Ozarks, is there?" she asked.

"Not commercially."

"Why not?"

"You drove through the mountains to get here. Can't you figure that out for yourself?"

She shifted positions on the swing, slipping her shoes off and tucking her feet beneath her. "The terrain is pretty rugged—lots of steep hills, ridges, gorges. But even the small valleys and relatively flat places I saw from the road weren't under cultivation. Why?"

"Poor soil. Dutchman's Valley is unusual. In a lot of places outside the valley, the topsoil is less than five inches deep. Under that is solid bedrock."

"But trees and grass and wildflowers grow there."

He gave her a long, steady look. "I can take you out in the woods here and show you trees growing out of what looks like solid rock. The roots go down through cracks in the rocks into the ground. As the trees grow and the root systems expand, they enlarge the cracks until one day the rock breaks apart."

"Will you?" At his blank look, she continued. "Will you show me?"

He should have kept his mouth shut, he thought grimly. He didn't have time to go traipsing off into the woods—or the desire to do it with her. He had made the mistake of coaxing Caroline into a hike with him once. She had fussed nonstop over the lack of easy trails, over the strenuous climbs and the difficult descents. She had fretted about the wild creatures they'd seen and had scared him half out of his wits with a bloodcurdling scream on spotting a harmless banded water snake, and all for what? To see a stupid waterfall? He had actually thought she would be interested in seeing a waterfall?

Annabeth read the reluctance in his expression and suppressed a disappointed sigh. "That's okay if you don't want to," she said nonchalantly. "If you don't mind, though, I would like to go back in there by myself. I would be very careful. I have a good sense of direction, so I wouldn't get lost." She knew she sounded hopeful, knew her voice—if not her words—was all but begging him for permission. Not that it really mattered. If he said no, she would wander off, anyway. Before she left Arkansas, she would know these hills in every season.

"There are other dangers besides getting lost."

"I know. I could fall and break my leg. I could run into a copperhead or a cottonmouth. I could walk through poison ivy or get scared by a bat or fall into a prickly pear cactus. I could get stung by a scorpion or run into a black bear or—" At his exasperated look, she broke off and laughed. "I'm not totally ignorant of the dangers of the mountains, Josiah. I may have been born and raised in a city, but I've lived in mountains before." And, she added to herself, she was conceived right here in *these* mountains. She came from good mountain people. Maybe, genetically, that counted for something.

He stood up and returned the rocker to its original location. "Lunch wasn't necessary," he said, avoiding her gaze. Then, after a moment, he added, "But thanks, anyway."

He gathered his dishes, and she took her own. Stacking them on top of her notebook, she offered an easy goodbye. She was at the bottom of the steps when he spoke again. "Saturday morning. Nine o'clock. Wear jeans and long sleeves and boots."

Turning, she acknowledged him with a wave and a smile. He responded with a tight-lipped look, then disappeared inside.

Yesterday's spell of loneliness had left her wondering if she'd made the right choice to come here. It was likely that her father would have no interest in meeting her, even more likely that his family had no idea she even existed. Surely he was married now, probably with children of his own. He'd probably had a nice, comfortable life for the last thirty years, one that he wouldn't want shaken up by the illegitimate daughter he'd never known.

But this afternoon everything looked bright again. So far, the weather was gorgeous—those warm, sunny days that smelled of crackling leaves and autumn's fires. She was making headway on the mill so that soon it would be as snug and cozy as could be, and Josiah was taking her into the woods to show her some sights. Although, beautiful as the Ozarks were, nothing, she suspected, that he might show her could be quite as pleasing to look at as *he* was.

At the mill, she scraped the leftovers from lunch into Emerson's food dish, then set the dishes on the table inside. Before going to bed last night, she had finished the worst of the sweeping. Another round with the broom this morning had left everything as dust-free as it was going to get. After a trip into town this morning to get the ingredients for lunch, she had cleaned the mill from top to bottom, using a worn dishrag on the windows and table, a mop gliding across the wood planks of the floor. With the help of a pan of water heated on the hot plate, she had even managed a sponge bath before heading over to Josiah's.

The scent of pine cleaner, far more pungent than the sweet scent in the forests, greeted her as she stepped inside. Soon that would fade, and the fragrance of the potpourri she had set out in baskets and bowls would fill the air. It was her favorite mix, made right here in Arkansas, and it smelled of cinnamon and cloves.

Unloading the car took the first part of her afternoon. All her clothes—jeans and shorts and skirts, blouses, T-shirts and sweaters—were stuffed into only two suitcases. Shoes filled another small bag—sturdy hiking boots, leather and canvas flats and sandals—and toiletries were loaded into another. Everything else crammed into the car was intended for living or work. Dishes, cookware, utensils. Her futon bed, rolled tight and squeezed in on top of everything else. Quilts and rugs, mostly handmade and gifts from subjects of her previous works. Reference books on the Ozarks, on farming and folktales, on mountain communities and old-time cultures. Her camera and camcorder, along with a tripod that fit both, and her microcassette recorders. Boxes of film, video and cassette tapes and batteries. Notebooks and pens, maps, copies of articles from the Little Rock library, copies of every census conducted in Dutchman's Valley.

Somewhere in one of those boxes was information on her father.

And on Josiah Miller.

She wasn't sure which one she would look up first.

When everything was unloaded and her car no longer scraped bottom, she changed clothes, locked up the mill and headed into town. Miss Hilda had invited her over this afternoon for a tour of the town, followed by a look around her garage. She had furniture she thought Annabeth might be able to use, and, with the only place to sit in the mill being the stair steps, Annabeth wasn't too proud to accept.

It was nearly five miles into town, most of it along a winding dirt road. The undergrowth was heavy, almost impenetrable in places, although from time to time she caught glimpses of what lay beyond—of a glade, tiny and dotted with a few fading wildflowers and thin grass. A log cabin, situated in a stand of oak and hickory, its roof gone now, its walls tilting inward. What once might have been a cultivated field, being reclaimed now by red cedars. A stream, appearing from a rock face above and cutting a path through a narrow gorge for twenty yards before disappearing into the rock again.

It was a beautiful place. A beautiful place to be connected to.

Dutchman's Corner, the only town located within the valley, was small and none too prosperous. Although the surrounding mountains were as lovely here as elsewhere in the Ozarks, the Corner, as the locals called it, had never been able to bring the tourists in. There were places just as beautiful and more easily accessible with many more of the conveniences today's vacationers demanded. The Corner had no motels, only three gas stations and two restaurants.

Medical care was available every other Friday at the clinic on the corner. There was a bank, a small one that still closed early on Wednesdays, and one grocery store. Insurance, real estate, a five-and-dime and the drugstore all shared the same space, and the feed store also dealt in tractors, hardware and auto parts.

And they had a library.

Miss Hilda was the only librarian the Corner had ever known. In fact, she had founded it herself, according to the letter of introduction she had sent Annabeth. She had taught school and loaned out her own books until she had persuaded the town to commit to a real, honest-to-God library. They had provided the space—once a café—and she had supplied the first books. Through years of careful budgeting and shameless begging, she had built up a library that any town would be proud to call its own.

A bell tinkled when Annabeth opened the door, announcing her arrival. The building had changed little in its renovation from a restaurant to a library. Money had been tight, so the black-and-white tile floor remained. So did the lunch counter, a wide slab of Formica, curving from one end down the length of the building and fronted by red vinyl bar stools. Even a couple of the booths remained, serving as tables for reading and studying. The library was by no means traditional, but it had a charm all its own.

Miss Hilda was cataloguing the stack of books Annabeth had dropped off yesterday. They had been gifts from her mother, a librarian herself, and her stepfather the professor, along with a few volumes from her own personal collection at home. The old lady worked by hand, her writing as graceful and perfect as the penmanship Annabeth had studied—but never mastered—in elementary school. Pausing, she greeted Annabeth with a smile. "Since you didn't come back here yesterday afternoon, I assume you charmed Josiah out of the mill."

Annabeth slid onto one of the bar stools and watched. "I don't believe my neighbor and landlord is a man to be easily charmed."

"Any man can be easily charmed by the right woman," Miss Hilda said archly. "Although I'm not sure about Josiah. He's become such a recluse in the last few years." Then, once she'd piqued Annabeth's curiosity, she went on. "Is the place livable?"

Someday, Annabeth promised herself, she would find out why her neighbor had become a recluse. As soon as she knew Miss Hilda well enough to ask without seeming forward or pushy. "It will be once I'm finished. I have running water, electricity and a wood stove. What more could I ask for?"

"A kitchen? A bathtub? A hot-water heater?"

Annabeth laughed. "Do I look so helpless and naive? So spoiled to the modern conveniences?"

Miss Hilda gave her a long look, from the top of her head all the way—by stepping around the counter—to the bottoms of her canvas-shod feet. "Yes, dear, you do. Now . . . are you ready for the tour?"

When she nodded, Miss Hilda placed a Back Soon sign on the door and led the way out. They walked down one side of the street, the old lady pointing out various businesses, divulging one bit of information or another. When they reached the edge of town, they crossed the road and started back along the other side.

"What was the first business here?" Annabeth asked, watching her step on the broken sidewalk between glances around.

"The mill. That was built by Josiah Miller in the 1840s. He was our Josiah's great-great-great-grandfather. There's an interesting story behind his coming here. What do you think of when you hear the name Josiah?"

Annabeth's smile was secretive. Now the name gave her an immediate impression of strength, of a handsome face and powerful hands and expressive eyes. But, putting him out of her mind, she concentrated on the name alone and found an answer. "A sea captain." On a long-ago trip up the New England coast, it had seemed that every other legendary sea captain she had come across had been named Josiah.

"Precisely. The original Josiah Miller was a sea captain, and quite a prosperous one. He sailed first out of Boston, and later Savannah. He married in Savannah, a Southern beauty with eyes of blue and hair as black as night. He loved his wife dearly, and she him. It was said they couldn't bear to be apart, and so she took to sailing with him on his voyages."

The old lady paused to clear her throat, and Annabeth understood more clearly why she'd taken such an immediate liking to her. Despite the differences in their ages, they had much in common: a love of their homes, their families and history. They also shared one more passion: they both loved telling stories. Miss Hilda was a natural for it.

"On one such voyage," she continued, "a fierce storm came up, and it was feared that the ship would go down with all aboard. Captain Miller sent his wife below, but she was frightened, and she wanted to return to him on deck. But just as she stepped onto the deck, a great wave hit the ship, and it washed her overboard. Her body was never found. She was the only one lost." Miss Hilda's voice had grown soft and regretful over the death of a woman she'd never known. "The captain was so overcome with grief that he never went to sea again. He couldn't bear even living near the water. One day he walked away—just left his home and his ships and his business. He traveled until he came to Dutchman's Valley, far from the ocean that had claimed his love's life, and he stayed here."

"And mourned his wife the rest of his life?"

Miss Hilda cleared her throat again. "Actually, no—at least, not so you would notice. He married again not long after he built the mill, and he and his second wife had nine children."

Annabeth laughed even as she filed the details of the story away for future reference. Growing serious again, she wondered if something similar had happened to *our Josiah*, as Miss Hilda had referred to him. Maybe he had lost his love.

Maybe she had died, or maybe she had merely left him for someone new, for someplace better. Heartache could certainly account for that sadness she had noticed. The power of love—in her oh-so-experienced opinion, she gently mocked herself—was vastly underrated by most people. Losing it had made drunks of teetotalers and weepers of stoics—had even turned Josiah's own ancestor from a man surely bound to the sea to a landlocked farmer. It had led to suicide, murder and worse. It could easily turn someone's life upside down.

And winning a new love could set things right again.

"So what do you think of your landlord?" Miss Hilda asked.

Annabeth watched their reflections in the store windows they were passing before quietly answering, "I think he's very sad."

Miss Hilda gave a satisfied shake of her head. "I think you're very perceptive." But that was all she said. She didn't offer any explanations, any hints as to what adversity had given Josiah that look. Instead, she asked another question. "How do you intend to get started on your research?"

"By picking your brain," Annabeth replied, softening the flippancy with a gentle smile. "Looking around. Driving some of these back roads. I have some information that the library in Little Rock provided, and I intend to start going through that. And, hopefully, sometime soon you could introduce me to a few people."

"In another two weeks or so, weather permitting, we'll be having our fall festival. It's an annual event, scheduled between Halloween and Thanksgiving. It isn't anything fancy—I'm sure you've seen the same sort of thing elsewhere—but almost everyone in the valley comes. There are food and crafts booths, games for the children, music and dancing. With your permission, this year I'll reserve a space for a storytelling booth. That would be a lovely way, I think, for you to get acquainted with the children and maybe even some of the older folks, too."

"That sounds like fun." She had found storytelling an effective introduction in the past. Children were drawn to the stories and the way she told them; teenagers came out of curiosity. Their parents took a little more time to win over, but were easier by far than the grandparents and great-grandparents. Unlike Miss Hilda, most older folks were generally polite, although distant, until they decided she could be trusted. She was never exactly sure what brought them to that decision—whether it was her gradual acceptance into their communities, whether they took her on faith because others were doing so, or whether, after testing and judging her, they determined that her interest was sincere, her curiosity definitely harmless and maybe even helpful.

It was probably a little of all that, plus a desire to keep the old ways alive. As their grandchildren and their grandchildren's children ventured out of the mountains and into the high-tech life of the big cities, so much was being forgotten—traditions, history, crafts, beliefs. By cooperating with her and others like her, they were ensuring that a part of them would live on after they were gone.

And, contrary to Josiah's opinion, there were people who cared about keeping the old ways alive. As she had told him yesterday, as life today grew more difficult, a lot of people turned to the past. Life hadn't been easier then, but it had been simpler and more satisfying. Knowledge—and consideration—of right and wrong, respect for your elders, love for your country, personal responsibility, the work ethic—those things had been an everyday part of life fifty or a hundred years ago. People hadn't had to worry about their children turning to drugs, alcohol or a life of crime; they hadn't had to fear their unmarried daughters would have babies and go on welfare. They had worked hard, yes—had often struggled and barely scraped by—but they'd had security, too. They'd had extended families and neighbors who had helped out when times got hard. They'd had strength, courage and strong moral values. They'd had a love of family, God and country that could see them through.

A lot of people today envied that. A lot wanted to find it for themselves.

Miss Hilda still talking, they passed the library again and stopped at the first house they came to. It sat on the northwest corner of the intersection, with the bank, a gas station and the feed store on the remaining three corners. It was a simple place, two stories with a wide porch and an American flag flying from the rail. Miss Hilda had been born in the valley, Annabeth knew, and had left only to attend college. Her husband, Albert, had been a farmer until he was called to serve in the army in World War II. He had come back minus one leg and taken a job working in the bank, where he had remained until his death six years ago. Their children were grown now, and gone, too. Their son had married the eldest Matthews girl and lived up on Turkey Knob, one of the mountains that ringed the north end of the valley, and their daughter had gone off to college and had never come back.

That was a story Annabeth had heard all too many times before. Unless you had money, life in the mountains could be hard—harsh weather and hard work, with little to show for it but a few conveniences and even fewer luxuries. It certainly could make city life seem appealing.

It had worked the reverse for her. Annabeth had been born in one city, had lived since she was five in another. Yet she had no doubt that, if it weren't for her family, she would have already relocated to some quiet, peaceful mountain home. Of course, she was lucky enough to have job skills that didn't leave her at the mercy of the weather, that didn't require her to engage in hard physical labor to earn a living. She had a master's degree in education, and she had her writing. There wasn't much money to be made in nonfiction, at least not her kind, but she liked to dabble in fiction, too. Maybe someday she would make the change. She believed in her writing ability, and she was a storyteller at heart. And, after all, what was fiction but the telling—the *skillful* telling—of stories?

Miss Hilda took her out to the garage, which served as a catchall for old furniture, old clothes and old memories. "Look around," she invited, taking up a position near the door. "You can take whatever you want. And, of course, you'll need this." She patted the old refrigerator beside her, an old-fashioned kind with the motor on top, so short that Annabeth would have to stoop to see inside it. "I had Tony Walker—that's one of Josiah's cousins—come over and have a look at it yesterday afternoon. It may be old, but it works fine."

It took Annabeth only a few minutes to make her selections: a wicker love seat, a twig armchair, a scarred walnut desk and its accompanying chair. "I appreciate your generosity, Miss Hilda," she said, going to stand beside her in the doorway. "Can you recommend someone I could hire to take all this out to the mill?"

"Oh, you don't need to hire anyone, dear." She gestured toward the feed store across the street. "Call Josiah over here. He can take it home for you."

Turning, she saw her neighbor climbing out of a pickup truck almost as battered and done-in as her poor Bug. One part of her didn't want to impose on him, but it would be an imposition no matter who she asked, so why not ask the man who at least had gotten some money and a home-cooked meal from her? "I'll be right back," she told Miss Hilda before starting across the street.

He had almost reached the door by the time she got to the edge of the graveled lot. When she called his name, he came to a slow stop, then even more slowly turned to face her. There was such a look on his face—surprise, she thought, mixed with aggravation—that it slowed her own steps. Was he annoyed that it was her, or—recluse that Miss Hilda said he was—was he unused to being spoken to in town? Did he make a habit of being unsociable, and if so, why?

"Are you busy?" she asked, then immediately grimaced. He was a farmer. The times when he *wasn't* busy were rare.

He ignored her idiot question. "What do you want?"

"Miss Hilda's loaning me some furniture for the mill."

When he didn't say anything, she tried a tentative smile. "I can handle the chairs and love seat, but the refrigerator and the desk won't fit in my car." She expected the image of that—her little VW with the top down and the antique refrigerator and heavy wooden desk upended in the backseat—to at least make him smile. It didn't.

Josiah gave the empty bed of his truck a narrow-eyed glance. He had come here for supplies—supplies that probably wouldn't fit once he'd loaded the truck with her stuff. That meant he would have to make a second trip into town. He tried to avoid unnecessary trips whenever possible.

He should send her to the station to see his cousin Tony. Tony had a truck, newer and nicer than this one, and he had a weakness for pretty blondes. Like Annabeth.

Like Caroline.

He *should* send her to Tony...but he wasn't going to. No doubt his cousin would come around soon enough, but damned if he was going to make it easy for him. "Get in," he said with a gesture toward the truck.

She didn't comment on the strength it took to open the passenger door or grimace when she saw the state of the truck inside. Caroline had hated it, had hated that everything was dirty and grimy, that the upholstery was torn, that the rubber mats on the floor had long since worn through to bare metal underneath. For the last couple of years of their marriage, she had wanted to get rid of this truck and buy a new car—a *car,* not a truck, not something that could be of any use on the farm. Wherever she was now, he would bet she had herself a new car.

And Kylie.

Damn her, she had Kylie.

The engine coughed and sputtered when he turned the key, but finally it caught. They drove the short distance in silence; then Annabeth climbed out to give him directions when he backed into the narrow driveway. She was all he saw in his rearview mirror—not the garage, not Miss Hilda, not any of a dozen other things that he knew were reflected—and he took a moment to look.

Her hair was pulled back on both sides with combs, making her look younger, somehow more innocent. The clothes helped with that, too. Gone were the bright yellow shorts and the snug-fitting blouse. Now she wore a loose white blouse that tied at her waist and a skirt in pale blue that was long and full and hid her legs. Perversely, knowing that he was the only one around who had seen those legs—damn near all of them—he liked the change.

When she signaled him to stop, he did and walked around to join the two women in back. Miss Hilda greeted him in that tone that never let him forget she had been his teacher in third grade and again in seventh, eighth and tenth. He gave her a polite nod, then started toward the refrigerator.

"You'll need help with that, won't you?" Miss Hilda asked. "Wait just a minute and I'll walk over and ask Tony—"

He interrupted her, not caring how rude he was. "No, thanks."

"Well, how about Stuart at the bank?"

Abruptly Annabeth stepped forward. "I can help, Miss Hilda. Between the two of us, we can manage."

Josiah gave her an idly curious look. If he were a suspicious sort, he might think she was no more anxious to have Stuart Dothan over here than he was to see Tony. It couldn't be because she had already met the man and decided she didn't like him. *Everyone* liked Stuart. He was intelligent, fair, hard-working and a good friend.

He was also closing in on sixty—a much friendlier age, in Josiah's opinion, than Tony's thirty-two.

"You think you can handle this?" he asked, skeptically looking at her over the top of the refrigerator.

"I'm stronger than I look," she retorted with a smile.

Maybe not stronger, he decided, his gaze moving down the column of her neck to her shoulders and her arms. But more capable. More determined. And—one quality he admired in anyone—willing to try.

The refrigerator wasn't heavy, not compared to bigger, fancier models. Although he took most of the weight when they lifted it into the bed of the truck, he wasn't surprised that Annabeth supported her end.

The desk went in next. Solid walnut, it was much heavier and required careful maneuvering and an assist from Miss Hilda to get it inside. The chairs and the love seat, as Annabeth had said earlier, were easy to handle. And, as he had expected, there was no room left for the building supplies he needed to pick up.

"Are you going straight home?" Annabeth asked as he got into the truck again.

He nodded.

"I'll get my car at the library and meet you there. Thanks, Josiah."

He didn't offer her a ride to the library—it wouldn't save her but a minute or two—and he didn't return her wave as he pulled out of the driveway.

Somehow, her moving into the mill seemed more real now that she was collecting furniture. It had been different yesterday and this morning, when all she'd had was what would fit in her car. That would make leaving so much easier—just put it all back in its boxes, load those boxes into the car and she would be gone.

But furniture... That suggested permanence. The unwillingness to accept the possibility that the mill wasn't meant for wintering over. The refusal to consider the possibility that she wouldn't last three months, much less the whole year.

Judging from what he'd seen already, he had himself a neighbor, and the sooner he got used to that, the better.

That was easier said than done. Getting used to Annabeth Gibbs might prove to be a dangerous thing. She had been there less than two days, and he was already starting to look for her. When he had come into town, even though he had seen that her car was gone, he had still given the mill and her sorry excuse for a pet a searching look. He'd spent far more time than he could spare thinking about her. That sounded harmless enough, but it wasn't *just* thinking. He was thinking about how pretty she was. About how her hair looked as if it had been dusted with gold. About how women he'd known would kill to have legs that long or a smile that bright or a voice that husky. About how naturally she smiled and how easily she laughed.

God, how long had it been since *he* had laughed?

He pulled into the clearing in front of the mill, lowered the tailgate and sat down to wait. The dog waddled over and sat down nearby, then, with a thump of his tail, edged a little closer until his fat belly was draped over Josiah's boot. "You're too lazy to even bark at a stranger, aren't you?" he murmured, shifting his foot side to side so the leather scratched the dog's belly. "You've got it made. She feeds you and pets you and takes you from place to place with her."

The dog just looked at him, as satisfied an animal as Josiah had ever seen, then closed his eyes.

He was in sorry shape, Josiah decided, watching the ripples in the pond from the waterwheel, when he found himself envious of a dog. While he had no interest in going anywhere outside this valley, he wouldn't mind having Annabeth feed him, not if this afternoon's lunch was any indication of her talents. Hell, he wouldn't mind a little petting, either. Just a few touches, a few caresses—something to remind him how soft and smooth a woman's skin could be, how gentle a woman's touch could be. Caroline's touches there at the end had been hurried, impatient, angry. She had been so angry—not just with him, but with the world.

In contrast, he thought as the little car chugged to a stop nearby, Annabeth looked as if she'd never been angry a day in her life. He had never known anyone so sunny, so warm and *alive*.

She unlocked the mill door, then came over and gave her dog a nudge with one foot. "Go away, Emerson."

"Emerson?"

"He's named for the poet."

He gave her a dry look. "Right. I always name my animals after poets."

He pulled his foot from beneath the dog, stood up and handed the twig chair to her. A fine example of mountain folk craft, it was old, not too heavy and not too pretty, either. It seemed that everyone he knew had one of these tucked away somewhere—the best place, in his opinion, being out of sight. But rich city folks would pay a fortune for this one and any others they could scrounge up. He wasn't sure why. Maybe owning one gave them some make-believe connection to a past that had never been theirs in the first place, or maybe they saw the pieces merely as investments. In the last five or ten years, the prices for genuine folk arts and crafts had skyrocketed. Or maybe they simply followed the trends. As soon as mountain crafts went out of style again, the quilts, baskets and twig furniture would disappear from the cities again.

He took the wicker love seat and followed her inside. The mill smelled of cleaner and spices, an odd combination but a definite improvement over the musty, stale air of yesterday. The place was clean, too, really clean, for the first time since he was a boy.

She had set up a kitchen in the corner that his grandfather had used as an office. With the addition of Miss Hilda's refrigerator, she would be all set there. The loft upstairs, he assumed, would do duty as her bedroom. Quilts draped the railings on both sides, offering privacy for the upstairs and an unusual sort of wall decor for downstairs.

Leaving her to decide on locations for the furniture, he returned to the truck for the desk chair and then again for the desk itself. Emerson had roused himself to move into the shade provided by the tailgate, but other than that, showed no signs of life at his approach. He had maneuvered the desk to the back of the truck when she joined him again.

"How are we going to do this without one of us getting hurt?"

She smiled that damnable smile. "We'll manage."

"We wouldn't have managed to get it in here without Miss Hilda's help," he reminded her.

"Maybe we should have called your cousin Tony."

He scowled at her. So she had picked up on his reluctance to have Tony around. "Maybe we should have called Stuart."

Still smiling, she gave him a cool nod, acknowledging her own reluctance back at Miss Hilda's to call on the banker for help. She didn't offer an explanation, though, and he, who had quit caring for explanations more than three years ago, realized he wanted one now. He wanted to ask if she knew Stuart, and if so, when and how they had met; if not, why she hadn't wanted to meet him today.

But he didn't ask. It was none of his business, and unlike too many others in the valley, he didn't poke into things that didn't concern him.

"We don't need any help," she announced, hands on her hips. "At Miss Hilda's, we had to lift it up into the truck. All we have to do here is get it down without letting it fall on our feet. And if we can't carry it, I have some old blankets. We can turn it end over end."

Without comment, he turned the desk sideways and pushed it to the very edge of the tailgate so they would take the weight of the heavier side first. The muscles in her arms strained—slender as she was, she did have some muscle— and so did his own as he moved to take more of the load. It wasn't as easy as she had made it sound—the longer they supported it, the lower her end got to the ground—but they made it to the narrow porch just before she had to let go. He lifted each end over the threshold, then together they slid it across to the location she'd chosen.

"I'm stronger than I look," she remarked with more than a hint of smugness as she leaned against the opposite end of the desk.

"You're short of breath, and your face is pink." But pink was too simple a word to adequately describe her flush. *Rosy* fit far better, the delicate shade of the rose verbena that bloomed along the creek banks.

She didn't take offense. "I'm a little out of shape. I'll get stronger."

He refused to look at her, refused to make the obvious comment that, as far as he could tell, there was absolutely nothing wrong with her shape. But he didn't need to look at her to see again the rounded breasts, the slender waist, the nice hips, the long, lean legs. Her image was firmly fixed in his mind.

It had been a long time since he'd been preoccupied with a woman's body—not since Caroline had entered her fourth or fifth month of pregnancy and it had seemed that her body was changing daily. That had fascinated him. He had been fascinated, too, when they had first begun dating, when for months she had primly allowed him no more than a kiss, when he'd had to rely on his imagination and his meager experience with his high school sweetheart for satisfaction.

But he could easily become preoccupied with Annabeth's body—could picture exactly how she looked underneath those clothes, could imagine the shape of her breasts, the delicate shading of her nipples, the softness of her stomach. He could all too easily imagine those legs entwined with his.

Startled by the faint desire curling in his belly, he abruptly stood up and headed outside. He hadn't experienced desire for a woman in months—in years. Occasionally, when he wasn't too bone-tired from work, he would find himself with a case of good old-fashioned lust, with the purely physical need to relieve himself with some warm body. But to actually want a woman, a particular, flesh-and-blood, approaching-him-now woman... That was something he'd thought Caroline might have destroyed forever.

But obviously not.

They unloaded the refrigerator without too much trouble and moved it against the wall near the table. Once it was plugged in, running and starting to cool, he headed for the door, intending to escape to the solitude of the farm. But, of course, she couldn't let him go that easily.

"Since I won't be here that long, can I have my mail delivered to your box?"

"I don't care." He walked out the door, all too aware of her soft footsteps behind him and crossed the clearing to his truck.

"Why don't you like your cousin?"

He stopped after opening the door and turned to face her. She was flushing again, this time from embarrassment at her tactless question rather than from exertion. She would look the same, he knew, his muscles clenching painfully, in bed after making love, only hotter. Hot and sweaty and sweetly, lazily satisfied.

Deliberately he looked away to the cool, stream-fed pool behind her. "Why don't you like Stuart?" he countered.

"I've never met him."

"Well, I *have* met Tony. I'm entitled to dislike him."

"Why?"

He returned his gaze to her warily. "That's between Tony and me. It's none of *your* business."

"Have you ever been married?"

Now it was *his* face that was hot, though not with embarrassment. With anger, sudden and swift, that she thought she had the right to ask him that question. With shame that someone in town would tell her their version of his marriage—of his failures—if she asked. With frustration that, sure as the sun rose each morning, she *would* ask.

He gave the door a slam, and it caught with a solid thud. Hands clenched at his sides, he asked, "Have *you* been married?"

"No."

"Why not? Couldn't find anyone you wanted?" He lowered his voice, made it meaner. "Or couldn't find anyone who wanted you?"

"A little of both, I guess."

"Why? What did they find wrong with you? Did they want someone prettier? Someone quieter? Someone not so nosy?" He paused, but not long enough for her to respond. "Maybe the men in South Carolina aren't so different from here, after all. Maybe they prefer their women a little more settled, a little less foolish and a lot less aggressive. Maybe they prefer a woman who acts like a woman, who minds her own business and doesn't force her way in where she's not wanted.''

For the first time since she had walked up to his house yesterday at lunch, her smile was completely, utterly erased. She held his gaze for a long time, her brown eyes dark and suspiciously damp; then she smiled a tight little smile that was anything but pleasant and quietly agreed, ''No, they're not so different, after all. Thank you for your help, Josiah. Don't worry that I'll ask again. Next time I'll call your cousin Tony.''

And with that, she left him, walking away stiffly, stepping over the dog to get inside the mill and closing the door behind her.

No, they're not so different, after all. What did that mean? he wondered bleakly. That they all wanted the kind of woman she wasn't, as he had implied?

More likely that a bastard was a bastard no matter where he called home.

And being a first-class bastard was one of the few things Josiah excelled at.

He looked at the mill. In spite of the afternoon's warmth, the door remained closed and probably would until long after she was sure he was gone, but the windows were open. After a moment he heard music from inside—not country or rock, as he would have expected, but mountain music. Twangy banjo, mournful harmonica, untuned guitar. It had to be a tape—the hills made radio reception almost impossible to come by, and he couldn't imagine any station finding a commercial market for this music. He wondered what she was doing as she listened to it. Just sitting and waiting for him to drive away? Unpacking? Working?

It was none of his business. Just as she had no right to delve into his life, hers was off-limits to him. The only thing he could do was what he insisted he wanted from her: leave her in peace.

He wondered if he would ever find it as easily as she did. Somehow he didn't think so.

Chapter 3

Annabeth didn't hold grudges.

She had been that way as long as she could remember—even way back in kindergarten when one pretty little ringleted girl had made fun of her in front of the whole class because she didn't have a daddy and never had. She had punched the girl in the nose, also in front of the whole class—a reasonable response, she had thought at the time and still thought now. When her mother was called to the school, Annabeth had asked why she didn't have a father like the rest of the kids.

She did, Lynette had told her as she'd dried her tears. He was a nice man, and he lived far away in Arkansas and his name was Stuart. Satisfied with her mother's answer, Annabeth had gone back to class and apologized to the pretty little girl, and they had been best friends the rest of the year.

She had also forgiven her stepfather's mother for treating her differently from her other grandchildren—her *real* grandchildren, the old woman had called them—in the beginning. She had forgiven her cousin in high school for stealing her boyfriend, had forgiven her boyfriend for preferring her dainty Southern belle of a cousin over her. She had forgiven her college boyfriend for breaking her heart— and over the same cousin!—and had forgiven the last man in her life for doing it, too, and had remained friends with both of them.

Holding a grudge against Josiah for what he'd said Thursday afternoon wasn't even worth the effort.

When Emerson announced his arrival Saturday morning with a snuffle and a snort, Annabeth was waiting, dressed in jeans and a long-sleeved hot-pink sweatshirt over a lighter T-shirt and wearing, as he had instructed, a pair of hiking boots. "I wasn't sure you would show up," she announced as she slipped a couple of rolls of film into her pockets, then slung her camera over one shoulder.

He wasn't amused by her careless greeting. "I said I would take you, didn't I?" he asked with a scowl.

"Ah, a man of his word. You would be amazed at how many people make promises, then conveniently forget them."

"No, I wouldn't," he replied crossly as she took two granola bars from the moving box that served as her cupboard and tossed them to him.

"Put those in your pockets, would you?"

Catching the snacks, he tucked them both into the breast pocket of his shirt. He followed her outside and waited while she locked up, then started toward the woods behind the mill. When he noticed Emerson tagging along, he stopped. "It gets too rough back in there for him."

"He has no intentions of going back in there. When he gets to the first uphill slope, he'll waddle back to the mill and find a nice sunny place to relax."

With a shrug, Josiah started again, and she fell in step behind him. It wasn't a bad place to be, she decided with a private smile. His flannel shirt accentuated the broadness of his shoulders, and his jeans, just tight enough to invite a second look—and maybe a third and a fourth—emphasized his narrow waist and muscular thighs.

He was undoubtedly the best sight she'd seen in these mountains yet.

"Where are we going?"

"You wanted to see a tree growing out of a rock." He swept a low branch aside and held it until she passed. "Why the camera? Surely the state's not paying you to take pictures, too."

"Nope, these are for me. To refresh my memory when I start writing. To put on my walls when I'm finished."

"Exactly what is it you're planning to write?"

"Papers and articles for the state that will go into their archives somewhere—"

"To never be seen again," he interrupted dryly.

"Maybe. But the book will be. People will read it."

"A book." The glance he gave her over his shoulder was skeptical. "You really think you can sell a book about this valley."

"I already have," she said smugly. "I've written two similar books, one on Virginia and North Carolina and one on West Virginia. Does that make you any more impressed with me?"

She was coming to expect that dry, it's-best-if-I-stay-quiet look of his. This time it made her laugh. "What kind of trees are these?" She was better than most at identifying trees, but not when their leaves lay brown and crackly on the ground.

"White oak. Blackjack. Hickory. Maple. Willow." He pointed to a specimen of each one. "In the hollows you'll find river birches, which normally don't grow in this part of the country. Near some of the creeks you can find beeches, and in the bogs there are tupelos."

"It smells wonderful out here. I can't wait to see it in spring when everything's green again and the wildflowers are blooming. Or next fall when the leaves change."

He gave her another of those looks. "You think you'll last till spring?"

"You do take the negative view of things, don't you?" she asked. When he started to reply, she stopped him. "And don't say it's because you're a farmer. I'm sure you have your reasons for such pessimism, but the state of agriculture—excuse me, agri*business*—in this country today is probably the least of them." After a moment's silence to concentrate on climbing the small, rocky ledge he had just ascended without breaking his stride, she thoughtfully remarked, "I think you're just grouchy."

Grudgingly he extended his hand and hauled her to the top. "Maybe I've just been in a bad mood for the last three years."

She wanted to ask what had happened three years ago, wanted to ask it so badly that she had to literally bite her tongue to stop herself. And he expected her to ask—she saw it in the sudden wariness in his eyes, felt it in the tension in his hand. He expected her to force her way into a place—his past—where she had no business and wasn't wanted, and if she did, she would only confirm the worst that he already thought of her.

Slowly she freed her hand from his, tore her gaze from his and turned in a slow circle, admiring the scenery and catching her breath. "What kind of rock is this?" she asked, gesturing with an open palm to the rock faces and outcroppings around them.

"Mostly sandstone and limestone. Some granite over there." His voice, like hers, was a little out of kilter. Not quite normal. Relieved. "The path is this way."

She turned to see him walking toward the left. "What path?" she teased as she followed. "I may be from the city, but I know a trail when I see one, and you aren't following one. You're just lucky enough to know where you're going."

They climbed a few hundred feet, descended into a steep gorge, climbed out again and followed a ridge a short distance before going down again. After a solid hour of walking, she estimated they hadn't traveled more than three quarters of a mile, as the proverbial crow flew. But crows flew horizontally, and most of their mileage had been vertical, so she gave herself credit for double that distance.

"There," Josiah said, stopping at last and gesturing ahead.

Annabeth walked around him to look. They were on a spur, a narrow projection tapering out into a valley deep below. Just ahead, soil and trees gave way to a great outcropping of sandstone that formed a rough arrow point before dropping off in a sheer cliff on both sides, and right in the middle of the sandstone grew a blackjack oak, a scrubby, stunted little tree. She walked around it, locating where each of the roots curved down through fissures in the stone. Moving to the edge of the stone, she bent to look over, only to have a powerful hand catch hold of her sweatshirt and pull her back.

She gave Josiah a reproving look. "I only wanted to see how far it was to the ground."

"Falling and breaking your neck isn't a good way to find out. It's about forty feet down from here."

Tugging at her sweatshirt to straighten it, she turned back to the tree. "So those roots go down forty feet to reach soil."

"More than that. This rock isn't just sitting on the ground below. It goes some distance below the surface."

"Says something about the will to survive, doesn't it?" She walked back a few yards and removed the lens cap from her camera. After sinking to her knees on the stone and snapping a few pictures of the tree—really an ugly little thing in spite of its will to survive—she asked, "Can I take your picture?"

"No."

"Why not? Afraid it would steal your soul?" She focused on him, but kept her finger away from the shutter release. "Some people believe that, you know—that if you take their picture, it steals their souls and they'll never find peace when they die."

The look that came across his face was exquisite—dark and haunted and filled with pain so pure she could almost feel it. "Who says I have a soul to steal?" he whispered before turning away.

She sat motionless, nothing in the viewfinder now but hills and trees and thin blue sky. When she realized she was holding her breath, she released it in a great rush, and that made her tremble. She couldn't remember a time when she'd wanted so badly to offer comfort . . . or a time when she'd known so certainly that she couldn't. She didn't even know what was wrong; how could she make it right?

But something *was* wrong. He was carrying a terrible sorrow, one that threatened to destroy him from the inside out. She wished she knew what it was, wished she could do something, say something to ease the pain.

But she couldn't. No matter how attractive she found him, no matter how much she enjoyed his company, they were still little more than acquaintances—unwilling acquaintances, on his part, at least. She didn't have the right to probe into his problems, to force confidences that he didn't want to share. She had no rights at all.

Finally she rose from the rock and went after him. He was sitting, his back to her, on a sloping boulder back where the sandstone met the spur. She approached noisily, not wanting to startle him, and set her camera down beside him.

"I hear water," she said after a moment.

He gestured down through the trees. "Dancing Creek runs through here. The spring that feeds it is back in there."

"Dancing Creek? Is that the creek that provides the mill's water?"

Giving her a quick glance, he nodded.

"I like that name. Can we see it?"

That earned her one of those looks. "You can see it outside the mill anytime."

"Can we go to the spring? Is it far from here?"

"The falls are right over there. The spring is another half mile from there."

She looked in the direction he pointed but couldn't make out anything but trees and, high on the south side of a distant hill, a miniature glade. But the waterfall must be what she was hearing, either that or a long series of riffles, so it couldn't be too far. "Can we go there?" she asked again.

Finally he shifted on the rock to face her. "Why?"

"Why not?" She offered her most appealing smile. "We've come this far. It would be a shame to go back now without seeing the waterfalls and the spring. And I've been good, haven't I? I haven't needed help or complained or talked too much—at least, no more than usual."

"Aren't you tired?"

"Of course. But it's not much further, and—"

"And if you're so certain you're going to stick around, you can come back some other time."

She was too disappointed to argue, since she suspected his reluctance to go on had to do with *her.* She obviously wasn't his favorite person; just because he'd been angry the other day didn't mean he didn't believe the things he'd said. He thought she was foolish, pushy and nosy, not pretty enough, not settled enough and not feminine enough—in general, an unwanted pain in the neck. These few hours had probably exceeded his tolerance for her company, and they still had to get home from here.

"Oh, hell," Josiah muttered, sliding to the ground and heading toward the path in the rocks that would lead them to the gorge below. When had he become such a sucker? Why did he care if the delight she'd found in the name of the creek had disappeared from her face? Why should the disappointment in those big brown eyes make any difference to him?

Finding no answers, he concentrated instead on the trail that wound down through the rocks to the gorge below. He moved quickly so he wouldn't have to see that self-satisfied look she was bound to be wearing now that she'd gotten her way. But when she stopped him, he saw that she didn't look satisfied at all. She looked troubled instead. Chastened.

"You don't have to do this. We can go back now."

He looked down at her hand, which rested on his forearm. It was small, soft, warm, her fingers long and thin, their nails clipped short and unpolished. Capable hands to be so small. Strong, too. Graceful. Fine.

And affecting. Even after she pulled her hand away, he fancied he could still feel its imprint—could still feel its warmth, its softness, its strength. There was a part of him that wanted to feel it again, wanted to feel her hands anywhere she wanted to place them, wanted to feel them especially—

Refusing to finish the thought, he swung away and started down the trail. "We've come this far."

This time they truly were on a trail, narrow, slipping and sliding. In summer this was a good place to find snakes, curled up to catch the morning sun or lingering in the shadows of the rocks. It wasn't far from here that Caroline had seen the banded water snake on their one trip out here. Her scream and subsequent thrashing and rustling had probably unnerved any and all wildlife within a square mile and had sent the snake rushing away to safety.

But Annabeth didn't seem like the type to scream.

Except maybe with sexual pleasure.

Glowering at the wayward direction of his thoughts, he stopped at the bottom of the trail and turned to wait on her. She scrambled down the last few yards, her feet slipping and sending a shower of dirt and pebbles down; then she released her tight grip on her camera and looked back up at the trail. "With a little more room to maneuver and an old cardboard box for a sled, wouldn't that be a hoot?"

"How old are you?"

His question was as blunt as any she had asked him, but she didn't seem to mind. "Thirty," she answered without hesitation. "I know. I take foolish pleasure in childish things."

Not foolish. Pleasure was never foolish, he thought, no matter where you found it. And not childish, either. Maybe child*like*—but there was a world of difference between the two.

She took the lead this time, and he let her. From here it was a simple matter of following the streambed a few thousand feet to the waterfalls. They weren't spectacular falls—

the creek was too small for that—but they were pretty enough, and they were his.

The trail from this direction came upon the falls suddenly—round a thirty-foot-tall hunk of granite, and you were in front of them. Annabeth came to an abrupt stop, staring and saying nothing.

He waited for her response, knowing that if it was anything similar to Caroline's, he would take it personally. *This is it?* Caroline had asked after one look. *You dragged me all the way back here to see this stupid waterfall? I thought you said it was something special.* What would have constituted "special" to Caroline? he wondered. A two-hundred-store, multilevel shopping mall. A fifty-bucks-a-meal restaurant. A grocery, convenience or liquor store on every corner.

Finally Annabeth spoke on an exhalation of breath. "Oh, Josiah, this is beautiful."

The faint sense of pride he felt was ridiculous. He owned the land, but he'd had no hand in creating this place. He couldn't take any responsibility for it. He shouldn't take pride in it.

But he did.

And it was the first time in a very long time that he'd taken pride in anything.

There were rocks all around, most big enough to stretch out on. She went to stand on one sunny, flat table rock, and Josiah followed her, concentrating on not watching her while she watched the falls.

"Can you ever swim in this water?"

"If you're brave enough, or hot enough. The temperature in the creek is pretty constant, somewhere around fifty-eight degrees. In the pools like this, though, if they get enough sunlight in the summer, they'll warm up a few degrees."

As if his mention of the sun reminded her, she bent to set the camera down, then began tugging at her sweatshirt. This time he couldn't resist watching, especially when the untucked T-shirt underneath decided to follow the heavier garment up. The clingy pink fabric cleared the waistband of her jeans, then slid further to reveal an inch, two, three of skin. By now her head and arms were lost inside the sweatshirt, and her midriff, along with a thin strip of pale ivory-shaded bra, was exposed.

Nonchalantly, as if it were no big deal, as if he saw such sights on a regular basis, as if he didn't have a sudden desire to see a whole lot more, he reached out, caught hold of the hem of her T-shirt and tugged it down. "Oh, thanks," she remarked as she emerged from the sweatshirt, her hair tumbling back down. She straightened her T-shirt, then tied the other shirt by its sleeves around her waist.

Oh, thanks. As if she hadn't realized and hadn't much cared that she was about to pull her T-shirt off with the other one. As if she hadn't just given him a more intimate glimpse of a woman's body than he'd had in more than three years.

Damn, but he was in sorry shape.

She picked up her camera again and snapped a few pictures, then let it hang loosely by the strap as she gracefully lowered herself to the rock. "Do you have family in the valley besides your cousin?"

"Some." He chose to sit a few feet away, where the rushing water had carved a natural bench from the soft stone.

"Your parents?"

"My father is dead, and when he died, my mother moved to Fort Smith to take care of my grandmother."

"And you're an only child who hasn't yet married and produced children of your own to carry on the family name."

He gave her a long look. Was this a sneakier way of getting an answer to her question two days ago about marriage? Or was it idle curiosity or, worse, business? "Considering I'm not much interested in this book you're planning to write, I'm not sure I should even talk to you," he remarked.

"Why?"

"I wouldn't care to pick up a copy and see anything I've said written there."

She returned his look evenly, only with a hint of a smile. "Do you have any secrets?"

Secrets. No, he didn't have any of those. Everyone in the valley knew everything there was to know about him. They knew his troubles with the farm and his troubles with Caroline. They recognized his despair over losing part of his land, knew that losing Kylie had been almost more than he could bear.

Outsiders wouldn't see his problems as anything unusual. Farmers lost their land on a depressingly regular basis. Divorces happened all the time. Court-ordered visitation agreements failed all too often. There was nothing at all out of the ordinary about his troubles.

But he didn't want them—didn't want his life—included in her book. He didn't want his failures put down on paper for the entertainment of anyone with the price of the book.

When he didn't answer her question, Annabeth gave in to the smile. "I won't write anything about you that you don't want written. I would like to use you as a source—you know an awful lot about the valley—but there doesn't have to be anything personal."

He wasn't sure he believed her. His trusting nature had disappeared about the same time Caroline had, and he saw no reason to find it again for a woman who reminded him entirely too much of Caroline.

"So...are you an only child?"

"Are *you?*"

If he expected his counterquestion to annoy her, he would be disappointed. Instead, she seemed pleased that he had asked. "I've got one brother and two sisters. They're all younger than I am—Bradley is twenty-one, Bonnie is nineteen and Christie is eighteen."

"Why the big age difference?"

"I'm illegitimate," she acknowledged with a shrug. "My mother didn't marry my stepfather until I was six. Three years later they started their own family."

She said it so carelessly, as if it didn't matter. He wondered if that were the case, wondered how it could *not* matter. Maybe in the city no one cared. Maybe, surrounded by hundreds of thousands of people, no one ever knew. But here in the valley, even in the 1990s, illegitimacy still carried a stigma. It was still considered a shameful thing.

But Annabeth didn't seem ashamed. She didn't seem any the worse for it. She certainly hadn't suffered for it.

"My stepfather has always treated me as if I were his own," she went on. "I don't even normally refer him to as my stepfather. At home, he's just Daddy."

"What about your other father?"

Abruptly she looked away, focusing her gaze on the waterfalls. "I haven't met him," she said flatly. Then, just as suddenly, she looked back at him. "In another five minutes my stomach's going to start growling. Do you want to skip the springs and head back and have lunch at the mill?"

Back at the bluff he'd been ready to do just that: cut the hike short, head back and bring an end to this time with her. Now he wanted more. He wanted to ask more questions, nosy questions, questions that were none of his business. He wanted to sit awhile longer here in the sun and listen to the water underlying the husky, soft sound of her voice. He wanted to look at her, to study her, to figure out why, when she was so wrong for this place, this valley and him, at this moment she seemed so right.

How long had it been since he'd wanted any company at all? How much longer since he'd wanted a woman's company? How long since he'd wanted to waste the better part of his day doing nothing but looking at and listening to a pretty woman from the city?

She had stood up, brushed off her clothes and shouldered her camera once again and was heading along the rocks to the bank before he finally agreed to her suggestion. "Sure."

He could forget about the springs for today. He had plenty of other things to occupy his mind.

And they all had to do with two subjects.

Annabeth.

And trouble.

* * *

As the wind rattled the panes in the window above her desk, Annabeth put her pen down, closed the folder she'd been studying and sat back in her chair. It was Friday, her tenth day in Dutchman's Valley. She had read just about everything ever written on the valley and its residents. She had talked to Miss Hilda several times, had made pages of notes and had ventured into town a couple of times for supplies and a moment's friendly chat with the store clerks. She had identified the major families and started on their genealogical charts, filling in births, deaths, marriages and children. Before she finished, she would know the dry history—the names, dates and figures—better than the families themselves.

Now she was ready to start on the interesting stuff—the interviews. Meeting people. Making friends.

She knew it wouldn't happen immediately. Few people would open up to her as easily as Miss Hilda had. Most would be like Josiah, suspicious of her interest, unwilling to trust a stranger with something so personal as the details of their lives.

She could have told Josiah on Saturday that her interest in him was purely personal, and it would have been more or less the truth. The state's interest in this project was simple: they wanted a bare-bones history of the settlement of the valley. Knowing that a struggling farmer named Josiah Miller, great-great-great-grandson of the original Josiah Miller, owned so many acres of land on Route 3 would be enough for them.

It was nowhere near enough for her.

She wondered how much *would* be enough.

More, she suspected, than she would get.

More than he would ever want to give.

Rising from her desk, she stretched, then headed upstairs to the loft. There she changed from sweatpants and shirt to jeans and a sweater. It was a chilly day, a reminder that winter, with its snow and ice and frigid temperatures, was fast approaching. She loved winter--loved the cold blast of the wind and the gray skies and the snow. She loved the foods—spicy chili and steaming beef stew—that everyone cooked when it was cold. She even loved the clothes—sweatpants and fleece-lined shirts, thick socks and snuggly sweaters, jackets and coats and scarves and gloves. She loved being all cozy and snug and warm when it was freezing outside.

But she had to do something about the heat before the temperatures dropped to freezing. The Franklin stove was cleaned and ready to go, but she hadn't yet seen to the fuel—firewood. There were a few pieces stacked at the end of the mill, but they were so ancient that they would bring only one great flame and a moment's warmth before crumbling into ash. She knew she could buy wood somewhere, but there was a part of her that wanted to provide at least a portion of it herself, just to prove—to herself or to others?—that she could. Maybe if Josiah didn't mind... He surely had the trees to spare.

She was on her way to the car when the steady sound of a hammer caught her attention. He had been working on the barn roof all this week. All too often she had found excuses to wander upstairs to the loft where she could see him from one window. Those were about the only times she *had* seen him since their hike Saturday. She had gone over once to deliver some fresh-baked cookies, but his truck had been gone and so she had left them, securely wrapped, on the back step.

She wasn't quite sure why she hadn't gone over other times, times when she'd known for sure that he was home. Because he already thought her pushy? Because he preferred his women less aggressive and more feminine? Because just once she would like for *him* to be the one to approach *her*?

But she went over there now, bypassing her car and crossing the road to his rutted driveway. She had a legitimate tenant-to-landlord question to ask, along with a neighborly offer.

The chickens announced her arrival before she had a chance to. By the time she stopped near the barn, he was already watching her and waiting.

"I'm going into town," she called, shielding her eyes. "Do you need anything?"

"No, thanks."

"I also have a favor to ask of you."

He didn't speak but simply waited for her to go on.

"Can I come up there?" she asked. Her neck was starting to stiffen from being tilted so far back, and she really preferred conversations where she could actually make out the expression on the other person's face.

"That's your favor?" he asked dryly.

"Of course not."

"Do heights bother you?" Before she could answer, he raised his hand to stop her. "Of course not. The ladder's around back."

By the time she'd circled the barn and climbed the ladder to the top, he was waiting to help her up the last step. While she caught her breath and her bearings, she held onto his hand—a little too tight, she realized when she saw his suspicious look. "You're not afraid of heights, are you?" he asked again, seeking reassurance.

She laughed and let go of him. "No, I'm not. You've got quite a view from up here." Stretched out as far as she could see to the south and for a fair distance to the east were his fields, plowed under now and awaiting next spring's planting. Pockets of trees dotted the land until the cultivated area gave way to forest, similar to the land surrounding the mill.

"So what's your favor?"

He started back to where he'd been working, and, moving gingerly, she followed him. "I noticed when we were in the woods Saturday that there are quite a few downed trees."

He picked up a hammer and a handful of nails. "And?"

"I was wondering if I could use them for firewood. I can do the cutting and splitting myself, and I would pay you a fair price."

After a long, measuring look, he began hammering shingles into place. "I suppose you know how to use a chain saw and an ax."

"I've done it before."

"And you're stronger than you look."

She shrugged even though he wasn't looking to see it.

"You know you could buy firewood with a lot less hassle in town."

"The only hassle is in dealing with you. What is it with you, Josiah?" she asked, not even mildly annoyed, although she sounded it. "Are you not capable of giving a simple yes-or-no answer?"

"I'm not sure I'm capable of dealing with a woman who thinks living in an abandoned old sawmill makes sense, or who thinks it's natural to cut and split her own firewood, or who doesn't think twice about climbing onto the barn roof just to chat."

Annabeth sat down at the peak of the roof, her feet braced above the last completed row of shingles, her hands clasped around her knees. "Your wife didn't do any of those things, did she?" she asked, her voice very quiet, her breathing very shallow.

It was just a hunch, a guess that a man who refused to admit whether he'd been married before either had come close but been left at the church or had managed the marrying part but not the till-death-do-us-part part. And her guess was confirmed by the sudden, dark look he gave her.

She wished she had kept her mouth shut. He looked angry, suspicious, hurt and ashamed all at the same time. Slowly he set the hammer down, returned the nails to the box and sat back on his heels to face her. "You been asking questions about me in town?" His voice was even quieter than hers had been, his breathing more controlled.

"No." All she managed was a whisper, so she cleared her throat and tried again. "No, Josiah, I haven't."

"Then how do you know about Caroline?"

Caroline. It was a pretty name, one that brought with it images of delicate, oh-so-feminine beauty. Of a woman who knew how to act like a lady. Of a woman who didn't enjoy doing a man's work or sliding down a dirt path, who didn't climb onto barns or know the business end of a chain saw.

Of a woman Josiah must have loved very much.

She looked away from him to a pasture below, where a horse grazed all alone. "It was just a guess," she said flatly.

"A guess."

She was used to being viewed with skepticism, to having her motives questioned and everything she said doubted. She knew that gaining a person's trust was often a slow, drawn-out process. Still, the disbelief in his voice stung.

"I would have found out, anyway, when I start going through the marriage and divorce records," she pointed out. "That's what the state wants from me, Josiah."

All those emotions slowly faded from his eyes, leaving them blank and hard. "So I was married. Now I'm not. Satisfied? Or do you want all the nasty details?"

Yes, she did. She was ashamed of herself for it, but she did want to know. She wanted to know if the end of his marriage was responsible for the three-year-long bad mood he claimed to be suffering. She wanted to know who Caroline was, where he had met her, how long they had been married. She wanted to know what had happened, if his marriage had been ended by death or divorce.

She wanted to know if he still loved her. If he ever might stop.

But she couldn't ask. If she did, it would destroy any chance of ever earning Josiah's trust.

When a moment passed in silence, followed by another and another, he finally returned to his work. He positioned a shingle, nailed it in place and reached for another. "You can have all the wood you need from my supply," he offered ungraciously.

She didn't say anything. After a moment, she got up and started toward the ladder at the opposite end.

"Annabeth?"

Still silent, she turned toward him.

"My marriage is personal. It's none of your business."

And business, she thought regretfully, was all they had between them. The business of her renting the mill from him. The business of being neighbors. The state's business. But in his opinion, there was nothing personal between them at all.

She made that first step onto the ladder, wishing briefly for a steadying hand as her foot sought the rung and found nothing but air. Then she found the step and quickly made her way to the ground.

On the drive into town, she forced Josiah out of her mind and concentrated instead on this afternoon's meeting. It might be utter foolishness, she knew, but she was going to the bank. She was going to introduce herself to the owner and president. To Stuart Dothan.

To her father.

She hadn't yet decided exactly what she would tell him. Somehow it seemed dishonest to hide her true identity from him, and she was a very honest person. On the other hand, knowing that she was his daughter might very well make him hostile. He had wanted no part of her or her mother thirty years ago. Why should he feel any differently now?

She had learned a little about the Dothan family in her preliminary research. They had settled in the valley in the mid-1800s, not long after Captain Miller. They had come from Ohio and had immediately set about forming the ragged settlement into a town and creating a market for their goods. Although one Dothan a few generations ago had tried his hand at farming and logging, primarily they had been businessmen. For a long time they had owned every business in the Corner, with the exception of the blacksmith's shop and the sawmill. Now their holdings were down to the bank, the grocery store and a share of the feed store, which left Stuart the most prosperous man in the valley.

She parked her car in front of the bank and went inside. It wasn't big—just two teller windows and a single desk, along with two private offices in back. The desk was unmanned, but one of the tellers politely escorted her back to

Stuart's office, leaving her alone and unannounced in the doorway.

Swallowing hard, she stopped just inside and for a moment merely looked. All these years she'd had images of how her father should look—tall and strong, handsome, with graying hair and laughing eyes. He should be warm and affectionate, friendly and loving. He should regret that he had dismissed his twenty-two-year-old pregnant lover, that he had sent her away to give birth by herself, to raise his child by herself. He should regret that he'd never known his daughter, that he had never seen her, that he didn't even know whether she was alive.

Well, Stuart Dothan was tall, handsome, gray-haired. He did have nice eyes—brown, a shade darker than her own. He looked like a nice man, a man everyone would call friend. But he didn't look as if he had any regrets—none so deep, at least, that they left any mark. He looked comfortable and at ease with himself. As if he wouldn't change a thing in his life.

She was trembling, she realized, and her palms were damp. Nervously she shoved them into the pockets of her sweater as she studied him. She wondered what color his hair had been before it had gone gray. Maybe blond, like her own? She had never asked her mother, had never asked for many details about her father at all, but at every family gathering, with every family portrait, she had wondered. Seeing herself—the only fair-skinned blonde in a black-haired, dark-eyed family—she had always wondered.

And now here he was. The man who, with her mother, had given her life. Her other father, as Josiah had called him, distinguishing him from the one who had given her a lifetime of love.

What had drawn her mother to this man thirty-one years ago? What had made her cancel her plans to spend the rest of the summer after college graduation traveling around the country and spend those weeks here instead? What had made her fall in love with this man?

He was entering figures into the computer that took up a large portion of his work space when finally he noticed her. Offering a warm smile, he got to his feet. "I'm sorry. I didn't see you there. Come in. Have a seat."

Annabeth obeyed.

"I'm Stuart Dothan. And, since we don't get many strangers in town, you must be our historian. I was wondering when I would get a chance to meet you."

When he extended his hand, she hesitantly accepted it. It felt strange shaking hands with her father, even stranger that he didn't know that he was. All he saw in looking at her was a stranger. A historian. He didn't see his own child.

But he had never wanted to see his own child.

"I'm Annabeth Gibbs."

He sat down again and pushed a sheaf of papers to one side. "I suppose it's sexist of me, but when I hear the word *historian*, I think of a wrinkled old man with white hair. You're a lovely young lady."

Maybe a familiar young lady? she wanted to ask. Didn't he see some resemblance to his mother or his sister, maybe to a cousin or an aunt? "Thank you, Mr. Dothan." Her voice wasn't steady, and neither were her hands. She clasped them tightly in her lap, then took a deep breath. "I won't keep you long today. You know why I've come to the valley. I would like to set up a time when you and I can talk in detail about your family and the role they've played in Dutchman's Valley, along with your own contributions."

"I can be available anytime that's convenient for you. That's one of the advantages of being your own boss." He said that last with a self-deprecating smile that she judged as sincere. He might well be the wealthiest person in the valley, but he didn't seem superior or condescending about it. "I'm glad to see someone finally expressing an interest in the valley. We're so isolated up here that sometimes we feel forgotten. Tell me, how did the state come to choose you?"

Her own smile, just starting, began slipping. No one had asked that question yet—not Miss Hilda and certainly not Josiah. Neither of them had found it odd that, with all the talent in their own state, an outsider had been brought in for this particular project. She could lie and attribute the grant to her previous projects... No, she couldn't, she admitted. She rarely lied—she didn't want to expend the energy required to keep stories straight—and never about important things. Never about her work.

"They didn't choose me," she said at last, forming each word carefully. "The project was my idea, but the state government is providing the financing."

"I hadn't realized that. I just assumed they had hired you. Now why would a young woman from...where was it I heard? North Carolina?"

"South Carolina." She swallowed hard. "By way of Alabama."

His expression remained unchanged. Maybe he had never known her mother was living in Alabama at the time of their affair...although Annabeth knew Lynette had given him her address before she'd left the valley all those years ago. In case he changed his mind. In case he ever decided to see his daughter.

Maybe he had forgotten.

Or, more likely, maybe he had never cared.

"So why would a pretty young girl from South Carolina by way of Alabama be interested in a place like Dutchman's Valley?"

She had given a great deal of thought to what she would tell him when they met, but she'd been unable to make any decisions. Now the choice came entirely too easily. The words, prompted by some darker emotion that she couldn't name, came out before she had even really thought about them. "Curiosity. My mother spent part of a summer here over thirty years ago. She thought it was the most beautiful place she had ever seen."

There was a moment's sharp silence following her reply. The temperature in the room seemed to drop a few degrees, and she swore she could feel her welcome slipping away bit by bit. Slowly the friendliness faded from his face, taking a bit of color along with it, and shadows darkened his eyes.

His scowl was every bit as potent as his smile, and it silently damned her and painted him with his own guilt. Maybe he had forgotten about her mother coming from Alabama. Maybe he had forgotten *her*. But he remembered his affair with Lynette.

With no more than a look, he admitted that much.

Moving very carefully, very precisely, he folded his hands together on the desk top. They were pampered hands, she thought, the skin smooth, the nails neatly trimmed, with a well-worn gold band on his fourth finger. They reminded her of her stepfather's hands—curious, when nothing else about him brought her stepfather to mind. Hands that did nothing more strenuous than lifting a book or typing on a computer. Hands with fewer calluses than her own.

"What was your mother's name?" There was no emotion in his voice, just a blank *waiting*. Waiting to have his suspicions confirmed. Waiting to hear news he had never wanted to hear.

"Lynette Bingham."

The blankness slowly gave way to a sort of perverse satisfaction that she had given the proper answer. "And what exactly is it that you want from me?"

He wasn't pleased or interested, not at all curious. He was face-to-face with his grown daughter for the first time in his life, and all he had to show, all he felt, was icy suspicion and distrust.

Her mother had tried to warn her, but Annabeth had blithely refused to listen. She wasn't looking for recognition or acknowledgment, she had insisted. She didn't want a relationship with her father; she merely wanted to know about that side of her family, that part of her history.

And all that was true. She couldn't possibly love any father more than she loved her stepfather. As she'd told Josiah, at home she never referred to Frank Gibbs as her stepfather. He was Daddy, the man who had read her bedtime stories and tucked her in at night. The man who had helped her overcome her fear of thunderstorms, who had taught her to play baseball, who had loved her and encouraged her to try anything and everything. No one could ever take his place in her life or in her love.

But it still hurt that Stuart didn't have any response other than this. It hurt that he wasn't even willing to get to know her before condemning her. It hurt that, without even knowing her, he could hate being her father so much.

"I don't want anything from you except information," she replied quietly. "I came here to do a job, and—"

"What will it take to make you leave?"

Sighing softly, she glanced around the office. Lavishly decorated, it would fit perfectly in any high-rent business district. For the town of Dutchman's Corner, it was downright luxurious. So the Dothan family had money, and Stuart wasn't above using it to get his own way. She wondered idly if he had tried to pay her mother to leave all those years ago. Had he offered her money to get out of his life, or had he merely sent her away with anger? "I'm not leaving until my research is done. I don't want your money or your attention or your affection. Just your cooperation."

It was clear in his eyes that he didn't believe her. "I'll write you a check—"

"I don't want it," she repeated, rising to her feet. "I'd just like to make an appointment when we could talk—"

This time *he* interrupted. "Who else have you told?"

"No one."

"No one?" he echoed. "Not even Hilda?"

She gave him a small, cynical smile. "My work here depends on being accepted by the people I'm trying to write about. Announcing that I'm your illegitimate daughter isn't going to make that acceptance come any easier. On the contrary, it will make people look at me more harshly. I dealt with the fact of my illegitimacy years ago. I'm not ashamed of it, but it's nothing to be proud of, either." She paused briefly. "I have a family—a father who loves me very much, who claims me as his own. I have sisters and a brother and grandparents and cousins. I don't need anything from you except your cooperation on this project. Will I get that?"

"Not in this lifetime!" he swore, rising from his chair.

"Fine. Then I'll get the information elsewhere—from your neighbors and your friends and your family. And you can explain to your wife and everyone else why you refuse to help."

Bracing his hands on the desk top, he leaned menacingly toward her. "You stay away from my wife and family," he insisted heatedly.

Did *family* include children? she wondered wistfully. Brothers and sisters? She would give almost anything to know, but she didn't ask. She didn't relax her control one bit. "Then work with me."

Slowly he sank down again, settling back in the chair and fixing a hostile stare on her. "I want your promise you won't tell anyone in the valley who you are."

"You have it," she replied without hesitation. She had no problems with that. Neither Miss Hilda nor Josiah suspected that she had any ties of her own to this valley, and she wasn't going to volunteer the information. She wasn't going to make herself the subject of gossip.

She wasn't going to claim a father who wanted no part of her.

"How do I know I can trust you?"

"I believe you extracted a similar promise from my mother. She's kept it for more than thirty years." A promise that Lynette would never tell anyone in the valley that he had fathered her child. A promise that she would never seek anything from him—not a name for her baby, not child support, not any sort of relationship between him and Annabeth. "I'm my mother's daughter, Stuart. I keep my promises."

After another distrustful look, he finally drew an appointment book from a drawer. "I can schedule a few hours next Tuesday afternoon," he offered grudgingly. "Will that be enough?"

She thought of the hundreds of hours of interviews she would need for this book and smiled faintly. "It'll be a start. What time?"

"One o'clock."

"I'll be here. Thank you." With a nod, she left the office, closing the door quietly behind her. She was trembling from the inside out, and the shakes didn't begin to ease until she was outside in the bright afternoon sunshine.

Had she just made a serious mistake in telling Stuart the truth? she wondered. Maybe. Probably. She hadn't meant to, but the words had just come of their own accord. Maybe it was because her mother had always placed such tremendous value on honesty, or maybe because she placed a high premium on it herself. She was too open to ever get away with telling lies.

Oh, well, if she had screwed up, she would just have to deal with it. Better that Stuart learn the truth and get angry now than to find out later, after they'd gotten better acquainted, after she discovered whether or not she liked the man, whether or not they could be friends.

She was about to get into her car when a hand-lettered sign across the street caught her attention. Firewood For Sale had long ago been painted on a square of plywood that was nailed to what looked like a piece of mop handle and stuck into the ground at the edge of the gas-station driveway. Slamming her door again, she crossed the street and went inside.

The mechanic and sole attendant was in the garage working on a shiny green pickup. Only the lower half of his body was visible under the hood, although she could hear his voice, low and annoyed, as he issued a string of curses. Circling around to the other side of the truck, she rested her hands on the fender and cleared her throat. "Excuse me."

Startled, he jerked up, banged his head and dropped his wrench. When he first met her gaze, he was scowling, but that quickly gave way to an appraisal of whatever he was able to see and an appreciative smile of the sort she had learned to beware of before she was fifteen.

"Well, well. It's the stranger in town."

She didn't offer an introduction. She rarely bothered to get acquainted with men who looked at women the way this one did. "The sign out front says Firewood For Sale."

"It does?" He glanced out through the garage doors, though he didn't take his eyes off her nearly long enough to even locate the tilting sign, much less read it. "Yeah, old Leon—he's the station owner—sells firewood for a little extra cash."

"Where can I find old Leon?"

"You got a truck?"

"No, I don't."

"Leon doesn't deliver anymore. He cuts it, but you have to pick it up yourself." He wiped his hands on a greasy rag, then slowly came around the truck. Annabeth resisted the urge to back away. "Now, for the right incentive, I could be convinced to deliver it for you. Why, I'd even stack it up right close to the mill for you."

"And what would that incentive be, Mr. . . . ."

"Walker. You can call me Tony."

"You're Josiah's cousin."

He took a step back, and the phony charm slid away. "Guilty." Then, with a rueful look, he added, "As far as Josiah's concerned, I'll always be guilty."

She didn't ask of what. Even though the curiosity was about to eat her alive. Even though it was a sure bet she would learn a lot more from Tony Walker than Josiah would ever tell her.

"About the wood . . ."

He grinned. "I'll be neighborly. I'll deliver and stack it for nothing. You can consider it a gesture of welcome to the valley."

She gave him a long look, from the dark hair and dark eyes so like Josiah's to his all-too-easy grin to the baggy coveralls that couldn't hide an all-too-nice body. "I don't care much for gestures, Mr. Walker. I'd rather hire you to do the job for me."

"I said I'd do it for nothing. You want to spend a little extra money? Give it to Leon. He never asks for as much as the stuff is worth."

His suggestion revised her opinion of him a notch upward. "Thank you. I will. Where can I find him?"

"Follow Sycamore Street until it runs into a dirt road. It's the last house on the right before it dead-ends. Tell him I'll pick it up for you in the morning."

"Thanks." She was almost out the door when he spoke again.

"Why didn't you ask Josiah to help you with this?"

She considered their brief conversation on the roof this afternoon. All she had wanted was to ask two simple questions: *Do you want anything from town?* and *Can I use that downed wood?* What had gone wrong? How had they wound up talking about his wife? How had a reasonably friendly conversation degenerated into anger and distrust and shame?

"You did ask, didn't you? And he turned you down. When I heard that he'd let you move into the mill, I thought maybe..." He broke off with a sigh. "I'll let you in on a little secret— What's your name? Beth?"

"Annabeth."

"The next time you want Josiah to do something for you and he says no, just tell him that you're going to ask me instead. I guarantee, that will change his mind. Cousin Josiah has this need to protect pretty ladies from me."

Of course, that roused her curiosity, too. She wished she wouldn't feel sneaky asking about Josiah behind his back. She wished she didn't feel obligated to find out whatever she learned about him from the man himself. She wished she could pull up a chair and ask Tony all her questions without feeling guilty for it later.

But she couldn't. She couldn't even consider it without feeling guilty.

And so she turned the conversation from Josiah to safer ground. "Do I need protection from you, Mr. Walker?" she asked coolly.

He gave her another appraising look, but this one didn't feel quite so insulting. This time he seemed to be looking at her as a person rather than merely a woman. "No," he replied with a grin. "No, ma'am, I don't believe you do."

Chapter 4

Josiah stood at the living-room window and gazed across the barren yard to the mill. It was another cool morning, the sun shining bright but offering little warmth. But it wasn't winter yet. By eleven the chill would be gone, and it would be a pleasant afternoon for working outside or taking a walk or sitting beside the millpond.

Apparently, Annabeth didn't want to wait for pleasant. She was sitting out there now, Miss Hilda's twig chair pulled onto a patch of yellowed grass, with her lazy mutt at her feet and a pile of books on her lap. Something about her pose struck him as expectant. Maybe she was waiting for company. But who besides Miss Hilda would drive all the way out here to see her? Who did Annabeth know yet besides the librarian and him?

Maybe she was waiting for *him*. That wasn't as conceited as it sounded. She had come around often enough in the last week and a half, even though he hadn't always been welcoming. Maybe she figured now it was his turn to make the effort, and her sitting outside certainly made it easier. It made the prospect of going visiting more appealing.

Besides, he had business, too. There was the plate from those cookies she'd baked to return, and arrangements to make for the firewood. She needed to choose a place for him to stack it before he took it over.

And those were simply excuses. Truth was, he couldn't think of a nicer way to spend a cool Saturday morning than sitting beside the millpond with Annabeth Gibbs.

Turning away from the window, he glanced around the room. His time would be better spent working. If he couldn't find enough farm chores to keep him busy, there was plenty of work here. The whole house needed cleaning—not just picking up and vacuuming, but a full-blown, top-to-bottom spring cleaning, even if it was November. Except for the kitchen and his bedroom, most of the place had a dreary, dismal unlived-in look. As if one long-ago day, its residents had gotten up and walked away, leaving everything behind.

Which was pretty much what had happened. Oh, Caroline had taken plenty with her—clothes and jewelry, books and mementos, the china her parents had given them when they got married and the cookware his parents had bought. She had taken the crystal wineglasses they had received from her friends, the television with its unwatchable reception and his stereo.

She had shown more discretion in packing for Kylie. She had taken just the clothes the baby could wear at that time, her playpen but not the crib, her bottles and teething rings and only the toys that could fit into one small box. The rest of their daughter's belongings, she had left where they were. Toys in the living room, baby-sized dishes in the kitchen, outgrown clothes in the closet, the crib and everything else in the nursery.

For a time he had taken to sleeping on the floor in the nursery, covered with Kylie's quilts, her flat little pillow under his head. Then he had limited his time in there to a few hours in the evening, sitting in the rocker in the dark before heading to his room for bed.

Now he didn't go in there at all. He didn't touch any of the toys left behind. When he opened the kitchen cabinet, he didn't look at the little dishes in their corner on the shelf. When he looked for a can of something to heat for dinner, he ignored the jars of baby food in the cupboard. He pretended she had never lived here.

No doubt, he should clean. He should give the house a thorough cleaning, should remove any sign of Kylie and Caroline from the house as thoroughly as they had been removed from his life. He should dispose of Caroline's wedding ring, still sitting in the dust, should take down every picture of her that hung on the walls. He should dismantle Kylie's crib and changing table and give them to someone who could use them. He should donate her baby clothes, too, and her quilts and blankets and all her toys. He should strip the pastel paint off the rocker in her room and set it, the wood bare, in the sun to weather and turn gray. He should paint over the pale yellow walls, should take down the lacy curtains, should make the room as dark as it was now airy.

He should.

But not today.

His footsteps echoing through the empty house, he went into the kitchen and took the heavy stoneware plate from the dish drainer. Letting himself out the back door, he headed for the mill.

The dog noticed him first, waddling over to meet him at the edge of the clearing. Josiah bent to scratch his head, then looked up to find Annabeth watching. She didn't offer a greeting, but she didn't look as if she wanted him to go away, either. That was something.

Rising slowly, he approached her, not stopping until he was only a few feet away. "I brought your plate back," he said unnecessarily. "Thanks for the cookies."

"You can set it inside."

He waited a moment for something else—another look, another word—but she turned her attention back to her books. His jaw tightening with disappointment, he started toward the mill. He was halfway there when she did speak again.

"There's fresh coffee in the pot, sugar on the counter and cream in the refrigerator. Help yourself."

When he glanced back, though, she was still reading.

She had scavenged an old plank of wood from somewhere and had installed it above the worktable for a shelf. Covered with lace-edged napkins—no, old-fashioned handkerchiefs, he saw—it served as her cupboard, holding dinner plates, saucers, bowls, glasses and coffee mugs. Service for four. He placed the plate he carried on top of the others, then took down a mug and filled it with coffee.

When he'd delivered her furniture last week—had helped deliver it, he corrected—he hadn't paid too much attention to what she'd done in here. Of course, then he'd been too busy paying attention to *her*. Now, as he stirred sugar and cream into his coffee, he looked around. Lace curtains hung at the windows, tied back by ribbons adorned with wooden cutouts of prettily painted wildflowers. The worn love seat was covered with a quilt and held several small pillows for extra comfort, and a half-dozen hand-loomed rugs were scattered around the room.

Pictures hung on the walls, too—family photographs alongside her own pictures. There were mountains and valleys, flowers and trees, oceans and beaches and thoughtful, powerful black-and-white portraits of people. Mountain people. An old woman, probably called aunt or granny by everyone she knew, family or not. A small girl, her black hair clumsily cut, wearing no shoes and a plain cotton shift and a streak of dirt across her cheek, staring with ageless dark eyes into the camera. An elderly couple, the old man in overalls and a work shirt, the woman in her best dress, surrounded by their children, grandchildren and great-grandchildren, married probably fifty years or more and still holding hands.

He sighed softly. It was supposed to have been that way for his grandparents, for his parents and for Caroline and him. Unbroken ties, big families, love and commitment and forever. But his grandparents were all dead, except for his mother's mother, who no longer knew her own family. His parents had intended to have a large family, but he'd been the only child they had ever managed, and his father had died five years before the birth of his only grandchild.

It was just as well. Losing Kylie would have broken his heart, just as it had broken Josiah's.

Going outside again, he leaned against the hitching rail and sipped his coffee. It was rich and strong, the way it should be, and not bitter, the way he always made it. Before Annabeth left, after learning everything there was to know about them, maybe he would ask her to teach him to make coffee like this.

"You have some nice pictures."

She nodded a polite thanks.

"I like the ones of the people. The black-and-whites." He had looked at the others, the color photographs of her family, only long enough to see that she appeared in only one group shot. That had been long enough to suspect, even if he hadn't already known, that she didn't quite fit in. She had done nothing when the picture was snapped to draw attention to herself—in fact, she had looked rather pensive and quiet, while her mother laughed and her younger sisters had mugged for the camera—and she had been dressed the same as the others, the women all in white dresses, the men in white trousers and shirts. Still, she had stood out. The only blonde in a black-haired family. The only spot of sunlight on a dark day.

How many people back in South Carolina knew that the laughing man with his arm possessively around Annabeth's shoulders wasn't her father? How many suspected? She had treated the issue so lightly last weekend, but did it ever bother her that she didn't belong to him in the one way that counted to most people?

"Are you being lazy today?" she asked, closing her books at last and turning her full attention to him.

"Even God took a day of rest."

Her smile came slowly, reluctantly. "I wasn't sure you had a sense of humor."

"I used to." He wondered whether she would ask the obvious question—*What happened to it?*—but she didn't. But silence didn't come easily to her. She drew her lower lip between her teeth, then finally released it with a sigh.

With his coffee mug, he gestured toward her books. "What's all that?"

"Folktales. Fairy tales. Tales of witches and goblins and ghosts."

"What do they have to do with your work?"

"Not much yet. I do hope to collect some folktales from this region and compare them to versions heard elsewhere. Mostly, though, these are for my other job."

"What other job?"

"Storytelling. Miss Hilda has asked me to do some stories at the autumn festival next weekend."

"Storytelling," he repeated. "Like around the campfire?"

She nodded.

"Back in South Carolina you can sit around telling stories to little kids and call it a job?"

She ignored his skepticism. "Actually, I call it fun. Although I'm doing it for free here, often I do get paid for it—not a lot, but I'm not doing it for the money, anyway. I like it."

Unswayed by her enthusiasm, he just shook his head. Storytelling hardly seemed a proper activity for an adult. Reading a bedtime story to your kid—that was fine. He had read to Kylie from the time she'd come home from the hospital. It had been his favorite time of the day, a quiet time for just him and his little girl, for getting to know each other. But to spend an entire afternoon telling tales to kids who weren't your own, for nothing more than entertainment, seemed like a waste to him.

Even without the storytelling, spending an entire afternoon with kids was more than he could manage.

She left the books on the chair and came to stand in front of him. She was wearing another of those long skirts and a plain white blouse, with a fine quilted shawl in shades of lavender and dusky rose and shadowy blue wrapped around her shoulders. "I can see you're not impressed, but that's only because you've never heard *my* stories. Would you like to hear one? I can tell you about ghostly hitchhikers and headless horsemen. Or how about ghosts guarding treasures for black-hearted pirates? Haunted houses, warnings from the grave, undying love or things that go bump in the night?"

She was, at the same time, both serious and teasing, tempting and gently taunting. And he was surely tempted, no doubt. To return her enchanting smile. To listen to one of her stories. To catch hold of the long fringe swaying from her shawl and pull her closer. To continue listening to her soft, expressive voice and to silence her with a kiss. To forget the ways she reminded him of Caroline—superficial likenesses, for the most part—and to remember the ways she could make him feel.

Less weary.

Amused.

Alive.

Aroused.

The good Lord help him, he was tempted.

Reading something in his face—the path his thoughts had taken? he wondered—she fell silent and stood not quite still only a few feet or so in front of him. He watched her, and she watched him, and he thought about how long it had been since he'd indulged in a kiss, just a kiss, and what the consequences would be for him, for her, for *them*.

Because Annabeth wasn't a woman to kiss lightly, and he had been alone for so long that for him there could be no such thing as *just* a kiss. But he wasn't ready for anything more. Less than two weeks ago he'd had to decide if he even wanted to continue living. It was too soon to even think about getting involved with someone—especially with a woman from the city. A woman who wouldn't be here more than a year. A woman who, even superficially, made him think of Caroline.

Still, it would be nice, wouldn't it, just to touch more than her hand? To be that close to someone once again even for only the length of a kiss? To have that kind of emotional connection?

She moved a step closer. Why not? he wondered without surprise. Hadn't she made most of the gestures so far? But before he could respond, before he could do anything more than lift one hand from the hitching rail, the sound of a powerful engine cut through the morning stillness.

Annabeth sighed softly, cursing the timing. "A word of warning, Josiah," she said regretfully. "That's going to be your cousin Tony. He's delivering a load of firewood for me."

But he wasn't paying attention to her. Instead he was watching the road as the truck came into view. As Tony pulled past the clearing, then began backing in, Josiah shifted his gaze to her. "I told you you could have whatever you needed."

"I didn't want you to *give* me anything," she reminded him. "I wanted permission to cut my own wood."

"Why?" he asked sharply. He was all tense now, she saw—his forehead wrinkled, his jaw held tight, his fingers gripping the rail. "To prove that you could?"

"Yes. I have to live here on my own terms. I ask for help when I need it, but I have to know that I can take care of myself."

"You didn't cut this wood yourself."

"No, but I paid for it. Would you have let me pay for yours?"

He didn't answer. Once again, he was paying no attention to her. With another sigh, Annabeth turned away and walked to the truck to greet Tony as he climbed out. He was wearing boots, jeans and a work shirt, identical except in color to Josiah's. He was shorter, leaner, but side by side, the two men could pass for brothers. Feuding brothers.

"I didn't know he would be here," Tony said softly.

"The surprise is mutual. Thanks for bringing the wood out."

"Where do you want it?"

She hadn't taken time to consider a location. She needed someplace relatively close to the mill, someplace relatively sheltered. There was a big oak tree only twenty feet away, but its leafless branches wouldn't do much to keep the rain off. What she needed was a shed, which would require lumber and supplies from town and her landlord's permission—and he wasn't looking real permissive at the moment. "Just dump it right here."

"I told you I would stack it for you."

Her smile was taut. "That's not necessary." After a glance at Josiah, she added, "I'll figure out where to put it and stack it myself this afternoon."

"It won't take long—"

She interrupted him with another smile. "I appreciate it, Tony, but I'm perfectly capable of doing it myself. Let's not cause any problems here, okay? Come on, and I'll help you unload."

"I don't need any help." He swung into the back of the truck and, in short order, dumped the entire contents of the truck bed on the ground. After climbing down again and closing the tailgate, he turned toward his cousin at the rail. "Josiah."

He didn't say a word, didn't do more than give the smaller man a look of pure loathing.

"It's been over three years, Josiah," Tony said softly, miserably. "How long are you going to hate me?"

Josiah dumped the coffee left in his cup into the sandy dirt, where drops splattered on Tony's boots. Then he turned and went inside the mill.

For a long time Tony just stood there, his back to Annabeth, his shoulders rounded. Finally, his eyes dark and sad, he returned to the truck, where she waited. "Thanks," she said awkwardly, feeling as if she shouldn't be witness to the emotions he felt so strongly. "I'm sorry...."

"Yeah, everyone's sorry—except Josiah. We used to be best friends, ever since we were little kids, but he hasn't even spoken to me since she left. We're not the only ones to blame. It was his fault, too." He sighed heavily. "But he doesn't care about that. He doesn't care about much of anything besides hiding away out here and hating the world."

After a brief glance at the mill, Tony climbed into the truck and closed the door. Looking at her through the open window, he changed the subject. "I hear you'll have a booth at the festival next Saturday."

Inside the shawl where she was holding the ends together, Annabeth's hands were clenched tight. *He hasn't even spoken to me since she left.* She? Caroline? Was Tony somehow involved in the breakup of Josiah's marriage? Was that why best friends all their lives couldn't share a civil word now?

Forcing her attention back to the conversation, she smiled unsteadily. "That's right. Miss Hilda was supposed to arrange it for me."

"Storytelling, huh? Sounds like fun."

Stepping back as he started the engine, she wished Josiah shared his views. "Maybe I'll see you there."

"You can count on it—unless you bring my idiot of a cousin along. See you later."

She waved; then, when he was out of sight, she turned to face the mill. Josiah hadn't yet come out again, although she imagined he would now that Tony was gone. He would come out, cold and brusque and brushing her off, and would go home to do only God knew what in peace. Brood? Mope? Pout?

Well, he could do that. Even though she wished he would stay. Even though she wished they could have one of their pleasant conversations, with no dark undertones brought on by her questions or his suspicions, her shortcomings or his failures.

Even though she wished he would kiss her.

And the day that happened, she figured, he would welcome his cousin Tony with open arms, her father would proudly proclaim their true relationship, and gold would rain down from the heavens.

But Josiah would have let *her* kiss *him*. If Tony hadn't interrupted, if he hadn't gotten annoyed over her purchase of the wood and his cousin's appearance, she knew he would have let her kiss him.

Now the moment had been lost.

Maybe it would come again.

Maybe not.

She was standing near the woodpile, studying the lot and the ground around the mill, when Josiah finally came out again. Their gazes met and locked. His, as she had expected, was angry. With her? she wondered.

He moved to stand on the other side of the pile. "You need to stack this someplace."

She knew that. She liked neat, orderly stacks of wood around a house—liked the scent and the homey look, liked not having to reach into a jumbled pile where inhospitable little creatures had taken up residence. Still, she held the shawl tighter and asked, "Why?"

"Are you trying to be difficult?"

"Some folks would say I don't have to try. Some folks think I'm incredibly difficult by nature."

"I believe that."

She glanced down the road where Tony's green truck had disappeared. "Other folks think I'm awfully easy to get along with," she added, the slyness in her voice tempered by caution.

He glanced in the same direction, then back at her. "I believe that, too."

She studied him for a moment, then took a deep breath and plunged in. "Your cousin seems very sorry for whatever he did."

"He should be."

"You're not a very forgiving sort, are you?"

"No. Not at all."

"Don't you ever make mistakes, Josiah? Don't you ever do the wrong thing? Don't you ever strike out at someone or see something you want and take it or tell a lie because it's convenient?"

"No."

She circled the wood and stopped near him. "Then you're an extraordinary and fortunate man. But the rest of us, including your cousin, are just humans. We do the best we can, but sometimes that's not enough."

"Do you know what Tony did?"

"No." She could have stopped there, could have said nothing else, but she didn't. "I know it somehow involved Caroline."

He became very still and quiet, very carefully controlled, just as he had yesterday on the roof. The change made her want to call her words back, made her want to put this conversation to rest and talk about something—anything—else.

"Another lucky guess?" he asked, his voice threateningly low.

She swallowed hard. "No. He said you used to be best friends, but you haven't spoken to him since *she* left. I assume he meant Caroline."

For a long time he just looked at her, his expression somewhere between anger and disgust, pride and shame. So his wife had left him. She wanted to tell him it was no big deal. Marriages broke up every day. One spouse left and started a new life, and the one left behind dealt with it and went on, too. It was nothing to be ashamed of, nothing to wound your pride. It was nothing to be so protective of three years later.

Unless he still missed her.

Unless he found it impossible to deal with and go on with his own life.

Unless he still loved her.

Darn it, that wasn't something she could think about right now.

Feeling strangely hollow inside, she moved a step toward him. "I know you think I'm nosy, Josiah, and can't mind my own business, but I haven't been asking for information about you. If I did ask, I could get it. With the right questions, Tony would tell me everything and never realize that he was opening up to a stranger, and Miss Hilda would confirm it. But I don't work that way. Other than the fact that it took place, your marriage has nothing to do with my research. I won't deny that I'm interested because..." She offered him a small smile that brought no response. "Well, because I *am* nosy. And you're my neighbor. And I like you. But beyond the statistical data I need for the state, I won't be snooping around in your life. I give you my word."

A moment passed, then another, and still he said nothing. Unforgiving and untrusting. Her word meant nothing to him. Finally, with a sigh, she turned away and went into the mill.

Upstairs she changed into jeans and a T-shirt, then sat down on the steps to put on her boots. She had to do something with all that wood out front, and now that she had sent Tony away and had probably offended Josiah into leaving, she had to do it all alone.

He might have been offended, but he wasn't gone. As she came out of the mill, pulling on a pair of work gloves, she saw him standing at the end, looking off toward the stream. He didn't glance her way, but he knew she was there. "You need a woodshed."

"I know. I was going to ask permission—"

He gave her a sidelong look then that stopped her words. "I'll be tearing down the storage shed this week so I can put up another one. We can use the wood from that."

His look dared her to refuse, just as she had refused his offer of firewood, and for a moment she considered it. She could buy the materials relatively cheaply and put up the shed herself. She had a book on her desk that gave step-by-step instructions for simple construction. But the wood from his shed would be old and gray, a match for the mill itself, and in good enough condition to keep a winter's supply of firewood dry. And if, as his "we" implied, he was offering to help her build it, to spend a few more hours in her company, how could she consider turning him down?

"Thank you," she said. "Let me know when you're ready to tear it down, and I'll help." This time she was the one issuing an unspoken challenge, and just as she had backed down only seconds ago, so did he now.

"First thing Monday morning."

"Fine. I'll bring breakfast."

For a moment he looked as if he wanted to refuse, then thought better of it. Resting her gloved hands on her hips, she smiled triumphantly.

Her gesture pulled her T-shirt taut. Josiah had noticed the shirt when she'd first come out; now he couldn't help but pay it—and what it covered—closer attention. It was white and fit as perfectly as if designed just for her. The fabric was thin, well-washed, and clung to her shoulders, her breasts and the flat sweep of her midriff. There was a pastel beach scene advertising her home state and a legend scrawled in hot pink across it: *Beautiful Places, Smiling Faces.* For all he knew, South Carolina might be the most beautiful place in the world—although he doubted it could compete with his valley—but there couldn't be a sand-and-sea-oats scene anywhere in the state with the charms of *this* one.

Or a face, either, so smiling and beautiful and full of life. All those times he had thought of her as pretty, he had been wrong. *Pretty* was too simple, too bland, too easy a word to use with Annabeth. *Pretty* covered many things—the weather, the morning fog hanging low in the valley, a robin red against a vivid blue sky, the daffodils that bloomed every spring at the base of the mailbox.

And Caroline. Caroline had been pretty.

But Annabeth was beautiful.

Absolutely, undeniably, make-you-hurt-inside beautiful.

And hurt, he thought with a sudden bleakness that chilled him through to his soul, was one thing he already had enough of.

* * *

Monday morning was chilly enough for a jacket, more than chilly enough to make eating breakfast on the tailgate of his pickup uncomfortable, Josiah acknowledged as he reached for the last of Annabeth's sausage-and-biscuit sandwiches. He should have invited her into the house, but he couldn't. Because he hadn't cleaned it yet? Because he didn't want her intruding there? Because it was his own personal little hell, filled with memories of Caroline and Kylie, with the echoes of a lifetime of happiness and three years of sorrow?

He didn't know, didn't want to even think about it. He hadn't invited her inside, and she hadn't complained, and that was enough on the subject.

She sat across from him, leaning against the side wall of the truck bed, her legs stretched out so that her feet almost touched him. She was wearing sweatpants today, thick socks and tennis shoes, a T-shirt and a sweatshirt and a Windbreaker bearing what looked like a school logo on the left breast. "What's the Citadel?" he asked, watching as she broke a cinnamon roll in half and returned a portion to the plate between them.

"A military college in Charleston."

"What's your connection?"

"I used to date a guy who went there. This jacket is about all I got out of a two-year relationship."

"And what did he get?"

She grinned. "My love and devotion for two years. And my cousin. I introduced him to Cassie, and that was the end for us."

Abruptly he looked away. It was ironic that they had each lost someone special—her lover, his wife—to a cousin. Only he hadn't exactly lost Caroline to Tony. His cousin had just been a brief diversion on Caroline's way back to the city— someone to fill her hours while Josiah was working, someone to give her the attention she felt she was lacking, someone to sweet-talk into helping her sneak away from Josiah and the valley.

She would have made it, too, thanks to Tony, if Josiah hadn't come in from the fields in the middle of the afternoon. She would have taken his baby daughter and disappeared. He never would have suspected they were going. He never would have had a chance to tell Kylie goodbye.

He didn't know if Caroline had been sleeping with Tony, didn't know if that explained her lack of interest in sex with *him,* and he didn't much care. That, he could have accepted. But helping Caroline try to spirit Kylie away...

He would never forgive Tony for that.

"Where did you go to school?" he asked, putting Tony and Caroline and Kylie out of his mind. It was too bright, too clear, too promising a day to think about the past.

"The College of Charleston. Daddy—my stepfather—is a professor there."

"A professor of what?"

"History."

What else? So she'd come by the interest naturally. "Is Gibbs *his* name or the other one's?"

"His."

"So what did you get from your..." He let it trail off, unsure of which word to use, and she laughed.

"I used to get confused, too. Most people call the birth father the real father or the natural father, but there couldn't be anything more natural or real about my relationship with Daddy. I like what you said before. The other one." She grew serious then. "Brown eyes. As far as I know, that's the only thing he and I have in common."

And if her birth father's brown eyes were as pretty, as trusting and charming as hers, it was no wonder her mother had gotten sucked in. He had probably made promises, and she had probably believed them. And when she had found out she was pregnant, what had his response been? What was hers? Back in the early sixties, unwed mothers had been rare enough to create something of a scandal. Had she been pressured to have an illegal abortion or to give her baby up for adoption? Had she been sent away to give birth among strangers or counseled to marry someone—anyone—just to give her baby a name? Had her parents accepted their pretty little illegitimate brown-eyed granddaughter, or had they been ashamed of her?

He couldn't imagine anyone being ashamed of Annabeth. If he had met her thirteen years ago, before marrying Caroline, he probably would have fallen hard for her. She was beautiful. Her body was well worth fantasizing about in the lonely dark hours of the night. She was open and guileless, funny and warm and unselfish. She took pleasure in simple things and found hope in everything. What more could a man ask for?

Even if he had met her four years ago, he would have been interested. Things had gone bad with Caroline by then. He had been working endlessly long days for rarely even enough money to pay his debts and little or no profit. He had come home each night to a wife who wouldn't speak to him or who only argued with him. To a wife who hated living on a farm, hated being broke, hated being away from the bustle of the city, hated the demands a newborn placed on her time, who most of all hated *him*. Oh, yes, he definitely would have been interested in Annabeth then. He wouldn't have done anything about it—being unfaithful to his wife even when he'd suspected her of the same sin had simply been out of the question—but he would have been tempted.

As he was tempted now. He needed some light in his life. He needed a reason besides work to get up in the morning. He wanted to be the man he'd been before things had gone wrong with Caroline. He wanted to rediscover the pleasure he'd found in life then—in a newborn calf or a fiery sunset, in a walk in the woods, in watching the rain from the shelter of the porch, in making angels in the snow and discovering the first blooms of spring breaking through the crust of that snow. He wanted to remember how it felt to laugh and what it was like to face each day with hope instead of grim determination.

For more than three years, he had sought solitude. Like a dog that had been whipped, he'd wanted to slink away and lick his wounds in private. He had done such a thorough job of shutting people out that now, when he went into town, folks he had known all his life rarely gave him more than a cautious nod.

He was tired of his solitude.

He was lonely.

He wanted to live again.

And Annabeth could teach him how.

She finished the last of her coffee, then stood up and brushed the seat of her pants. When she jumped over the side to the ground, the truck barely shook with her slight weight. "Have you already cleaned out the shed?" she asked, wandering that way.

"Yes." He recapped the Thermos, then joined her at the shed. She could walk right in; he had to duck his head to clear the low opening. Watching from inside, she laughed.

"Obviously you didn't build this."

"My grandfather did. He was five foot eight, and he didn't want to use one more foot of board than was absolutely necessary. I was taller than him before I was fourteen."

She moved in a slow circle around the perimeter of the shed, her shoes making scuffing sounds on the cement floor. Pausing in front of the lone window, a dirty, four-paned square in the east wall, she asked, "Do you remember him well?"

Even through the dirt, the sun touched her hair and warmed her face. She looked so pretty that he had to look away.

"Yeah, I do. He was a strong man. They used to have a lot of socials in town back when he was young. He worked the fields all day and danced all night—but only with my grandmother. He always wore faded denim overalls and a plaid flannel shirt and beat-up old work boots. I never saw him in anything else, not even at his funeral. His hair was gray from as early as I can remember, and it was always slicked back from the caps he wore."

Gimme caps, they were called: giveaways with advertising for this feed store or that chemical manufacturer. Josiah had several around the place, but his grandfather had worn only the John Deere freebies. His neck had been burnt red, and his eyes were wicked blue. He had played the fiddle and chewed tobacco and made knives in his spare time, and he had loved Josiah's grandmother with a passion that had never faded.

"How old were you when he died?" Annabeth asked softly.

"Sixteen. My grandmother died the year before, and he just didn't see much sense in going on without her. They had been married nearly sixty years."

She leaned against the wall, bracing her elbows on the windowsill. "That seems like a long time to be with one person, doesn't it? But when I was researching my other two books, I found it wasn't that uncommon. I talked to so many people who had been married fifty and sixty and seventy years."

"Things were done differently back then." Ducking his head, he left the shed again, going to the tools he'd gathered from the workshop before Annabeth arrived. "We'll take the roof off first," he said, offering her the smaller of the hammers and a nail claw.

"It's not really so different now," she disagreed, tucking the tools under her arm while she put on her gloves. "Both my mother's and my stepfather's parents have been married for more than fifty years. It's just that divorce is so easy these days."

He gave her a sharp look. "I doubt that divorce is ever really easy," he said, his voice as soft as his look had been harsh, before turning away to climb one of the ladders braced against the end of the shed,

The shed had only three walls of its own, with the outside wall of the barn providing the rear wall. It was under six feet high at the front, but sloped to more than seven feet at the back. It was so rickety that when he reached the top of the ladder, the wood creaked in protest. When he was a boy and the roof had needed repairs, he'd thought nothing of crawling out on it. But the shed hadn't been so ancient then, and he'd been smaller. If he climbed out on it today, he could expect to find himself on the concrete slab below. It was a good thing Annabeth was so eager to help.

"How long were you and Caroline married?" she asked when she appeared at the opposite side of the roof.

A few weeks ago he wouldn't even admit to having been married. Only a few days ago he had told her his marriage was none of her business. Now he ignored the twinge of discomfort her question brought and, his voice flat, answered. "Ten years."

"That's a long time."

"It was supposed to be a whole lot longer."

She looked at him for a long, still moment, then turned to the task at hand. She worked mostly in silence for a while, all her concentration on the job she was doing, and she worked methodically, needing no help from him and asking for advice only when she needed it. He liked that. Caroline had been one of those people with very definite ideas of men's work as opposed to women's. Women's work had included housework and cooking, caring for Kylie and doing laundry and weeding the flower beds. Everything else around the farm had been his responsibility. Because his grandmother had helped his grandfather and his mother had helped his father, he had assumed that Caroline would help *him*. She had wasted no time informing him that she was his wife, not his partner and certainly not his hired hand.

In all fairness to Caroline, he had overlooked one major difference between her and the women in his family: his mother and grandmother had been raised in the valley. They had done chores all their lives, had driven tractors and fed animals. They had planted and harvested and worked alongside their husbands. They had never known any other life.

Caroline's upbringing had been as different as could be. Her father had worked eight to five in an office; her mother had been a housewife and mother. External factors like weather and market prices had had no effect on their lifestyles. The only way high interest rates had affected them was in making their credit cards a little more expensive to use. She had never known what it was to do without, to make do. She had never done physical labor, had never even gotten dirty since she was a small child.

He had warned her, had tried to prepare her, but she had thought life on a farm sounded so wonderful, so idyllic. The reality of it had doomed their marriage from the start.

And here he was this morning, entertaining fantasies, considering needs and wants and temptations, that all centered on another city woman who thought life in this valley was wonderful. Another city woman who wouldn't last.

He was a fool.

When they reached the point where neither could accomplish anything more from the ladders, Annabeth matter-of-factly asked, "Do you think this shed will support my weight?"

He studied her from across the roof. "Do you want to find out?"

"It doesn't look like it will hold *you.*" She flashed him a smile. "But I'm a lot lighter than you."

Leaning forward, he tested it. The roof itself wasn't a problem; it was the weakened beams that supported it. Still, even though it groaned and shuddered beneath his weight, it held steady. To be on the safe side, though, he left the ladder and found a couple of sturdy timbers in the barn to shore up the roof and help support her weight.

While he watched from below, she finished removing the shingles and ripped off the last of the tar paper. On her knees in front of him, she grinned triumphantly. "I'm finished, and the building is still standing. But, not being one to press my luck, can you help me down here so I don't have to go all the way back to the ladder?"

He could have moved one of the ladders. It wouldn't have taken but a moment, and she could have come down by herself. But it didn't seem worth the effort, not when she had already scooted around to sit at the edge of the roof, her feet dangling over the side. Not when all he had to do was reach up and fit his hands around her waist. Not when she was so slender, so light, and placed less than a moment's strain on his muscles.

He lifted her from the roof and slowly lowered her to the ground, fully intending when he started to immediately release her. But, prodded by some perverse need for torment, he didn't just set her down and let go. Instead, he brought her into contact with his own body, slowly inching her closer, feeling the tingle in his nerves, the quiver in his muscles, as her legs touched his, her hips brushed his, her breasts pressed against his chest.

God help him, he hadn't held a woman in so long. He had almost forgotten the intriguing differences—the softness of her belly where his slowly strengthening erection pressed against her; the curve of her hips, so slender and delicate, yet so well suited for cradling him; and her breasts, not overly large but nicely rounded, flattening against the harder planes of his chest.

He had forgotten how good it felt to be aroused—unsteady and unsure, hungry and hard and intensely alive. She felt it, too. He could see it in her eyes, shadowy and dazed, could hear it in her ragged breathing, could feel it in her body, in her muscles that were knotted and tight. He could seduce her. He could fill this need, could fill this emptiness merely by filling *her*. He could crawl inside her so deep and for so long, could take her healing and her warmth and her soul, could satisfy these powerful demands of his body.

He could feel alive again.

With her, he could create life again.

He could create himself again.

She shifted against him, just enough to send new sensations rocketing through him, to make his muscles clench, to make his hardness swell more. Catching his breath, he whispered a warning—*Don't*—but his voice had no sound. She understood him anyway and moved somehow closer still, sliding her hands from his shoulders, where they had rested for balance, to around his neck. She was teasing him now, every movement a small torture, every brush an invitation, every whisper of a touch a challenge. He could seduce her, all right, but only because she was willing to be seduced. Only because *she* was already seducing *him*.

Meaning to kiss him, Annabeth rose onto her toes and leaned closer. He was watching her, his expression wary and aroused, needy and hungry and, yes, just a little bit afraid. She kept her gaze locked on his until she was too close, until he faded into a blur, until her mouth was only millimeters from his.

And then he stopped her.

He didn't abruptly push her away, didn't let go and step back and harshly reject her. His method was gentler, but just as effective. Raising his hands, he cupped her face in his callused palms, stopping her from moving any closer. He stroked the soft skin at her temples with the pad of his thumbs, his dark gaze all the while searching her face. Whatever he saw there wasn't enough, because finally, a look of regret softening his features, he untangled her hands from around his neck and walked away.

Annabeth closed her eyes on the tears that welled. She knew what he saw and what he wanted to see, knew what she was and what she wasn't.

She was foolish. Nosy. A woman from the city.

She wasn't pretty enough, wasn't feminine enough.

She wasn't what he wanted most of all.

She wasn't Caroline.

Chapter 5

"I understand you're living at the sawmill."

Annabeth had been gazing around the diner; now she brought her attention back to Stuart Dothan, seated in the booth across from her. She'd had lunch before she had driven into town for their appointment, but she had accepted when he'd invited her to join him. He had ordered meat loaf, mashed potatoes, green beans and coffee, and she had asked for apple pie and hot chocolate. There was a hard wind blowing outside today, bringing cold, gray skies into the valley. She needed something warm to thaw her inside.

"I haven't been out there in years, but I don't recall it being fit for anything."

"It's fine," she replied. "The building is sturdy and has plumbing and electricity, and the wood stove keeps the place warm. However—" she smiled a bit wistfully "—I surely would like to have a bathtub." Sponge baths were purely functional—they kept her clean—but they lacked the soothing comfort and luxury of a long soak in a hot tub. If she'd had a tub, she definitely would have been in it last night, although it was a toss-up as to which had hurt worse—her muscles from a day's unaccustomed labor or her ego after Josiah's rejection.

That little interlude there by the shed had ruined the rest of the day. There had been no more easy conversation, no more fun. She probably could have teased him out of his mood, but she'd had no desire to. She had felt too cheated, been too disappointed. Too hurt.

"What do you think of Josiah?"

The waitress served them, setting a steaming mug of chocolate in front of Annabeth. There were miniature marshmallows floating on top, slowly dissolving and adding their sweetness to the brew. She wrapped her hands around the heavy mug, letting the warmth seep into her fingers, and cautiously replied, "He's an interesting man."

"He's my wife's nephew."

She gave him a sharp look. So if step-relationships counted for anything, that made Josiah her step-cousin. In this situation, they didn't. Heavens, even her flesh-and-blood relationship with Stuart didn't count for anything, and she could guarantee his wife wouldn't be eager to take on the role of stepmother to his thirty-year-old bastard daughter.

"Josiah isn't a subject for your book," Stuart stated firmly. "Don't get the idea that he can be used that way."

Her gaze met his again and held. "I've never profiled anyone in one of my books without his permission, and I know how Josiah feels about the issue." After a brief pause, she added, "Don't get the idea you can dictate to me. I have my own guidelines to follow, and I don't need your approval."

After another brief silence, he said, "Hilda has several copies of your books in the library. I read one over the weekend—the first one that covers West Virginia."

She waited, not allowing herself to expect anything. She had learned with the publication of that first book not to solicit opinions. Her parents had thought it was wonderful, her sisters had liked it well enough, her brother had found it boring, and her friends had wondered aloud if it was all she had to show for several years' hard work.

He continued reluctantly, grudgingly. "I was quite impressed. You did a good job."

"I always do."

"It makes me feel somewhat better about your plans for our valley."

"Thank you." Withdrawing a small tape recorder from her purse, she set it on the table between them, pressing the record button. After giving the identifying information—day, date, time and place and Stuart's name—she said, "You mentioned earlier that your wife is Josiah's aunt. Is she a Miller?"

He gave the tape recorder a wary glance. "No, Mary Louise is a Walker. Josiah's mother—Kate—and Mary Louise are sisters."

"And Tony Walker's father is their brother."

Stuart almost smiled. "Of course, you've met Tony... which must not have set well with Josiah. Yes, Clint Walker is their younger brother. Kate is the oldest. In between her and Clint are Mary Louise, Martin, Bobby and Yvette."

She ignored the comment about Josiah and Tony. "How long have the Walkers been in Dutchman's Valley?"

"Mary Louise's grandparents settled here in the late 1800s. Their father died in a logging accident when they were nearly grown, and their mother moved to Fort Smith, where she had family. When Josiah's father died, Kate moved there to be near her mother. Bessie has Alzheimer's—doesn't even recognize Kate anymore. She's going to have to go into a nursing home eventually, but Kate's trying to hold that off. The others all still live in the valley."

It was a shame about Josiah's grandmother, Annabeth thought privately, but Kate should move back home. If her mother didn't recognize her now, then the old lady's needs could be met by anyone. Josiah, on the other hand, needed his mother's love and support.

Her attention on the tape recorder, she asked, "How long have you and Mary Louise been married?" Even though she wasn't watching him, peripherally she saw him look away. She kept her gaze on the tape counter, watching it slowly turn—five, six, seven, eight—recording nothing but silence.

Then he sighed heavily and replied, "Thirty-five years."

Annabeth felt a small shiver of shock, but still refused to look at him. So he had been married when he'd met her mother. Her mother had had an affair with him while his wife waited patiently at home.

She wished she had known. She wished Lynette had trusted her enough to divulge that one small, important detail. Maybe her mother had been ashamed. Maybe she hadn't wanted Annabeth to know that she was not only the illegitimate child of a man who wanted nothing to do with her, but that he was also married. Surely she hadn't wanted Annabeth to know that she had seduced another woman's husband.

Calling on every ounce of professionalism she possessed, she asked, "Do you have any children?" Not *other* children. She had promised in his office last week that she wouldn't tell anyone she was his daughter, and she intended to keep that promise, even with him. Any mention of their relationship, even between themselves, would have to come from him.

He sighed again, a sad, disappointed sound. "No," he said at last. "We couldn't. Mary Louise..."

Had been unable to have children, Annabeth finished. Had she known about Stuart's affair with Lynette? Did she have any idea that he had a child of his own, one that another woman had provided him? If so, she probably resented that child, and with good reason. If not, she didn't need to know.

"Do you have any old photographs of the town, of the businesses your family ran—anything that might help with my research?"

"I have some," he admitted, "along with some records and some journals. They're in my office at the house. You can . . . I'll bring them to the mill one evening this week."

"I would also like to see where your family first settled, where their businesses were located. I'd like to find out . . ." Her voice trailed off as the bell over the door tinkled and Josiah walked in. He gave the room a sweeping glance before his gaze settled on her and he started in her direction.

"Josiah," Stuart greeted him. "Join us for a cup of coffee?"

"No, thanks." To Annabeth, he said, "I'll start on that shed in the morning. You need to decide where you want it."

She found a smile somewhere inside, one that made her face hurt and her teeth ache. "Thanks, but I plan to start it this afternoon. I can handle it myself."

If she had thought he would be relieved to be free of that obligation, she was wrong. He merely looked annoyed. "You can't do it alone."

"Fine. If I need help, I'll ask for it."

"We'll start in the morning," he repeated, his jaw taut, his eyes narrowed.

She studied him for a moment, then slowly smiled again. "Still in a bad mood, Josiah?" she asked, a gentle note of teasing creeping into her voice. "All right. Tomorrow morning will be fine. I'll be waiting."

"The autumn festival is Saturday, Josiah," Stuart said once their business was concluded. "Will we see you there?"

He gave his uncle a sidelong glance. "I don't think so."

"You always enjoyed it in the past."

"Not this year." He started to leave, then hesitated. "Tell Aunt Mary Louise . . ."

After a moment, Stuart gave his nephew the affectionate sort of smile he ought to be giving his daughter. "I will."

Without so much as another look for Annabeth, Josiah left again. She was thinking about his exchange with Stuart, wondering how she could repeat the invitation to the festival in such a way that Josiah would find it difficult to refuse, when Stuart spoke. "Leave him alone, Annabeth."

She looked blankly at him.

"Josiah's had enough bad luck in the last few years to last a lifetime. You don't have to add to it."

"He's my landlord. My neighbor. Sort of a friend."

"If you want someone to amuse yourself with, go see Tony Walker. He likes pretty, young, flighty women. But Josiah doesn't need you in his life. He certainly doesn't need the grief you'll bring."

"You're wrong," she said coolly. "He *does* need someone. And from what I've seen in the time I've been here, no one around here cares."

"And *you* do." The sarcasm in his voice stung. "Don't make the mistake your mother made. Don't think you can come in here and make a place for yourself. Don't think you can rearrange everyone's lives to suit yourself. Josiah has had a tough time of the last few years, ever since—"

When he broke off, Annabeth filled in. "Since Caroline left."

He drew back, surprised. "He told you about Caroline?"

"Yes." Inwardly she squirmed at the firmness of her answer. He had told her a little about his marriage, so she hadn't exactly lied. Still, he'd told her precious little, and only after she had already guessed that he had been married. "I would never do anything that might hurt Josiah, Stuart. Beyond that . . ."

She offered him a challengingly cool smile. "I fail to see that my friendship with him is any of your business."

Annabeth stood back, hands on her hips, and studied the woodshed they had just completed. It had been a simple job, Josiah thought—squaring up the site so the corners would align, digging the postholes, setting the timbers that would provide support, framing the sides and adding the rafters, the roof and the siding. It wasn't large—only four by eight feet—or fancy—the mill provided the rear wall, and two sides sloped down to the open front—but it was adequate for Annabeth's needs.

It was enough to give her a look of pride.

"I like building things," she announced, adding her hammer to the rest of the tools in the truck. "Maybe I should have been a carpenter." With a quick grin, she asked, "Want some help when you build your new shed?"

He automatically started to say no, the way he had automatically brushed people off for three years. Instead, he hesitated, then asked a question of his own. "Won't that interfere with your work?"

"Oh, right. Like building this hasn't taken *you* away from *your* own work?"

"All right. I plan to start this afternoon."

Her grin turned into a full-fledged smile. "Great. Want some lunch? I have stew left over from last night's dinner."

"We need to stack the wood."

"We need to eat first." She pulled her gloves off and headed for the mill. Josiah hesitated only a moment, then followed her. Stacking the wood wasn't really a big priority, as long as they had it done before the next rain. They could do it later.

The door to the mill was open, Annabeth's dog lying square in the center. When Josiah bent to scratch his ears, the animal roused himself enough to stretch, then roll over onto his back. "This dog is worthless," he said, rubbing Emerson's belly. "Fat, lazy and ugly."

Annabeth removed a pot from the refrigerator and closed the door with her elbow. "He is not," she disagreed, then gave her pet a closer look. "Well, he is fat. And lazy. But we can't all be beautiful, can we, Emerson? And he's certainly not worthless."

"Name one positive thing about him."

She didn't need even a moment to consider it. "He doesn't get angry with me. He comes home every night, and he's happy to see me every morning. He doesn't make unreasonable demands, and he doesn't care how I look or how I act or what I say. He doesn't judge me by standards I can't meet. He accepts me the way I am. That's more than I can say for a lot of people, *you* included."

Straightening, Josiah leaned against the doorframe and watched her as she stirred the stew on the hot plate. "You think I don't accept you the way you are?" he asked curiously.

She gave him a long, steady look. "I think you wish I were Caroline."

Shoving away from the door, he approached her, stopping only a foot away. He studied her for a moment, taking note of the flush working in the cool morning air had given her, of the slightly parted set of her lips, of the solemn, ageless look in her brown eyes, and he responded with a carefully formed, simply stated, no-room-for-doubt answer.

"Not in a million years."

Then, before she could reply, he walked past her and into the bathroom, turning on the water in the sink, plunging his hands into the frigid flow, then reaching for a bar of soap. It was tinted pale blue and had a familiar sweet scent to it. Annabeth's scent, he realized. This was what he smelled whenever he let himself get close enough—not expensive perfume, but a bar of pale blue soap that could be had in any store for under a dollar.

He took plenty of time washing, rinsing until the water ran clear and longer still, until the coldness began to numb his fingers. Then he took almost as long drying, using a blue towel with a paisley heart appliquéd in the center. He didn't want any more questions, didn't want her to press that last topic of conversation any further. He didn't want her to ask if he still loved his ex-wife or if he wanted her back. He didn't want to think of Caroline at all.

When he finally came out again, she was pouring crackers into a cereal bowl. The stew was still in its pot, steam rising in little wisps, sending a fragrant aroma into the air. She glanced at him, but didn't speak, and neither did he. He simply wandered toward the other end of the room, pausing beside her desk.

A spiral-bound artist's pad, measuring sixteen by twenty inches, was open on the desk. It took only a moment to recognize the neatly lettered chart as a family tree. This one was for the Dothans, with much space left to fill in the blanks as she went along. There were numbers following the women's names; a flip of the page confirmed that the number three following Aunt Mary Louise's name was a reference to page three, or the Walker family tree; a similar number beside his mother's name referred him to the Miller chart.

It started with the first Josiah, his two wives and nine children and ended near the bottom with him, just as the Walker chart ended with Tony. His cousin had never been married, and for the first time Josiah wondered if it was because he had wanted Caroline for himself and no other woman would have suited. Once things had started going bad, Josiah would have gladly given her up...if not for Kylie.

There were no lines extending from Tony's name for marriage information, none for either of them for children. A penciled note opposite Josiah's name listed Caroline, along with a question mark indicating no further information.

There should be an entry underneath his name for his daughter, Josiah thought. Maybe she had disappeared from his life, but not from his heart. She deserved that much recognition.

But Annabeth couldn't recognize the daughter he'd kept secret. Eventually, of course, she would come across the information of Kylie's birth when she started combing through the records. That would be soon enough.

Coming to stand beside him, she offered him a glass of tea. He accepted it without looking at her. "You've filled in a lot of information."

"There's a lot left to learn."

That was true. This page, like the ones preceding it, probably like the ones following, had a lot of blanks. He knew some names that were missing, knew fewer dates. "I imagine official records here aren't as extensive as they are elsewhere."

"No, they're not. All too often in the early days, births and deaths weren't officially registered with the state. A long time ago, babies were born at home and old folks died there. People didn't worry about birth and death certificates. As isolated as the valley was, they didn't have much need for either one."

"A long time ago, huh?" he repeated, looking down at her. "I was born in the back bedroom of that house across the road—and it wasn't *that* long ago."

Her smile was pure delight. "You're kidding. Were you delivered by a midwife?"

He nodded. "An old lady from up on Whistler's Rock. Her name is Millicent Parks, but everyone calls her Aunt Millie. She delivered my father, too, and just about everyone else in the valley over the age of twenty-five and under the age of sixty."

"How old is she now?"

He shrugged. "Eighty? Eighty-five? I don't know. I haven't seen her in years. She doesn't get out much anymore."

"Do you think she would talk to me?" Annabeth asked, making a note of the name on a yellow pad.

Regretting he had even mentioned it, he shrugged. "I don't know. She's awfully old."

"Old doesn't mean useless, Josiah," Annabeth chided. "People shouldn't be written off as unimportant just because they're old. Elderly people add meaning to our lives. They can teach us more than we'll ever learn on our own."

He knew that, of course. Hadn't his own grandfather ranked right up there with his dad and Kylie as the most important people in his life?

"You're just being difficult," she said, going back to the corner to shut off the hot plate. "You don't want to be accused of cooperating with me. Judging from your uncle's reaction yesterday, I think folks in town would be scandalized if they knew how much I see of you. It wouldn't do much for your reputation as a grouchy old hermit if they knew you were in any way helping the busybody from the city, now would it?''

He turned to watch her dish up their lunch. "A grouchy old hermit? Is that how they think of me?"

"No." She reached for spoons from the shelf above the table, then gave him a sidelong look. "Miss Hilda and Stuart and Tony think of you as someone they care very much about who has had a very difficult time."

Feeling both a little embarrassed and a little shamed by her reply, he turned his attention back to her desk. He would have preferred to remain grouchy, at least in Annabeth's eyes. He didn't want her feeling sorry for him. He didn't want to see the same pity in her eyes that he was used to seeing in everyone else's.

They settled onto a handwoven rug in front of the wood stove to eat. Although last night's fire had long since burned down, the Franklin was still warm. He had just about forgotten the comforting, homey pleasure of a wood stove that no gas or electric heat could come near matching—the potent heat, the crackling sounds, the woodsy fragrance. In a place like this, really only one big room since the loft upstairs wasn't enclosed, nothing beat a fire for warmth.

"Tell me about the festival," Annabeth requested as she seasoned her stew with salt, pepper and hot pepper sauce.

"What's to tell? It's a typical small-town festival—food, booths, a few rides for the kids."

"What kind of food? What kind of booths? How many rides?"

He tried to remember the last one he'd been to. It would have been four years ago, when Kylie was only a few weeks old. Caroline hadn't wanted to take her—hadn't felt the festival was worthy of a few hours of their time—but he had insisted. This was the first opportunity for many of their family and friends to meet their daughter, and he had wanted to show her off. They would only stay an hour or so, he had promised Caroline, and she had grudgingly agreed.

By the time the next festival had come around, Caroline and Kylie were gone. He hadn't been to another since then.

"They'll have hot dogs, corn on the cob, roasted peanuts, apple and pecan and pumpkin pie. Cotton candy, candied and caramel apples and funnel cakes. There will be some craft booths—quilts, baskets, weaving, carving. There are usually quite a few people from outside the valley with money to spend. The rides are just for little kids—a merry-go-round, cars, a tiny Ferris wheel—and Jed Andrews always brings his Shetlands in for the pony ride."

"Don't you miss going?"

"I've seen it often enough," he said stubbornly. They'd been having the autumn festival as long as he could remember. In his three years away at college, he had always managed a trip home for it, had even brought Caroline once. She had thought it was quaint. *Quaint.* How long had it taken him to realize that, coming from her, that was less than a compliment?

"You could go with me."

He gave her a long, steady look. She made the suggestion so casually, but she refused to meet his gaze. Because he would see it wasn't casual? She had been there when he'd told Stuart he wasn't going. Had his uncle asked her to change his mind? "I'm not going."

"Why not? It would be fun."

"You think so? Fine, you go and enjoy it. But I'm not."

"It wouldn't hurt you to get into town from time to time, to see someone on a regular basis other than me."

"I was in town yesterday. I saw Stuart."

"And talked to him for all of thirty seconds."

"I saw Tony Saturday."

"And didn't speak to him at all."

"What difference does it make, Annabeth? You're going either way. You've got stories to tell." He gave the last phrase a decidedly unkind flavor that made her frown.

"I thought it would be nice to not have to go alone," she said, her voice cool, her expression slightly wounded. "But don't feel selfish. Miss Hilda will be there. I'm sure she'll be able to make a little time for me."

She was manipulating him. He knew the feeling far too well from all those years with Caroline to miss it now. She was trying to make him feel guilty and self-absorbed, trying to maneuver him into saying, "All right, damn it, I'll take you." But it wasn't going to work. He had no desire to attend the festival Saturday. He had no desire to see everyone in the valley gathered in one place. He had no desire whatsoever to see all those kids gathered in one place.

And absolutely nothing she could do would change his mind.

The festival was in full swing by the time Annabeth and Josiah arrived shortly after eleven Saturday morning. The highway that served as the Corner's main street was blocked off at both ends, and every side street was clogged with parked cars. Josiah found a space in front of the local school—grades kindergarten through twelve in one small square building—and they walked the block and a half to the festival.

She still wasn't sure how she had changed his mind about coming. They hadn't discussed the matter since Wednesday. Oh, she had asked him a few more questions—If the Corner had an autumn festival, was there also a spring festival? How did they celebrate the Fourth of July and Christmas? Was there any sort of Founder's Day celebration?—but she hadn't said one word to him about attending with her today. She hadn't tried to play on his sympathies, hadn't mentioned even once that she was a little nervous about going out on her own.

But yesterday, when they had finished the roof on his new storage shed, when she had put down her tools and stretched high to ease the kinks in her muscles, he had given her one of those hard, uncompromising looks and had done just that—compromised. "I'll go with you tomorrow," he said in a tough voice. "But I'm not introducing you to anyone."

And so here they were, standing on the corner in the middle of the festival, their senses assailed by sounds and sights and smells. The kiddie rides were to their left, bright colors and familiar old music. Demonstrations of weaving and quilting and candlemaking were going on, interspersed with booths selling the completed crafts.

Food was everywhere—she smelled spices and sweets and the tantalizing aroma of fried funnel cakes coated with powdered sugar. To their right was a stage for music, Josiah told her, and dancing later tonight. Would they be here for that? she wondered, thinking how pleasant it would be to glide around a dance floor—even a concrete one—in his arms. Deep in her heart, though, she knew wondering was all she would do. Getting him here was enough; he wasn't going to take her dancing, too.

Beyond the stage were more booths, the pony ride and, at the end, the storytelling booth. "Booth," she saw as they approached, was a polite name for the space she had been allotted. It was easily the simplest area in the festival, consisting only of bales of hay, loaned out by the feed store behind them. One sat at the front—a seat for her—and braced a hand-lettered sign, done all in gracious swirls and flourishes: Annabeth Gibbs, Storyteller—1 p.m., 3 p.m., 7 p.m. The other bales were arranged in loosely formed rows of seats.

"I love the smell of hay," she remarked, walking down the center aisle and stopping at the front. "Although I have to admit the idea of a roll in the hay always seemed terribly uncomfortable to me. It must be awfully prickly and dusty."

"It is," Josiah said as he stopped a few feet away.

His simple agreement surprised her. Sitting on the front bale, she gave him a wide-eyed look. "Were you ever that young, Josiah?"

"Once. A long time ago." He sat down across from her and pulled a straw from the bale, peeling the outer husk and sticking the end between his teeth. He looked at home surrounded by hay—after all, he was a farm boy. He looked handsome, too, she thought, in faded jeans and a cotton shirt the color of the sky overhead. "So what do you do here?" he asked, leaning back to rest his hands at the back corners of the bale, stretching out his legs and crossing his ankles in front of him.

He was definitely at home here, she thought, wishing for her camera. She would like to capture this image of him to keep forever.

But she didn't have her camera, and he had already told her once that she couldn't take his picture. With a wistful sigh, she answered his question. "First, I'll rearrange the bales. I don't want straight rows—that's too much like a classroom. A circle will do nicely. That way no one gets left out. Then, when the audience is ready—"

"Provided that there is one," he said dryly.

"There will be. I can charm any child on this street today—and most of their parents." She smiled slyly. "I guess you're an exception, though. You find me completely resistible."

He met her gaze but said nothing. She thought she saw a hint of amusement in his dark eyes, but it faded too quickly to be sure. She would like to see him amused, even at her expense. She would like to hear him laugh—heavens, would give a good part of her heart to even see him smile. She wanted that haunting air of anguish to disappear, wanted to see that he had dealt with his sorrow and was going on with his life, that he was going to be happy once again with his life.

But it wasn't going to happen today.

"So there you are, Annabeth." Miss Hilda, accompanied by several other ladies, joined them in the hay. "Why, Josiah, what a pleasure to see you here today."

He acknowledged her and the other ladies with a nod as he got to his feet. The last woman, though, got more than that. She got to kiss his cheek and give him a fond smile. Aunt Mary Louise? Annabeth wondered darkly.

"Annabeth, I want you to meet some of the Friends of the Library." Miss Hilda introduced each one of them with a little background information that Annabeth automatically filed away. Florence Griffith was the mayor's wife, and Peggy Sue McKinley was Miss Hilda's own niece. Sybil and

Celia Hinson, twin sisters who had never married, lived in the big yellow house down from Miss Hilda, and their little sister, Irene Schneider—sixty if she was a day—was the Corner's postmistress.

The sixth woman, the woman who had kissed Josiah, probably the youngest and definitely the prettiest of the group, *was* Mary Louise Dothan. Unlike the others, her hair showed more of the original black than gray, and her face was, for the most part, smooth of aging wrinkles. Hers was one of the older families in Dutchman's Valley, Miss Hilda was saying, and her husband, Stuart, owned several businesses in town, in addition to a small farm in the north part of the valley.

Hello, Mary Lou, Annabeth thought, the tune of an old song running through her mind. So this was her father's wife. Her stepmother. The woman Stuart had been married to when he'd had his affair with Annabeth's mother. The woman *she* had been forbidden to have any contact with.

She wasn't as pretty as Lynette, Annabeth thought, unashamedly biased, as she clasped the woman's hand. Where Lynette was petite and had a fragile look about her, Mary Louise was solid—not stocky, but never delicate. She looked capable, efficient, strong, and she had a no-nonsense approach. She shook Annabeth's hand firmly, gave her a measuring look, then said, "Welcome to Dutchman's Valley, Annabeth. I'm looking forward to getting to know you."

Really? Annabeth thought dryly. *Wish I could say the same.* "I've met your husband, Mrs. Dothan, and your nephews. The Dothan, Walker and Miller names keep popping up in my research."

"Our families have kept busy," she responded with a smile. "Any time you're free, come by the house. I have some old photographs you might be interested in and some stories to tell. And, you know, I really think you should meet Aunt Flo. She's my husband's aunt, in her early eighties and still just as sharp as a tack. I think she would enjoy talking to you. She's a great believer in passing on the old ways so they won't be forgotten."

Annabeth's smile felt frozen in place. "I'd love that, Mrs. Dothan." Aunt Flo. Stuart's aunt. *Her* great-aunt. Another family member to add to her very small pool of Dothan relatives.

"Oh, please, call me Mary Louise." She offered her own smile, a charmingly blunt one, then glanced at her nephew. "So tell me, Annabeth, how did you get Josiah to come today?"

Annabeth looked at him, too, but he was studiously avoiding their gazes. "I wish I could claim credit for it—I could work other miracles if I knew how—but he's here today of his own accord."

Mary Louise glanced from her to Josiah, then back again, subjecting her to another of those appraising looks. "Uh-huh," she agreed skeptically. "Well, I'll be back in time for one of your stories. Hilda's very excited that you agreed to do this. Josiah, be sure and come by the library's food booth. I've got some apple pies and a few gallons of my cider. I know that was always your favorite."

She left, trailed by the other ladies, leaving Annabeth and Josiah alone again. Giving the nearest bale of hay a shove with her foot, Annabeth remarked, "She's a little bit forceful."

"Uh-huh. And the sky is a little bit blue, the sun is a little bit bright, and you're a little bit cute."

She gave him another surprised look. His implication—that she was *a little bit cute* was an understatement—delighted her. She liked the idea that he thought she was a whole lot cute. Maybe even pretty? She could settle for that. Even though she would prefer take-his-breath-away beautiful, she could be happy with pretty.

He began pushing bales of hay to the side, and, laying her shawl at the front with the placard, she turned to help him. It took only a few minutes to rearrange the neat rows into a ragged circle, leaving an entrance in the middle.

That finished, they walked the entire length of the street, stopping at each crafts booth. Ignoring Josiah's quiet disapproval, she spoke to several of the artisans, explaining her interest in their particular talents and asking for a private demonstration sometime in the future. One or two were openly pleased and ready to set a date, one wary gentleman was noncommittal, and the rest offered tentative agreements. That was the best she could hope for.

"Hungry?" Josiah asked before they reached the kids' rides.

She flashed him a bright smile. "You bet. Where do we start?"

They got sausage dogs loaded with sweet peppers and sauteed onions and added roasted ears of corn and tall glasses of chilled cider, then headed back to the storytelling area to sit down. "Are you uncomfortable?" Annabeth asked as she settled on a bale of hay.

Her question immediately put him on guard. "Why do you ask?"

"A lot of people have been glad to see you, but you haven't encouraged anything more than a hello. These people are your friends."

They *used* to be his friends, Josiah thought grimly. Once they had been close friends and good neighbors. He had known everything about their lives, and they'd had the same knowledge about his own.

And that was why he wasn't very friendly. They knew all about his marriage to Caroline, all about his divorce. They knew that the divorce had almost killed him, that it had all but destroyed a great part of him. They knew about Kylie, knew that not seeing her had broken his heart, knew that living without her was a joyless way to live.

They knew too much. They pitied him.

"What kind of stories will you tell?" he asked, clumsily changing the subject.

Annabeth laughed. "Ouch. If you'd rather talk about my storytelling, then you must *really* not want to talk about your friends. But that's okay. I love to talk about myself."

That wasn't true, he thought, watching her. She wasn't exactly reticent in discussing herself, but she definitely preferred talking about others.

"I have a list of stories I might do today." She pulled it from a pocket deep in her skirt and offered it to him. "Of course, that's just some ideas. Sometimes I have requests for certain stories, and a lot of it depends on the audience. Little kids don't care for really scary stories as a rule, and adults sometimes feel insulted at simplistic children's stories. Love stories, of course, require a specific audience, usually teenagers or adults. Although," she added with a grin, "kids like them, too, if they involve ghosts or hauntings."

He looked at the list she'd given him. There weren't titles, just a few key words to bring each tale to mind. *Blackbeard's treasure. Ghost lights. Mystery ship. Haunted plantation. Hitchhiker. Yellow fever. Baker's daughters.*

Scary stories, kids' tales, love stories or ghosts. Like any normal child, he had enjoyed bedtime stories and ghost stories, but—like any normal child—he had outgrown them before he was ten.

He'd outgrown love stories, too.

"What kind of stories do you like?" Annabeth asked, almost as if she'd read his thoughts.

"I don't believe in fairy tales, witches or ghosts."

"What do you believe in?"

He considered it for a moment, then bleakly replied, "Nothing."

Without thinking, she reached across to clasp his hand. Without thinking, he let her. "That's not true," she disagreed. "You believe in the land or you wouldn't be working so hard to hold on to it. You believe in family. You believe in yourself."

"And you believe in it all, don't you? Ghosts and witches and love." She nodded so solemnly that he would have smiled if he could have remembered how. But he couldn't remember, and so he brushed her hand away, stood up and gathered the remains of their lunch. "It's almost time for your performance. I'll be around when it's over."

He started to walk away, but, of course, it wasn't that easy. Nothing with Annabeth, it seemed, ever was. She followed him, staying close to his side. "Will you give me the benefit of the doubt? Will you come and listen?"

Come and listen. From thirty feet away, he turned and looked back at the storytelling area. There were kids there now, a half dozen or so, sitting on the ground in the center of the circle. Maybe they were the only ones, along with their mothers seated on hay bales at the back, who would show up. Or maybe in the next eight or ten minutes, every other kid on the street would gather there.

Come and listen. He could do that. He could listen to her stories. It was a waste of time, but what better did he have to do today?

But not with those kids there. Even from this distance, he could hardly bear to look at them—at the pretty little girls with their long hair and soft voices and innocent smiles. If he got closer, he wouldn't be able to resist wondering if Kylie was as tall as this one, if her hair was the same color as that one. Did she prefer dresses and dolls and silken curls? Or was she more like that little tomboy there, with her hair cut boyishly short, wearing jeans and boots and a tiny six-shooter strapped to her hip?

Will you come and listen? Annabeth asked as if it were that simple: walk over to the circle, have a seat on a bale of hay and listen. Look at all those little girls and listen. Don't feel any pain, any regret or anger. Don't indulge in any guessing games. Just listen.

He couldn't do it.

He *couldn't*.

He turned his back on the group. "You go ahead. I'll be around when you're done."

"Come on, Josiah. One story—that's all I'm asking. Listen to one story and watch the kids, and then tell me that I'm wasting my time."

"Not today."

"Then, when? I don't know when I'll be doing this again. When, Josiah?"

Shamed by the beseeching note in her voice, he refused to look at her. "I don't know when, but not today."

She tried cajoling, offering him a charming smile, injecting a bit of teasing into her voice. "Why not? I guarantee you the best seat in the house. Small boys have been known to fight over who gets to sit beside me. Come on, Josiah. Give me fifteen minutes of your time. If I can't change your mind by then, I won't try again."

He glanced again briefly, very briefly, at the gathering, larger now as one o'clock drew nearer, then looked directly at her. He spoke very clearly, very precisely. "I'm not interested. Waste your time however you want. Just leave me out of it. Now... do you want to meet me somewhere when you're finished?"

The hurt darkening her eyes was so powerful that he could feel it deep inside himself. She stood very still for a long time, her face pale, her breathing shallow. Then, abruptly, she stood taller, drew her shawl closer and gave him an icy look. "No," she replied quietly. "I don't." Then, turning away in a whirl of clothing—long denim skirt, lacy shawl, frilly blouse—she walked away.

"Annabeth—" His muscles clenching tight, he muttered a curse. He wanted to go after her, to apologize and explain to her the real reason why he couldn't watch her work. He wanted to talk until that look in her eyes disappeared, until the color was back in her face, until the moment's pain was forgotten.

But the bell atop the Baptist church chimed the hour— one o'clock. Annabeth had already reached the circle of hay, and Miss Hilda was standing up to make the introduction.

It was too late.

As Caroline had once criticized, all he could offer was too little and too late.

Annabeth sat quietly, the old-fashioned shawl around her shoulders, her attention on the children in front of her while Miss Hilda spoke briefly about the history project and about Annabeth's previous works, and for a moment about the long-revered—and once nearly forgotten—art of storytell-ing. Revered? she thought cynically. Josiah certainly didn't see anything revered about it.

But there was no room in her mind for Josiah right now. She had a job to do, and she needed a clear head to do it. She would think about Josiah later. She would remember the pain later.

Finally the librarian gave the floor to Annabeth. She let a moment's silence pass until everyone's attention was on her; then she asked, "Halloween was a few weeks ago, wasn't it?"

A few children answered affirmatively.

"Did you go trick-or-treating?"

A few more voices chimed in.

"What did you dress up as?" she asked one small girl.

"An angel," came the soft reply.

"I was Batman," a red-haired boy spoke up. That brought a host of other answers: a soldier, a turtle, a clown, a princess.

"Did you dress up?" the redhead asked, only to be laughed down.

"Grown-ups don't dress up," one child admonished.

"Oh, grown-ups *do* dress up," Annabeth gently dis-agreed. "At least, I did. I was a witch." She had done an early Halloween program at a neighborhood community center before leaving to come here, and she'd gone in full costume—tattered black dress, pointy hat and her moth-er's tolerant black cat. The storytelling had used her entire repertoire of ghost and witch stories and had been a big hit. *So there, Josiah*.

"You couldn't be a witch," the angel disagreed impa-tiently. "At least, not a good one."

"Why not?"

"Witches are ugly," the angel stated.

"And they wear black capes."

"And ride brooms."

"And have great big noses with great big warts."

"And they laugh real scary-like."

"Like this?" Annabeth raised her arms and, substituting the shawl for a cape, cackled her best evil witch's cackle. A few of the smaller children just stared, but the others were admiring. Sound effects, she thought with satisfaction, always helped with children. "Do you like stories about witches and goblins and ghosts?"

After a chorus of yeses, she said, "I'm going to tell you a story that comes from my part of the country. I'm from South Carolina. That's way off on the other side of the country, right at the edge of the Atlantic Ocean."

"I went swimming in the ocean once," the angel said, then her smile slipped. "But the waves scared me."

"That's okay. Sometimes they scare me, too." Annabeth smiled at her, then glanced around the crowd. Outside the circle, she saw several small groups of people watching, but they made no effort to come in and join them.

There was no sign at all of Josiah.

"There once was an old man named John Smith, who lived not too far from where I live," she began. "One day he got so sick that he couldn't get out of bed. His wife sent for the doctor, but old Mr. Smith said, 'Why, there's nothing wrong with me.' 'You're dying, John,' the doctor said, but John Smith just laughed. 'T'ain't so,' he said, but the next day...'' She lowered her voice and slowed her words. "...John Smith was dead."

She looked at each small face, and each child looked back. This was what she liked best—the children.

"They put the old man in a coffin and had his funeral, and they buried him in the old graveyard. The next day, John Smith's neighbor was on his way into town, and he passed the graveyard, and he saw old John sitting there on the fence. 'I thought you were dead,' the neighbor said, and John just laughed. 'T'ain't so,' he replied. 'But they buried you over there,' the neighbor said, pointing to the brand-new grave. 'Well, I'm not buried, and I'm not dead,' John Smith said."

She went through the rest of the story, using her voice, her expressions and her body all as tools, leaning closer to this child, away from that one, laughing and frowning, letting her voice rise and fall, changing accents from one character to another. Her stepfather said that, at heart, she was a frustrated actor. Her mother insisted she was meant to be a mother, to tell these stories to her own children but settling for strangers' kids in the meantime. Annabeth thought they were probably both right.

"So, finally," she continued, "the people in town decided to hold another funeral. They called the preacher, and old John Smith's widow and children gathered around the grave. The preacher talked, and the people sang, and when they were finished, they put up a gravestone. 'Here lies John Smith,' it said, 'who died July 23, 1923.' And everybody went home. The next day there was old John again. He saw the gravestone, and he went to read it. He read it over and over. 'Here lies John Smith, who died July 23, 1923.' All this time people had been telling him he was dead, and every time old John had laughed and said, 'T'ain't so.' Now he read that gravestone one last time, and he scratched his head and said, 'Well . . . maybe it *is* so.' And he crawled into his grave, and no one has seen him ever since."

There was a moment's silence, then applause and requests for another one. She obliged with a chilling story about a headless horseman, one about an evil witch who was destroyed by a brave little girl and another about a mysterious ship floating off the coast of North Carolina. She talked until the smaller children got restless, until her throat was scratchy and dry, and then she stopped.

She sat there on the bale of hay, watching everyone leave, speaking politely to those who spoke to her, graciously thanking them for their compliments. The last to approach her was Mary Louise Dothan.

"You're very good."

"Thank you."

"Are you meeting Josiah now?"

Annabeth's smile faltered. "No. I imagine he's already gone."

"Oh, but he was here just a while ago—over by the bank, watching you. I saw him just a few minutes ago."

She looked up sharply, searching for a glimpse of him but finding nothing. No doubt he had been there—Mary Louise could surely identify her own nephew—but he was gone now.

"So...you said you were from South Carolina."

Slowly Annabeth shifted her gaze to the older woman. "Yes, from Charleston."

"I hear that's a lovely city."

"Yes, it is."

"You have family there?"

She nodded.

"Anyone special?"

Annabeth gave her a curious look. "My parents, brother and sisters. My grandparents, aunts and uncles and cousins."

"I mean a man."

No-nonsense, Annabeth reminded herself. That had been one of her first—and apparently most accurate—impressions of this woman. "No," she replied dryly. "There's no one special waiting for me."

"What do you think of our valley?"

"It's very beautiful."

"It's a wonderful place to live—if you don't mind giving up the bright lights of the city. It's really not as isolated as it seems. The roads are good, and there's a city within reasonable driving distance in any direction you care to go."

"I'm not interested in the nearby cities, Mrs. Dothan—Mary Louise," she corrected at the woman's gesture. "I'm here to study the valley."

"Yes, of course. But if you happened to stay longer than you planned..."

"And why would I decide to do that?"

"You're a bright woman—as bright and talented as you are pretty. I have two unmarried nephews. You figure it out."

No-nonsense and forceful, too, Annabeth reminded herself. How could she politely tell this woman that she wasn't at all interested in one of her nephews—and that the other wasn't at all interested in her? Rising from her seat, she smiled a little too brightly. "I'm glad you enjoyed the stories. I really would like to arrange a time when we could talk, and if you could set up a meeting for me with your husband's aunt..."

The older woman also stood up and offered her own smile. "How can I get in touch with you?"

"I'm at the mill most of the time."

"I'll let you know."

"Thank you, Mary Louise." Annabeth watched her walk away, then gave a sigh of relief at being allowed to escape so easily. The last thing she had expected from anyone here in the valley, especially her father's wife, was matchmaking. Who ever would have believed it?

It was well past dark when Josiah parked his truck at the end of the street and climbed out. The night air was cold, making him huddle deeper inside his jacket. The heater in the truck had stopped working again; sometime in the next week or two, before fall seriously turned to winter, he would have to find time to fix it.

For a moment he just stood there beside the truck. Much of the crowd was gone now. Those who remained were primarily valley people, squeezing every last bit of enjoyment from the day. The band on the stage wasn't too talented, but they made up for it in enthusiasm. The same could be said for the dancers, he thought, watching them, searching for a familiar length of blond hair.

He hadn't passed anyone on the road into town, so he knew Annabeth had to be here. He'd felt badly for leaving her here this afternoon. His mother had taught him better manners than that. No matter how angry he'd made her, no matter how helpless he'd felt, he should have at least offered her a ride home to get her car. He should have made arrangements with Miss Hilda or Stuart to give her a ride.

He should have done anything besides walk away and leave her there.

The storytelling booth was gone, the bales of hay returned to the feed store. The ponies were gone, too, loaded into Jed Andrews's trailer and trucked back out to the farm. All of the crafts had been packed up, some already taken away, others waiting for their owners to leave the dance and cart them home. The only activity now was around the stage—dancing and talking and laughing.

He saw her at last, sitting on the curb with several other women. A baby was asleep in her arms, and a small child snuggled close to her side, about to doze off himself. It was a scene he had witnessed every year—mothers watching each other's children so they could all participate in the dancing. When he had married Caroline, he had expected to someday see her sitting there with their own children. They had been foolish expectations, he knew now. Caroline never would have sat on the sidelines baby-sitting, and certainly not with someone else's kids, when she could be having fun instead.

But Annabeth didn't seem to mind. She looked as if she fit in there with the other women, some older than she, some younger, one a grandmother. She didn't mind that the children she cuddled weren't her own. She didn't mind that any man there would be happy to give her a twirl around the floor.

She *belonged*.

He was about to step out of the shadows and approach her when someone else beat him to it. Tony greeted all the women with a smile, but his attention was mostly on Annabeth. He offered her a hand, and she passed the baby to one woman. Another shifted the little boy so he leaned against her instead, and Annabeth took Tony's hand and got to her feet.

He wouldn't stand here and watch them dance, Josiah swore. Not when *he* wanted to be the one talking to her, holding her hand, holding *her*. He couldn't bear to watch

Tony put his arms around her, to see her smile at his cousin the way she smiled at *him*.

But they didn't go to the dance floor. Apparently Tony asked, but she shook her head, pulled her hand from his and folded her arms across her chest. She had to be cold, Josiah thought—her denim skirt and leather boots were probably warm enough, but the cotton shirt with the lace-edged collar and the openwork shawl weren't meant for warmth. But cold or not, if his cousin offered to warm her...

With a bleak sigh, Josiah drew deeper into the shadows. No matter what Tony did, *he* couldn't do anything. He couldn't interfere because he didn't have the right. If Tony put his arm around her, if he held her close or kissed her, if he took her home and spent the rest of the night warming her, Josiah couldn't do anything but hate him for it.

Sometimes, it seemed, that was what he did best.

Chapter 6

Annabeth was sweeping Monday morning when a Bronco turned into her driveway. Stopping in the doorway, she leaned on the broom and watched Stuart get out. Somehow, after seeing his office, she had expected him to drive something a little nicer, something in the luxury class. But then, four-wheel drive made sense in the mountains, especially in winter. She could just imagine her little Bug when the roads turned icy. Although she dearly loved the car, she had no doubt that dreams of a heavy truck and chains would be filling her snowy winter nights.

He took a box from the passenger seat and approached her, giving Emerson a vaguely amused look before turning a sterner expression her way. "I understand you met Mary Louise," he said in lieu of a greeting.

"Yes, I did."

"I told you to stay away from my family."

"She wants to talk to me. She has some tales to tell, and she wants to introduce me to your aunt Flo." She turned back to the sweeping, brushing the last of the dirt from the mill and starting on the narrow length of porch. "What would she think if I told her I wasn't interested?"

"You gave your word—"

She interrupted him with a harsh look. "I promised that I wouldn't reveal our true relationship to anyone in the valley. That still stands. I have no interest in breaking the truth to your wife."

For a moment, suspicion lingered in his eyes; then it gave way to resignation. "These are the papers I told you about."

Setting the broom against the wall, Annabeth took the box from him. "Do you have time to go over some of them with me?"

"I suppose so," he said grudgingly. "Let me get something from the truck."

She carried the box inside and set it on the sofa. The flaps were folded over and secured with a strip of tape. She peeled that off and had just glanced inside when Stuart crossed the threshold. What she intended as a quick glance at him turned into a long, steady, surprised look. "What is that?"

He set his load down near the stairs. "You said you would like to have a bathtub. This belonged to my—to your—to my grandmother."

Delighted, she circled around the tub. It was obviously old—she doubted such things were still being made today, certainly not on a routine basis—and the galvanized metal still showed distinct hammer marks. It was by no means big enough to stretch out in, but she could certainly soak when sore muscles or hurt feelings required it. One end had a graceful, high curve to support her back, and a small dish hung over the side to hold the soap. "Thank you," she said, already envisioning a long, hot soak by the stove tonight. "That was very thoughtful."

Embarrassed by her gratitude, he turned away. "The place looks a hundred times better than I thought it could."

"I told you it was sturdy."

"I used to come here when I was a kid and watch Josiah's grandfather work. In exchange for helping out here and there, he gave us scraps of wood left over for carving and whittling. I doubt there was a kid in the valley then who didn't own a wooden gun that came from his scrap lumber.''

Giving the tub a satisfied pat, Annabeth returned to the sofa and the box. Stuart continued to look around, gazing up at the quilts on the loft rail, fingering the delicate crocheted lace curtains at the window, winding up as she had known he would at the photographs.

For a long time, he said nothing—just stood there and looked. What was he thinking? she wondered. Did her mother have a special place in his memories, or had she been just one of numerous other women over the years?

''Lyn is still a beautiful woman,'' he remarked at last.

Lyn. No one had ever called her mother that, not her grandparents and certainly not her stepfather. Because that had been Stuart's pet name for her? ''Yes, she is,'' Annabeth agreed quietly.

He looked at the picture a moment longer, then turned away. ''You stand out.''

That statement was too obvious to bother agreeing with.

The twig chair creaked when he sat down in it. ''Your mother told you . . .''

''About your affair?'' She nodded. ''She forgot to mention, though, that you were married at the time. Did she know?''

He nodded.

And she hadn't cared. Oh, she might have felt a little remorse at the fact that she was seeing another woman's husband, but it hadn't stopped her from becoming lovers with him. Annabeth wondered what the attraction had been. What had been so strong between them that it had made her mother forget right and wrong, had made her father forget the wedding vows he'd taken only a few years earlier? Passion? Affection? Love?

Could it have been love? Their relationship had lasted less than one summer. Could love grow, then die, that quickly?

Desire, maybe. Pure, old-fashioned lust.

''Has it been . . . difficult for you?'' Stuart asked.

"What? Not having a father the first six years of my life? Standing out like a sore thumb in every family photograph, at every family get-together? Knowing from the time Bradley was born that, no matter how much Mama and Daddy loved me, I would never fit in quite the same way he did?" She knew she sounded bitter, but she wasn't, not really. It was a simple fact of life, Grandma Gibbs had long ago taught her. She didn't look like the others because she wasn't quite like the others, and nothing could change that. She could let it rule her life—could let it *ruin* her life—or she could accept, then forget about it. The choice was hers.

"No. I'm as happy and well-adjusted as they come."

"I'm sorry."

She carefully lifted a leather-bound journal from the box before glancing at him. "I'm not. If you and Mama hadn't met and..." She shrugged. "I wouldn't be here—and frankly, I like being here. I like life."

She held his gaze a moment longer before settling the journal on her lap and opening it. It smelled musty and old, and the date on the first page confirmed it: June 21, 1849. The paper was fragile, the ink fading, the handwriting carefully controlled.

"We reached the valley today," the first line began.

It's a beautiful place, not so different from Ohio...if one can overlook the mountains that surround the place. They are really hills, actually, but sharp ones, steep and jagged, with deep gorges and high ridges and water...such water! The streams run clear and cold, often dropping below ground before reappearing a few yards or even a few miles away. There is much familiar about this place, and much more that is new and strange. I find myself longing for home with all its familiarities, but immediately put a stop to such feelings. This is my home now. This is where we will live. This is where we will make our future.

"That was written by Emmalee Dothan," Stuart said. "She and Henry Dothan had been married three weeks when they left Ohio for Dutchman's Valley. She was the daughter of a prominent physician in Cincinnati. She would have been your great-great-great-grandmother."

Annabeth put the journal aside and took the next book, this one records for one of the businesses the Dothan family had engaged in. After thumbing through inventories and shipping records, payments and accounts, she reached for yet another. There was a wealth of information in the box, she discovered—journals, letters, ledgers, even dusty old photo albums. She could spend hours going through it all— later.

Now she returned everything, leaving Emmalee's journal on top, and drew her feet beneath her on the sofa. "I'll take good care of these things. I'll get them back to you as soon as I'm finished."

"Take your time." He shifted positions, then awkwardly stated, "Mary Louise tells me it was you who convinced Josiah to go to the festival Saturday."

For nearly two days now, Annabeth had refused to give Josiah any thought, because every time she did, the muscles in her neck got tight and she developed the beginnings of a headache. Memory of his flat-out rejection Saturday still hurt, along with the disappointment that he had never come back. Of course, he had offered to meet her after the stories, and she had turned him down. Still, she had remained convinced that he would return before the evening was over, if for no other reason than to take her home.

But he hadn't. She had been forced to beg a ride from Tony, and she hadn't seen Josiah since.

"I don't know why he went," she said guardedly.

"Mary Louise thinks you're a good influence on him."

"Did you tell her what *you* think?"

He ignored her reminder of their conversation in the diner last week, when he had warned her to stay away from Josiah. "I wish you could have known him five years ago. He was so different—easy-going, relaxed, always willing to lend a hand, such a pleasure to be around. They say that God never gives you more burdens than you can bear, but I wonder.... Josiah certainly got more than he could handle. Between the recession and the divorce and..." Abruptly he stopped, sighed and shook his head. "You were right last week. He *does* need a friend. But he doesn't need someone who's going to walk away in a few months' time."

"I'm here for a year," Annabeth said, then softly added, "At least." She could easily imagine herself extending that time. If her work required it. If she had a reason. If Josiah gave her a reason.

"A year is such a short interval in the span of a lifetime." Sighing again, he got to his feet. "You read over that stuff—make notes, copy whatever you want—and then I'll give you a tour of the valley that hits all the Dothan family highlights."

She walked to the door with him. "Thank you, Stuart."

His response was a slightly weary shrug. "It's your heritage, too."

She watched until he was gone, then returned to the sofa and the next entry, a few days later, in Emmalee Dothan's journal.

Henry has found some land, a valley within the valley. The land, he tells me, is rich and good for farming. I am not a farmer's wife, but everything is so distant. We must supplement our provisions however we can. Henry hunts for fresh meat—deer are plentiful, as are elk and black bear. I'm not anxious to taste bear, but the neighbors tell me the furs are well worth the hunt. There are also fish too numerous to count in the streams that cross our land, many of a type I have never seen before.

And so I shall learn to garden. I wish I had paid more attention to Cook's garden at home—no, in Ohio; this is home now. Mrs. Harris down the road has kindly offered me plantings from her own garden and seeds

for next year's. The time to plant is past, of course, but
I shall make do.

Annabeth stopped to get a pen and pad from her desk,
then settled on a tape recorder instead. She read the first
entries again, aloud this time, with the tape running. With
Stuart's permission, she might find a place to use passages
from Emmalee's journal in the book. Better to transcribe a
copy from tape than to subject the ancient paper to exces-
sive handling or copying.

She read on, often forgetting that this was research, work
and not necessarily pleasure. Emmalee had been an intelligent, articulate woman who loved her husband and had
come to love his land as much. She wrote often about
Henry, sometimes with the shyness of a young girl, sometimes with the admiration of a grown woman and, on occasion, with the passion of a wife. She wrote with pride
about her garden and the building of their house, about the
success of Henry's businesses and their friendships with the
few others in the valley.

And she wrote with love about the birth of their first
child, Jeffrey, and, a year later, their daughter, Amanda.
There were anecdotes about brother and sister, milestones
of walking and talking and first teeth documented, tales
about squabbles. When she wrote that she was expecting
their third child, she confided that life couldn't be better. "'I
have a husband I love dearly, a home I could never leave,
two children who bring me joy and another soon to be
born.'"

So it was with something of a shock that Annabeth turned
the next page and read the first line.

"'Jeffrey died today. I do believe my heart has broken.'"

"Annabeth."

She gave a start. Somehow, Josiah thought, she hadn't
heard his footsteps on the porch, hadn't heard his knock at
the open door. He had caught her last words, her voice thick

with tears, and had cowardly considered leaving again before she knew he was there, but curiosity—and something more—had stopped him.

He saw the diary, the tape recorder and the wetness in her eyes and realized what he had overheard. She was tearful over some misfortune that had happened long ago to some stranger who had died—judging from the age of the book—long before she was even born.

Sniffling, she turned off the tape, closed the journal and just sat there looking at him. He had come to apologize to her, but now that he was here, now that she was looking at him that way—without a smile or even a hint of welcome—he couldn't think of the words to say. Feeling like an idiot, he gestured to the galvanized tub. "I saw Stuart over here."

She didn't respond.

He stood there a moment, searching for some intelligent words, some effective way to say he was sorry and make her smile again. Coming up blank, he muttered, "Oh, hell, Annie," and turned to leave. He'd made it as far as the hitching post when she spoke his name.

She was standing in the doorway when he turned, her arms across her chest, her hands clasping her elbows. She wore jeans today, faded with a rip across the knee, and a ratty, too-big sweatshirt with the College of Charleston seal on it, but she looked as feminine and graceful in those clothes as she could in the finest lace gown.

She looked beautiful.

Sad and wary and beautiful.

"I want…" He exhaled deeply. He wanted a lot of things. To apologize and explain and get things back to normal between them. To make up for the way he'd acted Saturday. To hear her laugh again. Hell, he wanted to laugh with her.

When he didn't say anything right away, she reached behind her to close the door. "Let's take a walk."

Emerson followed as far as the road, then settled there to wait. Annabeth, hands in her pockets and head down, was leading; Josiah followed along when she turned to the east.

"I was reading about Emmalee Dothan," she announced, kicking up little puffs of dirt. "She was the wife of the first Dothan to settle in the valley. She and her husband had a little boy named Jeffrey who died."

She couldn't have given him a better lead-in to his explanation. Of course, Kylie wasn't dead—at least, he prayed every night that she wasn't; surely not even Caroline could be cruel enough to keep such information from him. But he understood the loss and the grief. Even though she'd had no children of her own, he suspected that Annabeth understood, too.

"About Saturday..."

She bent to pick up a stone, then sent it sailing into the trees. "Forget it."

"No. For the last three years everyone has been letting me get away with behavior that would shame my parents because they feel sorry for me. I keep telling myself I don't want their pity, but I certainly have played on it to get my way."

Finally she looked at him, her expression still disconcertingly somber. "Pity? Because of Caroline?"

"No." This time he was the one who picked up a rock and threw it—hurled it—away. It hit a tree with a resoundingly loud crack. "Because of Kylie."

Annabeth stopped in her tracks. "Kylie?"

He walked a few yards farther, then turned to face her. "My little girl. Caroline and I have a daughter named Kylie. She turned four the day before you came, and I haven't seen her in three years, three months and—" he sighed heavily, unsteadily "—a week or two. I can't deal with kids, Annabeth. I see them and I wonder if she looks like them or talks like them or acts like them. I feel helpless because I can't see her, and I get angry because she's not here with me where she belongs, and...Saturday I took it out on you."

The startled look slowly faded from her face and was replaced with not pity but sympathy. He'd been the recipient of both so many times that he easily recognized the fine line that separated them. "Oh, Josiah...where is she?"

"I don't know." He stared into the woods along the side of the road for a minute, then finally looked at her again. "When Caroline left here, she went back to Little Rock to live with her parents and to file for divorce. We agreed on the settlement and on visitation—she was very generous with the times I could see Kylie—but when I went to Little Rock for our first weekend . . . they were gone."

"And her parents wouldn't tell you where they'd gone?" She sounded dismayed and looked it, too, her brown eyes soft and shadowy.

"They claimed they didn't know. I don't know, maybe they didn't. Maybe she had sneaked out on them the way she tried to sneak out on me. About a month later, though, they left town, too. Her father quit his job without notice, they put the house up for sale and disappeared—no forwarding address, no nothing."

"And your lawyer couldn't do anything?"

Frustrated, he tugged his hand through his hair. "You've seen the farm, the house, the truck, the buildings. I didn't have money for a lawyer. Because we weren't fighting over anything, we just had one attorney—Caroline's. I saw him, but it didn't do any good. He'd done business with her family for years. If he had any loyalty, it was to them, not me."

Falling silent, he recalled that last meeting with the lawyer. If he knew where Caroline had gone, the man said, stressing the "if," but none too convincingly, all he could do was advise her to notify Josiah of her whereabouts and make arrangements for him to see Kylie. If Josiah wanted more than that, he should retain his own attorney.

"He told me to get a lawyer of my own. But it was just before harvest, and I was working eighteen-hour days. I didn't have the money or time to do anything. I didn't even know how to go about trying to find them."

"I'm sorry, Josiah." She sighed softly, wistfully. "I really am sorry."

"So am I—and about Saturday, too. I just couldn't face being around those kids. It hurts too much. I start wondering why all those people get to have their kids when I can't have mine, if they're better parents than I am, if they're more deserving than me, why I'm being punished.''

She moved toward him, and together they started walking again. ''Maybe someday Caroline will change her mind,'' she suggested, a hopeful note in her voice. ''Maybe, when Kylie is old enough to have questions about her father, Caroline will let you answer them.''

Optimistic, cheery and believing in a brighter future—that was Annabeth. He had been hopeful once himself. He had believed every morning when he got up that *this* might be the day Caroline brought Kylie back, and he had gone to bed every night, sore at heart because it hadn't happened. He had hoped long after hope had run out, had believed until faith had deserted him.

''It isn't going to happen. Caroline played me along. She let me believe everything was going to be all right, that even though Kylie wouldn't be here with me, I could still see her whenever I wanted, and all along she was just buying time so she could make her escape. She wanted me out of her life, and out of Kylie's life, and she's not going to invite me back in.''

''But people don't just simply disappear, Josiah. They're out there somewhere—not just Kylie, but Caroline, too, and her parents. Someone has to know where they are. Someone has to know how to find them. There must be something you can do.''

He gave her a sharply critical look. ''For God's sake, Annabeth, do you think I would live this way if I could do anything about it? From the time we found out Caroline was pregnant, that baby became the single most important thing in my life. She's the only person I've ever wholly, completely, unreservedly loved. I would give anything to have her back.''

She started to speak, thought better of it and closed her mouth, then softly, hesitantly blurted it out. ''Even your farm?''

Gazing down at her, he tried to smile, but it came out a twisted grimace instead. "Are you asking why I haven't sold my precious farm and used the money to find her?"

She flushed, which meant she had, of course, been thinking just that.

"Times have been tough for years. Farmers are going under every day. Anyone in the market for good land can pick it up for far less than it's worth. If I sold this place for the absolute best price I could get, I would still owe twice that amount. At least now I have an income. And who knows? Maybe things will get better and someday I'll actually make a profit. Maybe then I'll be able to afford to try to find them."

"So Caroline gets away with it." Disappointment shaded her voice. "She gets to take your daughter away from you. She gets to ignore a legal, binding agreement and live comfortably with her family God knows where, and you can't do anything about it."

"That's about it."

They walked in silence for a while, reaching the end of the road where a rough circle had been carved out of the shoulders of the road for a turnaround. A few beer cans and food wrappers littered the ground—this was a popular spot for parking with high school kids—and a lone sock, once bright pink but now faded and dirty, rested on one shoulder.

"How does someone lose only one sock?" Annabeth asked as they slowly turned to head back.

"She was in a hurry, I guess."

"To take off her socks? And how do you know it was a she?"

"Because none of the farm boys in this valley would wear socks that color—and the socks weren't all she was taking off."

There was a moment's sweet perplexity on her face; then suddenly, unexpectedly, she grinned. "Oh. Okay. A country road, a dead end, no neighbors close enough to notice or care. I get the picture."

"Where do kids go to make out in the city?"

"Depends on the city."

"In *your* city. Charleston."

"Well, it's not that big, so you can find deserted country roads there, too. And beaches. On a warm summer night with the tide coming in and a quarter moon up above, a sand dune is a very romantic place to be."

"Sounds even worse than a roll in the hay."

She laughed softly. "Suffice it to say you have to be very careful. Sand clings, you know."

He didn't have any firsthand experience on the subject, but he would like to find out. He would like to see her city, would like to see just how romantic her sand dunes could be. Maybe some winter, when she had gone back home and his work was slow...

With a scowl, he put a stop to that thought. He didn't want to think about her going home, didn't want to think about the mill being empty once more, about his life being even emptier than before.

"Annabeth—"

She interrupted him with a searching glance. "At the mill you called me Annie. Why?"

He hadn't realized it, but she was right. *Oh, hell, Annie.* It had just slipped out, born of frustration and need and guilt. "I don't know. Annabeth is a nice name, but it's kind of a mouthful. Annie is sweet. It fits you."

After another short silence, in a voice so soft he strained to hear it, she solemnly remarked, "I like it."

So did he, he thought just as solemnly. God help him, so did he.

While they'd been gone, Emerson had waddled a few yards farther from the mill and was sprawled in the grass beside the pond, his ears gone askew, his soulful eyes half-closed. "Have you ever watched when he lies down?" Josiah asked, crouching to pet the poor ugly thing. "He just sort of dissolves into the ground in one fat blob."

"You're a fine one to make fun of him," Annabeth admonished. "A farmer without a dog? That's unheard of. That's un-American."

"If I had a dog, he'd be a whole lot prettier than this one. And he would earn his keep."

Annabeth sat down on the other side of Emerson and smoothed his prickly coat. "He earns his keep," she said haughtily. "He loves me." Then, a complaining note entering her voice, she asked, "Why are you fixated on attractiveness? Your ex-wife is probably gorgeous, and I'm sure your daughter is the prettiest child ever seen, and you're not half-bad to look at yourself. But you can't judge people—or animals—on how they look. Some of us just don't measure up, but that doesn't mean we're not worthwhile."

That wasn't the first time she'd made similar statements. *We can't all be beautiful, can we, Emerson?* she had asked when defending the lazy mutt. *He doesn't care how I look.... He doesn't judge me by standards I can't meet. He accepts me the way I am. That's more than I can say for a lot of people,* you *included.*

When he looked at her, he saw that she was staring across the pond, her lower lip caught between her teeth, her cheeks rosy pink. Forgetting the dog, he moved around in front of her, compensating for the slope of the bank by balancing on his knees. "You're wrong, Annie," he said quietly. "Caroline is pretty, and Kylie is gorgeous, and I don't think I've scared anyone lately, but you . . . you are beautiful. And if I've made you feel less than worthwhile, I'm sorry."

Even though he was right in front of her, she avoided looking at him. Instead, she seemed to find the ground between them incredibly interesting. Josiah reached out, sliding his fingers beneath her chin and gently tilted her face up until she had no choice but to look at him. Her eyes were shadowy again, but this time there was no indignation, no dismay, no hurt. This time there was solemnity. Anticipation. Just the faintest hint of pleasure.

"You are beautiful," he repeated, his fingers shifting slightly to test the softness of her skin. "You remind me of the first warm spring morning, when the snow has melted and the cold has gone and everything is alive and new again.

When you wake up to a morning like that, you can't help but believe that everything's going to be all right.''

The corners of her mouth twitched, as if she really needed to smile but didn't think it appropriate. After a moment, though, the smile won out. ''No one's ever compared me to a morning before,'' she said softly. ''It sounds nice.''

He needed such mornings in his life—many of them. Maybe it really could make everything all right—starting each day like that. With Annie in the morning.

For a long moment, they just sat there—close but not close enough. Touching, but only in that one small way, his fingers beneath her chin. Then, slowly, hesitantly, wondering if he should do this and knowing he couldn't possibly stop, he leaned closer and touched his mouth to hers.

It wasn't a kiss—not that first contact. They both still had their eyes open, and they were both utterly motionless. It was just a touch, a simple, straightforward, nothing-intimate touch.

Then he closed his eyes and bent his head and coaxed her lips apart, testing, tasting. It had been so long, and she tasted so sweet, so warm and full of promise. She opened her mouth to him, welcoming his tongue, welcoming *him*, and he felt the old heat gathering and strengthening inside him. God, it had been so long, but it was familiar, deeply, intensely familiar. Arousal, desire, need. *Life*. For three years he had been dead, and with this one kiss, Annabeth was giving him life again.

Eyes still closed, he used his hands to see her, to stroke her face, her hair, to glide down her arms to her hands, resting limply in her lap, to slide over the well-worn softness of her sweatshirt, over the warm sweep of her midriff to her breasts.

She caught her breath when he brushed across her nipple—he heard it, felt it. His fingers ached for a more intimate caress. She was naked beneath the shirt; all he had to do was slip his hands beneath it and touch her, stroke her and give her pleasure.

He could give her pleasure.

Slowly he drew away. Opening her eyes, Annabeth met his gaze, wondering what he was looking for, what he was thinking. There was no denying what he was feeling. He was definitely aroused—his muscles taut, his body hard, his breathing uneven. But what was he thinking? What was he wishing? That she was Caroline?

No. This look—this kiss, this passion—was *hers.* Not Caroline's. He wanted *her.*

He touched her, his fingertips grazing her skin, circling the ribbed neck of her shirt, loosening the bands that held her hair in its braid, combing it out. His gaze locked with hers. He drew his hands down her body, almost but not quite touching her breasts, settling them at her waist. "I haven't done anything purely for pleasure in years," he murmured, his voice thick and hoarse.

So he hadn't had sex since Caroline. Some small part of her was surprised by the idea of a healthy, normal man voluntarily abstaining for so long, but the larger part of her wasn't. Josiah hadn't been healthy. Oh, physically he'd been fine, of course, but he'd been dealing with the disappearance of his beloved Kylie from his life.

I do believe my heart has broken.

No doubt, like Emmalee Dothan, *his* heart had been broken, too.

She wished she could put it back together for him, wished that she could somehow make everything all right for him. But she didn't know how, didn't know what to offer him, what to say to him. She didn't know what he wanted, what he needed, what he might be willing to accept from a city woman whose time in the valley was limited.

The dull pain that thought brought made her wonder about the condition of her own heart.

For the first time she reached out to touch him, cupping her hand to his face. His skin was smooth, browned by years of exposure to the sun. There were fine lines at the corners of his eyes, eyes that were darker than usual now, eyes that watched her so solemnly. When her fingertips brushed his mouth, he gave them a kiss of sorts, wet and gentle, making her smile.

Slowly, her heart pounding, her muscles trembling, she slid her hands around his neck. It was a funny thing about arousal, that something so good and pleasurable involved such pain. Her breasts ached, and her throat was tight. She had an uncomfortable feeling in her chest and a tingling, burning, badly-in-need-of-relief emptiness deep in her belly. And she wouldn't even think about the torment of the heat, frustrating and potent and damp, between her thighs.

She drew him closer, leaning back, her hands coaxing him down, down, until they were both on the ground, bodies touching, her thigh snugly between his, his hardness pressing against her. She raised both hands to his face, her thumbs stroking, her fingers urging him closer so she could kiss him. He cooperated, but only to a point. When their mouths met, it was he who controlled the kiss. He kissed her hungrily, hard, his tongue searching, stroking, filling, building needs and aches that demanded satisfaction. Her breasts were swollen, her nipples craving attention that she was about ready to plead for when slowly, so lightly that she first wondered if she imagined it, he slid his fingers beneath her shirt.

His hand was warm, his palm and fingers callused. It skimmed across her stomach, barely touching, then stroked her breast in slow, widespread caresses that ended on her nipple. This wasn't relief, she thought dazedly, feeling the tightness in her chest expand until breathing became difficult, feeling the sensations in her breast intensify until his barest touch made her tremble. This was torture—pure, relentless torture—and she wanted it to never end.

As if jinxed by her thoughts, once again he drew away, resting for a moment on one elbow. This time he looked as regretful as she felt. "Someone's coming," he said quietly.

If she listened hard, she could hear the sound of an engine, still some distance away. "I don't care," she said stubbornly, reaching for him again as he rose to his knees.

"You'll care if you get caught stretched out naked by the side of the road." He took her hands in both of his and pulled her up with him, supporting all her weight until they were both standing.

The motor was closer now. In another minute or so, the car would come around the last curve in the road. Annoyed, she found the rubber bands where he had dropped them, and she gathered her hair into a reasonably controlled ponytail. Before she turned to go, though, she laid her hand on his forearm. "Josiah, it's not fair," she said softly, seriously.

The corners of his mouth turned up in a semblance of a tiny—very tiny—smile. "There'll be other times."

"No. I mean about Kylie. It's not fair that Caroline could take her away like that."

His rare smile faded. "No, it isn't. But there's nothing I can do about it."

Maybe he was right, she thought as they started toward the mill just as the approaching truck came into sight. Maybe there was nothing he could do. He had other obligations—the farm, his creditors, earning a living. He had to work long hours, had to spend every extra bit of money he had on his debts or put it back into the farm. Maybe he just had to accept that Kylie was forever gone.

Maybe he had to give up hope.

But *she* didn't.

"It's Aunt Mary Louise," Josiah announced as the truck turned in at the mill.

So it was. The woman got out and leaned against the truck, watching them with a smug smile. "Can you spare the time to come over and talk with us?" Annabeth asked. Surely Mary Louise would be too subtle to attempt any matchmaking in Josiah's presence.

"I don't think that would be such a good idea," he said dryly.

Wondering why, she glanced at him; then her gaze was drawn surreptitiously lower. Tight jeans were a wonderful thing on a well-formed man. Women the world over loved a man in snug, faded denims; they left little to the imagination. For that very reason, when they reached Josiah's mailbox, he called a greeting to his aunt, said goodbye to Annabeth and turned into his driveway.

Annabeth continued to the mill, offering Mary Louise a vague smile and a polite greeting. "What can I do for you this morning?"

"No, it's what *I* can do for *you*." She watched Josiah until he was out of sight, then turned her sharp gaze on Annabeth. "Out for a stroll with my nephew this morning?"

"We were just talking."

"What does an attractive young couple like you two talk about when you're all alone?" With a sly smile, she continued before Annabeth could answer. "By the way, dear, you have grass in your hair."

Flushing, Annabeth combed her fingers through her hair and brushed loose a few long blades of tough, browned grass.

"I won't be difficult and tease you," Mary Louise said. "I came to tell you that Stuart's aunt Flo has agreed to see you. She sent me over with orders to take you to her house for lunch. Are you free?"

Annabeth thought longingly of Josiah somewhere over around his barn, of wandering over that way as soon as Mary Louise was gone and picking up where they'd left off. It wouldn't be a difficult position to duplicate—her mouth had been on his, his hand had been on her breast. She had been hot, and he had been hard.

But she suspected it wouldn't be quite so easy as picking up where they'd left off. They would have to start over, and that might take a little finesse. And how could she possibly turn down a command from Stuart's aunt Flo—from her own great-aunt Flo—to come for lunch and reminiscing?

"Of course," she replied with a smile, even though that was exactly the opposite of what she wanted to say. Even though listening to an old lady's nearly forgotten recollections was the last thing she wanted to do today. Even if that old lady was related to her. "Just let me get a few things."

She left the mill door open behind her and went straight to her desk, gathering supplies: notebook and pen, tape recorder, batteries and tapes, camera and camcorder and film.

She was loading everything into a backpack she had modified with sturdy cardboard shelves when Mary Louise, her attention on the bathtub, spoke from the doorway.

"I see my husband has already been here today. Odd that he didn't mention he was coming. I could have delivered that for him."

There was a curiously flat tone to her voice that made Annabeth pause. Was that jealousy? she wondered. Possessiveness? Disapproval? Maybe a little of all three. If she was aware of Stuart's long-ago affair, then wouldn't it be natural for her to be displeased with the knowledge that he had visited a strange woman in her home?

Or maybe it was nothing. Maybe it had been a simple statement of fact and Annabeth had read too much into it because of the secret she was keeping.

After zipping up the bag, she slung it over one shoulder by a webbed strap, then faced the older woman. "Your husband knows a great deal about the valley," Annabeth said evenly. "It's the older people I'm most interested in talking to, you know. They've lived so long, have experienced so much. They have so many stories to tell."

Mary Louise gave her a long, measuring look, then slowly smiled. "The older people," she repeated. "You make it sound as if we've got one foot in the grave, as if we're the ancient ones."

Annabeth's laugh was a little forced. "You're not even close," she admonished, politely ushering the woman from the mill and closing and locking the door behind her. "Growing up, the only elderly people I knew were my grandparents. At that time, sixty and seventy seemed incredibly old to me. But in the course of doing my research for the first two books, I met dozens of people in their seventies, eighties and nineties. I even interviewed a few people in North Carolina and Virginia who were over a hundred years old. They were still vital, still lucid, still enriching the lives of everyone around them.''

"Like Aunt Flo." Mary Louise walked to her truck, gesturing for Annabeth to follow. "You can come with me today, since I could never give you directions worth following. But pay attention to the way we go, because once Flo gets her hands on you, she's not going to let go until she's told you *everything*. And, honey," she said, smiling across the truck at her, "after eighty-some years of living, that's an awful lot."

Chapter 7

Friday evening brought cold winds that rattled the windowpanes and a heavy rain that, falling unchecked, would soon turn the road into a sea of mud. Josiah stood at the window in the darkened living room, staring alternately at the mill and the empty road between. The mill stood dark and Annabeth's banged-up old Bug was gone from its customary parking place.

Where was she?

She'd been going up to see Florene Hilliard every day this week, all the way to the top of Buzzard's Peak, but she made it home each evening before dark. She had said she would be home by five this evening, had invited him to dinner at six. A short while ago the clock in the hall had struck seven. Where was she?

Maybe she'd gotten absorbed in her talk with the old lady and had forgotten the time. That certainly wouldn't surprise him. But he had told her that it was supposed to rain, had warned her that that old mountain road and her low-slung little car weren't compatible in heavy rain.

A shiver passed through him. It was almost as cold inside the house as it was out. He hadn't turned on the heat when he'd come in from work two hours ago, since he hadn't been planning on spending the evening at home.

He hadn't seen much of Annabeth since Monday morning. While she'd been with Aunt Flo each day, he'd been spending far more time than was healthy fixing the heater on the truck and working on that old tractor of his. If he ever got a new John Deere, he swore he would set this one in a field and let it rust. But considering that the price of a new tractor could easily exceed the price of certain new homes, he was relatively certain he would never have a new one. He would make this one work until it absolutely couldn't be repaired anymore, and then he would go into debt even deeper to get a newer, though used, one and start all over again.

Just as surely as Aunt Flo was filling Annabeth's days, others were occupying her evenings. Stuart had been over there Tuesday, and Miss Hilda on Thursday. Josiah had gone over for a time Wednesday evening to deliver a few pieces of mail that had been in his box, but she had been preoccupied with that journal again. Although she had put it away and given him her full attention, he had felt as if he were intruding and had soon come home again.

He had been looking forward all day to this evening together. He wanted a chance to talk to her, a chance to kiss her again, a chance just to hold her.

"Oh, hell, who are you kidding?" he muttered aloud. He wanted *everything*. Intimacy. Passion. Pleasure. Fulfillment. He wanted so badly to make love to her that he had trouble sleeping at night. When he finally drifted off, it was to dreams of wanting her, dreams he awakened from hard, frustrated and supremely unsatisfied.

The hall clock chimed one time. She was now two and a half hours late, and the rain hadn't even considered letting up. Maybe the rain had started while she was still at Aunt Flo's, and the old woman hadn't let her leave. Or maybe it hadn't and she had left and got caught in it on the way. Maybe she was safe and dry and warm somewhere.

And maybe she wasn't.

Muttering a curse, he pushed away from the wall and headed for the back of the house. A fleece-lined jean jacket hung on a hook on the enclosed porch; next to it was a thick rubber slicker. He put on the jacket, then the slicker, dug his keys from his pocket and dashed through the rain to the truck. For once it chugged to life on the first try. Accelerating slowly, he pulled out of the muddy yard and maneuvered astride the ruts in the driveway to the road.

Buzzard's Peak was north of the Corner and, at two thousand feet, was the tallest of the mountains that encircled the valley. As the crow flew—or the buzzard, in this case—the Hilliard place was about twelve miles away, but the snaky curves in the road probably added another five miles to that distance.

Once he got on the highway, he picked up his speed, but the rain still slowed him down. Sometimes it fell straight down in sheets; others times the wind would catch it and blow it horizontally. Either way, it was hard to see.

He was halfway up the mountain and coming around a curve when his headlights picked up the car. It was on the side of the road, the right side against a weathered board fence, the left wheels half-buried in mud. Although the rain had long since washed away any evidence of what had happened, it wasn't hard to guess: coming around a hairpin curve from the other direction, the car had begun sliding and had kept on until something—in this case probably a combination of the fence and the mud—stopped it.

Josiah slowed to a stop beside the Bug. His heart pounding, he climbed out into the rain and immediately felt the mud grab at his boots. "Annabeth!" he shouted, but the wind carried his voice away. He hadn't been able to see inside the car when his lights swept across it. Maybe she wasn't there. Maybe she had walked back to Aunt Flo's and was waiting there...but Aunt Flo's was a good three more miles. In this rain and wind, in this cold, she might not make it.

Maybe she just hadn't heard him.

Or maybe she was hurt.

He slogged through the mud, grasped the handle and yanked the door open. A sodden, huddled shape in the front seat whirled around with a cry of fright, then just sort of dissolved against the seat in relief, much the way Emerson might have. "Josiah," she whispered.

Crouching beside the car, he cupped her face in his hands, turning it this way, then that, using the dim light to look for any sign of injury. Seeing none, he clasped her hands instead. "So you're the one who taught your lazy mutt how to do that," he said unsteadily.

Her face had been cold; so were her hands. Her clothes were wet, her teeth were chattering, and yet she still managed a smile. "Don't make fun of my dog," she warned him. Then, the smile fading as quickly as it had come, she forlornly said, "I'm cold, Josiah. Can we go home?"

Quickly he unsnapped his slicker, scooped her into his arms and covered her as much as possible. Shoving the door shut with his foot, he hurried to the truck and lifted her onto the seat, climbing in after her as soon as she scooted aside.

"Are you all right?" he asked, turning the newly repaired heater on high.

"Y-yes. Just t-terribly cold."

"What happened?"

"The road was so slick, and my car doesn't get very good traction. It started sliding, and nothing I could do helped. I'm afraid I tore down a section of that fence."

"Don't worry about it." Peering through the rain—heavier now, it seemed, than ever—he slowly moved the truck forward. There was a place up ahead, a wide spot in the road where, nearby, one of the Ozarks' countless springs bubbled to the surface. At one time or another—before their wells had been dug or when they'd gone dry—everyone who lived along this road had collected drinking water there.

When he reached the place, he pulled off the road. He rolled the window down a few inches for a breath of fresh air, left the engine running for the heat and slid across the seat. He shrugged out of his slicker, tossing it on the floor, and then removed his jacket. Annabeth protested, but he wrapped it tight around her. She stopped protesting when he lifted her onto his lap and held her close.

"You scared me," he admitted softly, stroking her damp hair.

"I didn't mean to..." she started to apologize, but he stopped her by putting a finger to her lips. Getting scared once in a while was a good thing. It meant you cared about something.

He hadn't been scared in a terrible long time.

Even with the heater on, even with his jacket and his arms around her, she was still shivering. It made her seem so small. So vulnerable.

"It was just starting to sprinkle when I left Aunt Flo's," she said, resting her head against his shoulder. "She had been telling me about the boy she wanted to marry when she was young, only her father wouldn't let her because he wasn't from the valley, and so they had run off together, and he left her alone and penniless in Memphis. It created such a scandal that she felt quite lucky when Burt Hilliard asked her to marry him a few years later. Anyway, I wanted to let her finish that before I left. It was already six-thirty, and she doesn't have a phone so I could call and tell you I was going to be late, which is all right since you don't have a phone, either."

When she stopped for breath, he cupped his palm to her face and asked again, "Are you sure you're all right?"

She nodded. "I didn't hit the steering wheel or anything. It was as if the accident happened in slow motion. The car just sort of gracefully slid across the road and into the ditch and came to rest against the fence. It almost would have been fun if it hadn't been scary. Oh, my poor car."

"Your car's probably fine."

She raised her head and gave him a look. Even though he couldn't see it, he could easily imagine it—dry and scolding. "That car hasn't been fine since it was five years old—which was a very, very long time ago. Sometimes the windows won't go down, and when they do, sometimes they won't go back up. The convertible top is cranky and ill-tempered, and there are dings and dents in every conceivable place. It has so many miles on it that the odometer couldn't count that high and so it quit trying. It has no airconditioning, and the heater only works on high. Always on high. Even in summer."

"Then if it's in such bad shape, a ride through the ditch and into a fence can't do too much more harm, can it?" He shifted her on his lap, drawing her legs closer. Her skirt was uncomfortably wet. If he had a blanket, he would strip off her clothes, wrap her up tight and share his body heat with her. But he didn't have a blanket, and stripping her naked would result in a much more intimate exchange of body heat than he intended.

Now was not the time for such thoughts, he admonished himself and moved to release her. "We'd better go home."

"Not yet. Give the rain a chance to let up. Hold me a little longer." She sighed softly, and he felt it against his throat. "I didn't know such darkness existed. I can feel you and hear you and touch you, but I can't see anything more than a shadow."

That was partly due to the rain—the clouds obscured the moon and stars—and partly to their location so far away from neighbors and lights, and to the canopy of trees, mostly evergreens, that met overhead. It was a little disconcerting, seeing nothing, but comfortable, too. Cozy.

"Why did you come looking for me?"

"I missed you. I was wor—"

She kissed him right in the middle of the word—an unexpected, sweet smack that ended almost as soon as it started. "Thank you."

Josiah was surprised . . . and instantly aroused, instantly hot. For a moment he sat motionless, barely even breathing, wishing he could see her face, wishing he could gauge exactly how innocent that kiss had been. Then he decided he didn't care, because there would be nothing innocent about his response.

He brushed her wet hair away and tilted her head back and fitted his mouth perfectly over hers. She responded with an immediacy—and an intensity—that was gratifying and answered his question. She wanted this, every bit as much as he did.

His tongue stroked hers, while his hands stroked down her body, moving unerringly to her breasts. Her shirt was damp and cool against her skin, but there was a steamy sort of warmth in the cocoon of his jacket around her. Feeding on her mouth, he unfastened each button and pushed the sodden fabric aside.

Her breasts were sweetly full in his hands, her nipples pressing hard against his palms. He was hungry to taste her, to kiss her soft flesh, to draw her nipple into his mouth, to suck it hard and make her moan. But she was already moaning, already whimpering as he pressed his hands hard against her, rubbing them slowly back and forth across her nipples.

Pulling his mouth from hers, he left a trail of kisses down her throat, then lifted her to sit astride him, so that, by merely ducking his head, he could kiss her breast, could take her nipple between his teeth, could gently bite and suck and tease it.

Annabeth pushed his jacket away, then struggled out of her shirt, dropping it to the floorboard. Only moments ago, she had been freezing; now the truck cab felt like a steam-bath. Where had all this heat come from? she wondered, then answered her own question with a lazy smile. From *them*. She was suddenly so hot that she just might ignite. Everywhere Josiah touched her—one hand on her hip, another on her back, his thighs pressed against hers, his mouth at her breast—she damn near burned.

He suckled first one breast, then the other, now gentle, now hard, creating the curiously opposing twin halves of arousal. Pleasure, now pain.

She was on her knees, unable to make contact with his body where she needed it most. Tugging him away with her hands in his hair, she sank down to sit on his lap again, rubbing slowly, sensuously, against his hardness, almost whimpering with need and frustration at the clothes that separated them.

Unable to reach her breasts when she held him so tight, he kissed her again, only this time it wasn't so much a kiss as an assault. Heated passion, desperate hunger, desire so thick and strong and hard that not even the torrential cold rain outside could dampen it. Annabeth couldn't remember ever feeling so wanted . . . or so needy herself.

She opened his shirt with far less finesse than he had managed hers and slid her hands inside, feeling him flinch at the coolness of her fingertips, hearing him groan at her feathery caresses. She wanted to touch him everywhere, and wanted it *now,* and to that end she set to work on his jeans—unfastening his belt, fumbling with the button, reaching for the zipper.

He caught her hands, tore his mouth from hers and drew in a ragged breath. "Annie, we need to go home," he protested hoarsely.

She kissed his jaw, his cheek, then his ear. "We need to make love."

"In the truck? We don't have any room."

She laughed throatily and traced the shape of his ear with her tongue. "Farm boys have been making love in trucks since the beginning of time."

"I'm not a boy."

Freeing her hands from his, she opened his zipper, slid her fingers gently inside and at last reached her goal, cradling him in her palm. He was heavy and hard, searing hot, and wickedly, sinfully ready. "Tell me about it." Then the teasing disappeared and was replaced by a plaintive appeal. "Oh, please, Josiah, I need you. . . ."

He looked at her for a moment—she felt his gaze—then cradled her face and gently kissed her. "I need you, too, Annie," he whispered solemnly.

Josiah removed his clothes and left Annabeth's to her. He heard the thud of her shoes, the rustle of her skirt, the slow, damp slide of her panties. There was something tantalizing about the sounds in the dark, something secret and erotic.

When his own clothes were gone, he reached for her, intending to lift her onto his lap, to slide her into place on his hardness, but naturally, being Annabeth, she had other ideas. They moved and shifted and bumped on the wide bench seat, him protesting, her simply laughing, until she was on her back and he was between her thighs and with one slow, thick, relentless thrust, he was inside her.

Her giggle died away unfinished as her body adjusted to his intrusion, stretching, tightening, relaxing. She hadn't been prepared, he thought regretfully, for the size of him, but she didn't seem to be in pain. She didn't stiffen or pull away, and her soft little gasp had seemed to consist more of satisfaction than pain. "Are you all right?" he whispered, resting his forehead on hers.

She moved experimentally, moving away, then taking him fully, deeply, again, and she laughed that delighted laugh again. "Not a boy at all, are you?" she teased. She stroked her fingers through his hair, then pulled him closer and kissed him slowly, lazily. "Oh, Josiah," she sighed. "I do need you."

He finished almost as quickly as any of those eager-for-the-experience teenage farm boys she had mentioned earlier, but Josiah didn't mind. This hadn't been the sort of take-your-time-and-savor-it lovemaking they would indulge in later. This had been a hot, fast storm of passion that had left them both trembling, stunned and satisfied. It had been incredible.

She was still now beneath him, her arms around his neck, her face pressed to his shoulder. Her breathing was steadier, slowing from the rapid, nearly tearful little gasps when he had filled her, and her muscles were relaxing, although from time to time a shudder still passed through her. He stroked her hair, then kissed her forehead, her cheeks, her nose. "Sweet, sweet Annie," he murmured as his mouth found hers.

She took his kiss not as a gentle, soothing finish, as he had intended, but with a shiver, with a low, interested moan, with a tightening of the muscles inside where she still sheathed him.

"We'd better get home before the road washes out."

"Does it do that?" she asked, her voice husky and enticing.

"Occasionally."

"That might be nice."

"No, it wouldn't." He gently disentangled himself from her, lifting away and moving her legs so he could sit on the seat. "I'd have to turn the motor off in a minute, and it would get very cold very quickly."

"Oh, but you could keep me warm."

He found a pile of clothing on the floor and identified each piece—her shirt, thin and still damp, his jeans, her skirt, also still damp, and his boots. Dressing in the cramped space was as awkward as undressing had been, but he managed and, after a moment's urging, so did Annabeth.

Funny. The space had been just as cramped—even more so—but making love hadn't seemed awkward at all.

Once he was reasonably dressed—his shirt wasn't tucked in, his belt was somewhere on the floor, and so were his socks—he turned his attention to leaving. The rain wasn't as heavy as it had been, but the road was still treacherous. He turned the truck around carefully, pulling forward, backing up, pulling forward again, hoping all the time that he wouldn't drive into a mudbank like the one that had caught Annabeth earlier. Finally they were heading back down into the valley. The truck slid a few times, but each time he managed to regain control before they reached the rain-swollen ditches.

As soon as they made it to the valley floor, he reached across the seat, catching hold of Annabeth's skirt and tugging until, with a laugh, she slid across to sit beside him. "Who is Sweet Annie?" she asked, resting her hand on his thigh, leaning her head against his arm on the back of the seat.

"You are. As sweet as honey on a hot summer day."

"Uh-huh. Right. You compared me to Sweet Annie my first day in the valley. You didn't know then just how sweet I could be. Who is she?"

Josiah thought of the story his grandfather had told him years ago—with a wink and a grin, when none of the women in the family were around—of the pass at the east end of the valley. Sweet Annie's Pass, named for a woman who had lived nearby. At the time, Josiah couldn't have been more than eight or ten years old. He hadn't completely understood what his grandfather was saying, and the old man had had better sense than to explain it in terms a child could understand. What was funny, he had wondered, about a woman being so well liked that the passage through the mountains where she lived had come to be named after her?

He had been fifteen or sixteen and taking shelter from a summer storm on the porch at the mill with Sallie Ann Andrews before he'd truly understood the significance of his grandfather's tale. Annabeth would probably love the story, but somehow he didn't think his connecting it to her would amuse her. Besides, it didn't matter. She was *his* Sweet Annie now, and making her own pass through his life.

"Is that invitation to dinner still open?" he asked, ignoring her question.

"I might be persuaded to throw something together."

"How about an invitation to spend the night?" His tone was serious, underlaid with more than a hint of nervousness. Shyness. They were back in town now where streetlights, few and far between, could give him a glimpse of her face, but he didn't look. He didn't want to second-guess her answer.

Laughing softly, she shifted on the seat so that she could whisper in his ear and, at the same time, insinuated her hand in a seductive caress between his thighs. "I think I could be persuaded."

For an instant he let himself concentrate on her bold touch and on the sweet pleasure that awaited him at the mill. Then, as the truck drifted over the center line, he pulled her hand away and forced his attention back to the road. "You're a dangerous woman, Annabeth Gibbs."

"Annie," she promptly insisted. "Call me Annie."

"Annie," he obliged.

Sweet Annie.

Annabeth sat back in the seat. She felt all warm and smug and incredibly satisfied inside. In spite of the rain and the cold and her poor little car, this was a good day, a wonderful day. The best in her life.

And the night promised to be even better.

She was going to stay in Dutchman's Valley forever. She was going to fall in love with Josiah— Going to? she wryly interrupted. She was already so close that one more tumble would send her crashing so deeply that she would be lost forever. She was going to love Josiah the rest of her life and even after, and someday he was going to come to love her, too.

Someday, she promised herself with a small smile, he was even going to tell her about Sweet Annie.

They parked outside the mill, and Josiah slipped on his jacket, leaving the waterproof slicker for her. Hand in hand, they raced across the puddle-soaked clearing to the porch, where a snoozy Emerson greeted them with a whine.

"Oh, Emerson." Annabeth hung the slicker on a hook, then gave Josiah the keys while she crouched to pet the dog. "It's a good thing I put that blanket out for you, isn't it?" she asked, scratching his ears, about the only part of the animal not covered by the worn yellow throw.

As soon as Josiah opened the door, Emerson shuffled inside and immediately settled at the side of the woodstove. She was tempted to follow—the mill was cold and unwelcoming—but, instead, she offered Josiah a deal. "You get the fire going, and I'll see about dinner as soon as I get changed."

Upstairs it took her only a moment to remove her sticky clothes, and ten times longer to decide what to put on instead. Would a nightgown be too forward? she wondered, then immediately discarded the idea. None of the bed clothes she'd brought with her—nightshirts all, flannel for winter and cotton for summer—could be considered in the slightest seductive. Should she choose something warm and snugly or pretty and feminine?

She settled on comfortable—blue jeans, fuzzy socks and a big white shirt, left unbuttoned at least two buttons too much. Downstairs, she took a moment in the bathroom to brush her hair and wash her hands, then she went into the kitchen.

She had planned to fix roast with all the trimmings, but it was much too late for that now. She was bent over, staring into the refrigerator, considering the possibilities, when Josiah wrapped his arm around her waist, pulled her bottom snug against his hips, against his arousal. With his free hand, he guided her into an upright position so he could nuzzle her neck and her ear.

Annabeth's fingers clenched around the door handle, then slowly, with a twitch, released it, and her entire body went limp. He was rubbing her breast now, not inside the shirt, which she had conveniently left open for just that activity, but through it, his hand big and brown against the bright white cotton.

"I thought you were hungry," she whispered, unable to find the breath to give her voice strength.

He turned her around and traced one finger down the open neck of her shirt until he reached the first fastened button, somewhere closer to her waist than her breasts. "Show me what you've done with the loft," he quietly demanded. "Show me where you sleep."

Kicking the refrigerator door shut, she took his hand and led him upstairs to the loft. "This is where I keep my clothes," she said, still breathy as she gestured to the stacks of handwoven baskets and the hooks on the walls.

He didn't look at the baskets, though, or the hooks and the hanging clothes they held. He merely looked at her in the dim light from below while he unbuttoned his shirt.

She cleared her throat. "These quilts are gifts from people I've interviewed over the years. I helped make that star quilt myself—all the crooked stitches are mine."

His shirt fell, and his jeans and briefs came off, too. She couldn't swallow, couldn't pull her gaze from him. She had been as intimate with him as two people could be, had held him in her hand, had felt him inside her, but she hadn't imagined... He was magnificent—muscular, strong, throbbing. Beautifully, enticingly magnificent.

"Those corn husk dolls..." Moisture was gathering between her thighs again, along with heat and hunger and helpless, achy need. They made it hard for her to think, hard to keep her mind focused, hard to make her mouth work. "They...uh, they're made by a lady in a...in a tiny little hamlet in North Carolina. She...she sells them...to gift shops and to tourists and supports a family of four kids...."

Still without looking away from her, he knelt and unfastened her jeans and pulled them off, along with her socks and her panties.

"But she...she wouldn't let me pay for... Oh, my."

That last bit ended in a startled sigh as he pressed a kiss to the tender inside of her thigh, biting, sucking. He could finish her right here, right now. Another kiss, a gentle stroke of his finger, and she would collapse in a quivering heap at his feet. But he didn't kiss her again, didn't part her thighs to stroke her. Instead, he stood up and wrapped his arms around her, lifting her so that his hardness rubbed her belly, then probed between her thighs, pushing through the blond curls to the heat underneath. She braced her hands on his shoulders, her breathing uneven and harsh, her muscles clenching and unclenching, waiting for him to lower her over him, to fill her so snugly again, to take her standing like this and make her weep.

But slowly he lowered her feet to the floor again and, for the first time, showed some interest in their surroundings. "So this is your bedroom."

Restraining a grin, she pounded one small fist against his chest. "I will punish you, Josiah Miller," she warned. "I will make you plead for mercy, and I won't show you any. I will be cruel and hard—''

In one fluid movement, he slid his hand between her thighs and filled her with two fingers, making her gasp and tremble and offer a tiny, wordless plea of her own. "Hard?" he echoed. "Honey, you're the sweetest, softest thing I've ever seen—and hot. You're going to catch on fire." He withdrew his fingers, moist now with her flavor, and offered her a devilishly innocent smile.

Annabeth returned the smile, then, without warning, began making her warning a reality. She didn't bother with a gentle seduction, although that held tremendous appeal, too—kissing him until he couldn't catch his breath, stroking him until his muscles trembled uncontrollably, coaxing his flat nipples erect with tender suckling, adding pleasure upon layer of pleasure until the slightest scrape of her nails made his flesh quiver, until the most innocent brush of her breast made him twitch. No, she would save all that for later, for one morning when she awoke before him and found him all warm and innocent and asleep at her side.

This time she got straight to the point. Before he could guess her intentions, she knelt in front of him and slowly, agonizingly slowly, kissed away the dampness that glistened on the tip of his arousal. When he groaned and moved his hips, she let him fill her mouth, taking all that she could, bathing his length, savoring the taste of him and herself, the heat and the incredible softness of the flesh that sheathed such hardness.

When the muscles in his thighs were taut and quivering, when Josiah knew he couldn't take one more minute of such torment, she pulled away, leaving him like that, and *sauntered,* damn her, to the mattress on the floor against one rail. She pulled the covers back and lay down, her hair tumbling over the lace-edged pillowcase, and offered him a sultry smile. "And this is where I sleep."

He lowered himself to the bed, parting her legs at the same time, and came up hard inside her, filling her in one stroke. She started to laugh, that sexy, throaty laugh, but he stopped it with his kiss, claiming her mouth as thoroughly as he'd claimed her body. The passion built quickly, subsided, then built again. He wanted to make it last forever, but his heart was thudding, his blood pumping, and sweet Annie was making the most tormenting, tantalizing movements beneath him.

When she finished, it was with a cry, her cheeks flushed, her breasts heaving, her muscles clutching at him. That was enough incentive—those tiny little spasms—to bring him to the edge. He strained against her, emptying himself into her, hot and heavy, and he held her tightly, so tightly, so that they might never slip apart.

His muscles finally easing, his body going soft inside hers, he moved to lie beside her, to gently turn her on her side and gather her close against him. For a long time, they were both silent—Annabeth watching the fire below, Josiah watching her.

For a man his age, he'd had remarkably little variety in his love life. There had been Sallie Ann Andrews, who had been as naive and inexperienced as he was, who had liked the kissing and the petting and everything else except the act itself, who had merely endured that part in exchange for the rest. There had been those three weekends his first year in college, with a girl as lonely and homesick for her family's farm in southern Arkansas as he had been for his. And there had been Caroline, who, at eighteen, had known far more about making love than he had.

But he knew enough to know that Annabeth was special.

He knew enough to know that he cared for her.

He knew enough to know that his life would be emptier than ever when she left.

But that wasn't exactly true. Of course he would miss her—even though her leaving was eleven months away, he already felt a little shiver of dread thinking about it. He would miss her laugh and her delightful smile. He would miss seeing her battered little car parked out front here. He would miss smelling the smoke from her fire when he stepped outside in the morning. He would miss talking to her and looking at her and, God help him, making love with her.

But it would be a bittersweet kind of missing. It wouldn't devastate him, the way missing Kylie had. It wouldn't leave him incapable of facing life. He would be richer for having known her.

She snuggled back against him, her cotton shirt soft against his chest. "Josiah?"

"Hmm."

She lifted his hand from her waist and pressed a kiss to it. "Thank you."

Thank you. He should be saying that, not her. She had saved his life. She had shown him how good it was to feel again. She had given him reason to want to live again.

She kissed his hand again, tracing the line of the scar that extended across the back. Holding it away from her a bit, she rubbed over the long scar, and then the smaller ones, then drew in her breath, preparing to speak. He stalled her with the answer to the question he knew she was about to ask.

"I was working on the tractor and smashed my hand pretty badly. I broke a few bones and got those scars."

"It must have been painful."

"Hmm." In fact, it had hurt like hell, but he had been grateful for the physical discomfort. It had, for a short time, taken his mind off his emotional wounds. Lying here naked with Annabeth was a much more pleasant way to accomplish the same thing.

"It must have been frightening, living alone the way you do." Abruptly, she rolled over to face him, turning in the tight space so that she was practically nose to nose with him. "You need a neighbor."

"I have one," he replied with a smile. "You can't get much more neighborly than this."

She stared at him so intensely for so long that he wondered if something was wrong. Then she raised her hand and touched his mouth with one finger. "It's good to see you smile," she whispered.

It felt good to smile, to know that he hadn't forgotten how. To know that life wasn't always bleak, as he'd believed for more than three years, and that his heart wasn't completely broken. And he had Annabeth to thank for that.

For teaching him.

For loving him.

For healing him.

Annabeth's car was out of commission the first part of the week while Tony Walker waited for parts to repair the damage she'd done on the mountain road. She took advantage of the lack of transportation by working at home, spending her days transcribing tapes, making notes and filling in blanks on the genealogical charts.

And spending her nights with Josiah.

They snuggled close on the not-quite-double-width bed, sharing their warmth, making love and talking. Sometimes they talked for hours, the mill lit only by the glow from the wood-burning stove. They talked about growing up, about families, about good times and bad times and hopes and dreams. Annabeth talked about disappointments, too, but Josiah didn't.

Of course, she already knew his greatest disappointment: living without Kylie. He rarely mentioned his daughter, and the few times he did, a great sadness darkened his eyes.

Other times they didn't talk at all. They were simply together—sometimes in bed, sometimes downstairs, sometimes touching, other times not. Those were sweet times.

Someday they would be sweet memories.

Wednesday afternoon was one such quiet time. Josiah had spent the morning digging postholes for the new pasture fence. They had eaten lunch together, as had become their habit, and now they were sitting outside beside the pond, Josiah obliging Emerson with a lengthy belly-scratching and Annabeth balancing a notebook on her lap. She was supposed to be making a list of questions that had arisen after her last interview with Aunt Flo, but it was such a pretty day and the sun was reflecting on the millpond and Josiah was entirely too close. Work seemed a sorrowful way to spend such a day.

"Look at that," she said softly, her gaze directed to the grass between them. A single yellowed blade was quivering in the still afternoon air, disturbed by some unseen force that left its neighbors untouched. "That means a fairy is dancing."

"I don't believe in fairies." He made the statement in the easy tone of voice she had come to associate with him these last few days—neutral, not hostile, and just a little bit amused.

"Why doesn't that surprise me?" she asked dryly. "Do you know that horses can see ghosts?"

"I don't believe in them, either."

"Horses?" she asked, her voice light with innocence.

With a scowl, he threw an acorn her way, but she deflected it in midair.

"Do you know that if you're building a fire and it goes out three times, it means you're bewitched?"

"Or your wood isn't seasoned."

"That the seventh son of a seventh son will be a healer? Or that a sudden silence in the midst of conversation means an angel is passing through?" She smiled smugly. "Or don't you believe in healers and angels, either?"

"I believe in healing," he acknowledged. "But you're about the closest thing to an angel I've ever seen."

Her cheeks flushed with pleasure, and she pretended to scratch something from the notebook in front of her. "Why, thank you. Now I can forget about searching for violet blossoms. Brewed into tea, they're said to cure a man of the grouchies."

"I'm not grouchy," he disagreed. "I'm just a realist."

"A cynic."

"A skeptic. You show me indisputable proof of a fairy, a ghost or a witch, sweetheart, and I'll believe."

She sighed dramatically and repeated, "A cynic. Can't you take anything on faith?"

"I accepted Caroline on faith, and look what it got me."

A little embarrassed, Annabeth looked away, then, strengthening her resolve, looked at him again. "What it got you was eight or nine nice years of marriage, a wife you loved and a daughter you adored. It wasn't all bad, Josiah. I'm sorry your marriage ended in divorce. I'm sorry Caroline left the state and took Kylie with her. But you had some good times. You have to have some good memories."

He gazed out across the pond for a time before finally facing her again. "Nope. Not one."

She made a *tsk*ing sound. "A cynic and a liar. I know you were very much in love with Caroline when you married her. I know you had great hopes for your future with her. I know you have some wonder-filled memories of finding out she was pregnant and watching her get bigger with your baby. I know you were thrilled when Kylie was born." She paused, and her voice softened. "And I know your heart was broken when she left."

Emerson was asleep now, his snores disturbing the quiet around them. Josiah gave him one last pat, then moved to sit closer to her. "Caroline wasn't even going to say goodbye," he said quietly. "She had everything all planned. I was supposed to come in from the fields that night to find them gone."

He fell silent, and Annabeth waited patiently, her knees drawn to her chest, her hands clasped around them.

"She planned it that way because of Kylie," he continued at last. "I wouldn't have tried to stop her. I don't think I would have cared much at all that she was leaving. But she knew I wouldn't want to let Kylie go. She was . . . my life."

Had Caroline been cruel? Annabeth wondered. Or just afraid? Surely she had known how deeply it would hurt Josiah to be denied a chance to tell his daughter goodbye. Had she, like so many people ending marriages, been deliberately spiteful and mean, or had she feared that he would stop her, that he would take Kylie from her and refuse to let her go? Had she been as reluctant to leave the baby behind as Josiah had been to let her go?

Annabeth didn't know. She didn't know enough about Caroline Miller to make such a verdict. She had to admit, though, that she was leaning toward spiteful. What else would explain Caroline's leaving Arkansas without telling Josiah? What else would explain her deliberately cutting him out of their baby's life?

"I came back from the fields early—the tractor had broken down—and the first thing I noticed was that Kylie's car seat was gone from the truck. I thought maybe Caroline was going into town with one of her friends, and that was why she'd taken the infant seat. Then I saw her and all the boxes and suitcases and the guilty look on her face—on their faces..."

On their faces. Obviously he wasn't talking about nine-month-old Kylie. Which meant... "Tony helped her leave."

He nodded.

"Is that why you haven't forgiven him?"

He sighed heavily. "He was probably having an affair with her. He had always flirted with her, always made such a big deal over her, but I thought it was harmless until...until things started going wrong. Until all Caroline and I could do was fight. She wasn't interested in making love with me or talking to me or spending time with me...and she spent a *lot* of time with Tony. The funny thing is, by that time I didn't care. I didn't care if she was sleeping with him or every other man in this valley under the age of seventy. But he was helping her take my little girl away from me— helping her sneak Kylie away while I was supposed to be off in the fields. You're right. I haven't forgiven him for that, and I don't think I ever will."

"You know he didn't mean to hurt you," she said softly.

He gave her a skewed look. "Helping my wife move out behind my back? Taking my baby away without telling me? Those things weren't meant to hurt?"

"Maybe he thought he was helping. You and Caroline obviously weren't happy. She wanted out, and she couldn't leave without Kylie."

He wasn't in the mood to be mollified. "If she was so anxious to leave, she could have told me. *I* would have helped her move."

"But you wouldn't have helped her take Kylie."

His expression turned as dark as the deep water in the middle of the pond. "No. I wouldn't have."

"But you couldn't raise a baby, not by yourself. With the work you do and the hours you keep, you couldn't possibly take care of a little girl, too," she pointed out gently. "Under the circumstances, if you and Caroline couldn't stay together, Kylie . . ." She hesitated, swallowed hard, then, with a silent prayer, finished what she'd been about to say. "Kylie was better off with her mother."

He sat motionless for a long time, staring into the distance, seeing nothing, she suspected, but his baby's face. Was anger building behind that blank look? Was he damning her for taking Caroline's side? Was he going to stand up in a moment, give her one of those cold, bitter looks and walk away?

But she was right, and he had to know it. If Kylie could have only one parent, Caroline was the better choice. He spent long hours at hard labor. A tractor or a barn or a fertilized field wasn't a safe place for a little girl. Tools, chemicals and animals were hardly the proper toys. But what choice would he have had? His mother had been in Fort Smith, her hands full caring for his grandmother. And he couldn't have afforded to hire a baby-sitter. He would have had to rely on the kindness of his relatives and friends, and that would have been a poor solution at best.

"Josiah . . ." She touched his arm gently. "I'm not saying that Kylie doesn't need you. A father's love is every bit as important as a mother's. But love was all you could give her. You could only be a father to her in the hours that you weren't working. Caroline could manage better."

He gave her a long, steady look. She was expecting anger, maybe even a reminder, as he'd given her before, that his personal life was none of her business. And if he said that, she vowed, she would punch him. His life *was* her business. The last month had made it so, and last Friday night had sealed it.

Then, wryly, he asked, "Are you going to allow me to hold on to any of my grudges, Annie?"

Her smile came swiftly and was filled with relief. "Holding grudges only hurts you, Josiah, and the people who care about you. If I were the type to hold grudges, I'd be holding more than a few against you, and we certainly wouldn't be talking like this."

He grinned. "Sounds a bit colder than what you *do* hold against me."

She poked him in the side with her elbow. "You're showing progress," she teased. "Next we'll work on your relationship with Tony."

An all-too-familiar frown replaced his grin. "Honey, you haven't got near enough time to deal with that."

"I have all the time in the world," she said softly. "The rest of my life."

He looked at her, then softly, deliberately pointed out, "Eleven months hardly constitutes the rest of your life."

"I can always stay longer," she replied just as softly, just as deliberately. "I can do my work anywhere, and I know I would like doing it in Dutchman's Valley."

"Your home is in South Carolina."

"My family is in South Carolina. My home is wherever I choose to make it." She hesitated, gathered courage. "I've been considering making it here."

He had no response to that. He didn't offer her encouragement, didn't show any pleasure, didn't tell her that she wasn't welcome. He just continued looking at her in that same quiet, measuring way. Half-afraid to breathe, she searched his face for some hint of what he was thinking, what he was feeling. All she found was exactly what she'd seen earlier when talking about fairies, ghosts and angels: skepticism. Doubt. Disbelief.

That was all right, she counseled herself, even though it didn't feel all right. He just needed time. When six months had passed and he saw that she was still here, when the year they had agreed on had ended and she stayed on, when she made it through this winter and the next one and the next, eventually he would have to believe her. Sooner or later he would have to see that she wasn't like Caroline. She hadn't come to the mountains expecting a storybook existence. She had lived under harsher conditions with fewer conveniences than even Josiah himself. She knew what she was suggesting, knew what life would be like in these mountains year in and year out.

She wouldn't go running home to the city.

Sometime in the future he would be forced to realize that. She could be patient until then.

Chapter 8

The sound of cars on the road drew Josiah's attention away from Annabeth. He recognized the familiar, peculiar sound of her Bug just before it came into sight around the curve. "There's Tony with your car," he announced, rising to his feet and offering her a hand up. "Speak of the devil...."

"Do you know if you speak of an angel, you'll hear the rustle of her wings?" she asked absently, brushing grass from her skirt.

More of her folklore. She knew more worthless—and fanciful—bits of information than anyone he'd ever known. "That's your skirt rustling, Annie," he disagreed as he guided her, his hand in the small of her back, up the bank to the clearing.

Tony parked the Bug close to the mill, and Mary Louise pulled in behind him. Good, Josiah thought grimly. Tony could bum a ride back to town with her instead of—as he had surely planned—asking Annabeth to take him.

His cousin got out of the car, offered a subdued greeting to Annabeth and a wary look to Josiah. Mary Louise was friendlier all around. "Good afternoon, Annabeth, Josiah. Well, nephew, I'm getting rather used to finding you over here instead of slaving away over at your place. Isn't this a lovely day to lazy along?"

When he didn't say anything beyond a guarded hello, Annabeth agreed, "It's a beautiful day. Tony, thanks for bringing my car out. Is everything okay?"

He patted a rusty fender. "She'll never be as good as new, but she's in at least as good shape as before your run-in with the fence."

"He," Annabeth corrected. "I know most men refer to cars as 'she,' but this one is male in spirit—cantankerous, obstinate and difficult to get along with."

"And you love it dearly," Mary Louise said with a laugh. "You couldn't ask for a more accurate description of the male of our species or the way we feel about them, could you? You know, Annabeth, I don't know what Aunt Flo was thinking, letting you leave her house with that rain on the way. With all her aches and pains, you know, she can forecast rain better than any meteorologist."

"She did suggest that I wait, but I—" She broke off, and a delicate pink crept into her cheeks. "I didn't listen. Um, Tony, let me get my purse and I'll write you a check for the repairs."

Josiah watched her walk inside, then Mary Louise called his attention to herself. "Tomorrow is Thanksgiving, and the family is gathering at our house, as usual. Will we see you there?"

He hadn't been to a family Thanksgiving dinner in at least five years. The last few years they were married, Caroline had insisted on visiting her parents in Little Rock, and the years after she'd left...well, he hadn't had much to be thankful for. But now the mere mention of the family get-together stirred a vaguely familiar feeling inside. Homesickness, he thought. He was living right here in the place where he had been born, but he felt homesick—for the people and the traditions and the routines that he'd turned his back on. For the sense of belonging he'd misplaced. For the love he'd rejected.

But if he accepted his aunt's invitation, where would that leave Annabeth? They hadn't discussed the holiday—it had just never come up—but he had assumed they would spend it together. She hadn't mentioned any other plans, any invitations. As much as one part of him wanted to be with his family, a stronger part wanted to stay with Annabeth. After all, he would have a lifetime of holidays to spend with the family, but only a year's worth with her.

He hesitated so long that Annabeth was back before he'd given Mary Louise an answer. His aunt looked from him to her, then, with a knowing smile, said, "Our families put on a big Thanksgiving Day celebration, Annabeth. We'd like to have you join us."

There was reluctance in Annabeth's eyes—because she really didn't want to go or because she didn't feel she would belong? he wondered. She smiled what must seem a perfectly ordinary smile to anyone who didn't know her well, but he could see the uneasiness behind it. "I appreciate the invitation, Mary Louise," she said graciously, "but Thanksgiving is a time for families. I would hate to intrude on that."

"With the Dothan and Walker families combined, there will be so many people there, no one will know you're not family," Tony pointed out.

That didn't make Annabeth feel any easier, Josiah noticed, although she was still smiling.

"And if you don't come, dear, Josiah won't," Mary Louise took over. "If you do, he'll have to bring you to ensure that you don't get lost on one of our country roads."

"You could just draw her a map," Josiah suggested.

"Why would I bother doing that when you could find your way to my house blindfolded?" Mary Louise asked innocently. "So...it's settled. We'll see you sometime around one o'clock." Thinking she'd gotten her way once again, his aunt started toward her truck. "Come along, Tony. I have a ton of cooking to do."

Tony pulled a greasy bill from his pocket and handed it, along with the keys, to Annabeth. While she wrote out the check, he approached Josiah. "If it makes a difference to you," he said quietly, "I can go someplace else tomorrow."

His first impulse was to ignore him, his second to tell him that it made a hell of a difference. But a warning glance from Annabeth made him swallow down the bitter words. Instead, avoiding looking at Tony, he replied, "No. It doesn't." The words were harsh, the tone cold, but he had spoken. For the first time in a very long time, he'd spoken to his cousin.

After a moment's hesitance, Tony turned away and accepted the check from Annabeth, then joined Mary Louise in the truck. His aunt waved merrily as she drove away.

Long after they were gone, Annabeth came to Josiah and, stretching onto her toes, pressed a kiss to his cheek. "You're a hard man, Josiah," she murmured, then turned away, but she was smiling when she said it.

Before she had come into his life, he *had* been hard. Life had made him that way. Now she was undoing that—tearing down his defenses, melting the ice inside him, making him warm again. But he needed to hold on to some small part of the hardness. He needed some bit of strength to see him through the next eleven months. He needed some of the pain to remind him that her stay in the valley—her stay in his life—was temporary. To remind him that he could like her, could enjoy spending time with her, could ache to make love with her. That he could want her and need her and care very, very deeply for her, but he couldn't love her.

He *couldn't*. The way things stood now, her leaving would be painful, but he could deal with it. He could survive it. But loving and losing her would finish what losing Kylie had started.

It would destroy him.

"When Mary Louise told me she had invited you to dinner today, I was certain you wouldn't come."

Annabeth, standing at a big picture window, glanced up and smiled as Stuart joined her. "Josiah says I'm pushy."

"He doesn't mean that as a compliment."

"I know." She turned her attention back to the view outside. "He wouldn't have come if I hadn't."

"So it's like that, is it?"

She didn't ask for an explanation. She had seen the curious looks, had heard the curious whispers, every time one of Josiah's relatives spotted the two of them together. She knew exactly what they were thinking: for the first time in too many years, he'd made an effort to be part of the family, and it must have something to do with her. She wished it were true, that she had that much influence on him, but it wasn't. It had simply been time for him to come out of seclusion. He had shut himself away for as long as his spirit could stand it, and now he had to get out, had to be with people who loved him.

Like her.

"What are you going to do when the year ends?" Stuart asked, keeping his voice soft so no one else could hear, but making no effort to disguise his dismay. "Leave like Caroline did?"

Annabeth watched the children playing outside, the girls in dresses in deference to the holiday, the boys in jeans and sneakers. Two small girls sat with their dolls on a swing beneath an arbor of grapevines, but the rest were involved in a rousing game of tag. She would prefer to be out there with them, she thought, with these children who didn't watch her with speculation or suspicion, with Josiah's small cousins and her own. Then she wouldn't be having this conversation with Stuart. She wouldn't be forced to say what she was about to say.

But she wasn't outside with the kids, and she did have to answer his question. Under the circumstances, he had a right to know her plans.

Clasping her hands together, she turned slightly to face him. "I haven't decided for certain yet," she said politely, "but I might not leave the valley next fall."

Stuart stared at her, disapproval sharpening his features. "Ever?"

She shook her head.

"You won't get anything from me. Do you understand? Not a—"

"I'm not considering staying because of you," she interrupted. "It's not even entirely because of Josiah. I've always thought I would wind up living in the mountains somewhere. I like this place. I like the people and the town. I like the hills. I love the peace. And…Josiah…" She didn't go any further. She wasn't going to put her emotions on display here for Stuart's satisfaction. What he believed, what he thought, didn't matter.

The wariness didn't fade from his eyes, or the sharp edges of anger from his face. "Come outside with me," he commanded, taking her by the arm and steering her toward a side door.

It was a pretty day, the sun shining, a nip in the air. It smelled of wildflowers and autumn, of fallen leaves and evergreens and woodsmoke. There had been a low fog this morning, the kind that hung close to the ground and had swirled around her feet when she let Emerson out. He had whined, then waddled off to take care of business, and she had waited, feeling the damp chill on her ankles and bare legs. When Emerson was finished and settled once again beside the stove, she had beat a hasty retreat to the loft, shed her robe and snuggled into bed again with Josiah, pressing her cold feet and legs against his for warmth. He hadn't even awakened, had just drawn her closer, pressed a kiss to her shoulder and slept on.

Oh, yes, she loved this place.

She loved *him.*

Stuart led the way across the yard, past the children playing, past a small grove of trees, redbuds and dogwoods that would flower in spring, to the banks of a stream that cut through the property. This one, Josiah had told her when they had crossed it on their way to the house, was called

Enchanted Creek. She loved the name, as he had known she would.

"Have you told Josiah that you intend to stay here?" Stuart demanded when they were a fair distance from the house.

"I told him that I might. That I could."

"And what did he say?"

She hesitated, remembering the doubt in Josiah's eyes. "Nothing."

"He was really excited by the idea, wasn't he?" Stuart asked sharply. "What if he doesn't want you here?"

She refused to think about that, refused to consider that maybe Josiah was just using her for his own needs, that he didn't feel something as real and strong and binding as what *she* felt for *him*. He wasn't that kind of person. He just hadn't yet learned to fully trust her. He hadn't realized how much he already trusted her. He never could have made love with her without having some faith that she wouldn't hurt him. He just hadn't yet recognized it as faith.

"Why do my plans have to revolve around you and Josiah?" she asked quietly. "I like this place. I could live here with or without Josiah and definitely without you."

"I wish you had never come here," he muttered, turning to face the stream. "I wish your mother had never come here."

"You pretended for thirty years that you didn't have a daughter," Annabeth reminded him. "Nothing has really changed. I don't want a daughter-father relationship with you. I don't care if we become friends. Don't cause any trouble for me, Stuart, and you have my word I won't cause any for you."

"Something *has* changed," he said with a heavy sigh. "You're here."

"You've ignored me all my life. Ignore me now. I don't care." But even though she spoke with utter certainty, she wondered if she was being truthful. Could she live the rest of her life only a few miles from the father who had never wanted her and not care? Could she face him on a regular basis for the next however many years he had, do business with him, socialize with him, and never reveal their true relationship to anyone? Could she truly never care that, even after meeting her, he wanted nothing to do with her?

Yes. If she had to.

Just as she could live here in the valley without Josiah.

If she had to.

"We have guests," Stuart said, his manner strained, his tone resigned.

Annabeth looked in the direction he gestured and, after a moment's search, found a small group of deer at the edge of the trees on the opposite side of the stream. "Aren't they beautiful?"

"Mary Louise doesn't think so. They get into her garden and eat her plants."

"Feeding the deer seems as good a reason for planting a garden as any other."

"I don't think my wife would agree." Stuart moved upstream to a bench set in a grassy area only a few feet from the water and sat down. "Have you read Emmalee's journal?"

"About half of it." After a moment's hesitation, she moved to sit at the opposite end of the small bench. "Is this the only journal she kept?"

"No, there are several others. Remind me, and you can take them with you today."

"She was a remarkable woman."

"Yes, she was. She was said to be very beautiful. Golden-haired and brown-eyed."

Hiding a triumphant smile, Annabeth fingered a strand of her own hair that had worked its way free from the French braid. Finally, someone she resembled! She couldn't lay claim to beautiful—although Josiah frequently told her she was—but at least she had the golden hair and brown eyes. That was more than she'd ever shared with any other relative she'd known in her entire life.

"This land here was settled by Matthew Dothan, Emmalee's third son. You know the first one, Jeffrey, died from a copperhead bite?"

She nodded. That had come in a later entry—months after the boy's death. Other than noting the birth of her third child, a son named Paul, Emmalee had written nothing in her journal for more than seven months. She had been unable to, she had explained when she started again. Caring for Henry, Amanda and Paul had been all that her grief would allow her. There had been no energy, no strength, no emotion, for writing.

"After Jeffrey, Amanda and Paul, there was another son, Matthew, then two more daughters, one of whom died at birth," Stuart went on. "Matthew married into this land, which he cleared for farming. He discovered that was harder work than he cared to do for the rest of his life, and he made more money selling the timber he'd cleared from the fields than he did from his first year's crops, so he bought into a logging company. It was a poor decision. If you've noticed the woods on Josiah's place, there's a wide variety of trees. It used to be that way here—white and black oak, hickory, black walnut, shortleaf pine. Some of those trees have come back here, but mostly we have acres and acres of blackjacks."

She remembered the scrubby little tree in the rock Josiah had shown her and realized that it was dominant here. "What was the timber used for?"

"Railroad ties mostly. The railroads were expanding across the country in Matthew's time, and there was a great demand for ties. Eventually, the boy got smart and started clearing other folks' land, but the damage had already been done here."

"So you're related to Emmalee through Matthew." And so was she. She filed that information away. It would make for interesting reading when she got to Matthew's birth in the journals.

"We've got descendants of all four of Emmalee's surviving children back there in the house."

"Do you still have family in Ohio?"

"I suppose we do, but no one's kept in touch in years. I couldn't give you a name or even a city to start looking in." He turned sideways to face her. "What made you decide to start doing this? Why aren't you teaching school somewhere and settled down and married?"

"What makes you think I should be teaching?"

"Because Hilda Franks says you have a master's degree in education."

Of course. Talk did get around. "I don't know," she replied in answer to his question. "I'm in this for a lot of reasons, I guess. My stepfather is a history professor, and he loves his work. And I grew up in Charleston. It's an old city and very proud of its past. You can find people there whose families have lived in the same place for ten generations. Everything is old and preserved and alive. And I'm curious. When I was a kid, I enjoyed going to the nursing homes with one group or another and listening to the old people. I always liked hearing my grandparents and, when I was small, my great-grandparents talk about their lives. I was the only kid in the family who didn't run the other way when one of them started with, 'When *I* was a boy...'"

She sighed softly. "One of the first people I ever interviewed in the Blue Ridge Mountains was an eighty-year-old lady who told me everything I wanted to know about her life. When I asked her why she was talking so freely to a stranger, she said that as long as she could pass these stories on to me, the life she had lived would never end. It would never be forgotten. And I think that's important. I think we never should forget."

After a moment's silence, Stuart touched her arm. It wasn't a domineering showing-her-where-to-go kind of touch, like when he'd taken hold and practically pulled her from the house, but gentler. Nicer. Darn near companionable, she thought. "We'd better go back now. If I know Mary Louise, she's decided it's about time for dessert."

Helping her to her feet, he added with an awkward little laugh, "And I try never to miss Mary Louise's dessert."

Josiah had talked to relatives, both his and Stuart's, he hadn't seen in far too long, but finally he'd gotten away for a while and was looking for Annabeth to see how she was dealing with the crowd. She'd had a hard time deciding to join him today, had suggested several times that he come without her since it was *his* family, after all. It wasn't until this morning, when he'd told her flatly that he wasn't coming if she didn't, that she had agreed.

They had gotten here just in time for a round of introductions before dinner. For the meal she had been claimed by Aunt Flo at the main table in the dining room, while Josiah had wound up in the kitchen with most of the men. Afterward he'd been kept too busy to talk to her. That had been all right for a while—after all, they would have the entire evening and the night alone together—but he was missing her. He just wanted to check on her.

A walk through the house revealed no sign of her. Finally he approached Mary Louise, standing with her arms folded across her chest, in front of the bay window in the side hall. "Aunt Mary Louise."

She barely glanced at him before turning her attention outside again. "I'm glad you came, Josiah."

"Thanks for inviting us. Listen, have you seen Annabeth?"

She raised one hand in a taut gesture before letting it rest on the other arm again. He followed her gaze outside to the yard where the kids were playing and past that to the creek. Annabeth and Stuart were there, just rising from the cedar bench Josiah had helped build years ago. She was laughing—a familiar sight—and Stuart was smiling as they stood up.

"She looks perfectly capable of standing up by herself," Mary Louise murmured beneath her breath.

Josiah looked closer and saw that his uncle's hand, where he had helped her up, remained on Annabeth's arm. It was a perfectly innocent touch...even if it did make Josiah wish he were the one touching her instead.

He wasn't exactly sure what to say about it. He knew Mary Louise was a jealous woman—and he'd heard whispers when he was a kid that Stuart had given her reason to be—but worrying about Annabeth was ridiculous. For one thing, she was spending so much time with *him* that there was no way she could be seeing anyone else. For another, Stuart loved his wife. And yet another, he was old enough to be Annabeth's father. What interest could she have—other than business—in a man his age?

"I wish she hadn't come."

"But, Aunt Mary Louise, you invited her."

"Because I wanted *you* here, and you seem to be more than a little sweet on her. I didn't think you would come if you couldn't bring her."

"I probably wouldn't have," he admitted.

For the first time she turned her attention fully on him. "You're not falling in love with her, are you? You know she's not going to stay here. You know she'll get what she wants and then leave, just like Caroline."

"Annabeth isn't like Caroline," he said quietly. They were both pretty, both blond, both from the city, but that was where the resemblance ended. Annabeth was warm, generous, giving freely of herself and her time. She cared about other people—didn't her choice of jobs show that? She could be living an easier life, working an easier job in the city, but she chose to spend long summers and hard winters in the mountains, in places with few of the comforts of home.

"Spoken like a truly objective man," Mary Louise retorted. "Show a man a pretty young face, and he'll act like a fool every time."

Hiding his irritation with her words, Josiah wondered which part it was that bothered his aunt most about Annabeth—that she was pretty... or that she was young?

She was definitely both. Leaving Stuart so that she could join the kids in their games, laughing delightedly at their antics, she looked younger than her years. With her hair pulled back in a fancy braid and wearing soft leather boots, a full denim skirt with a ruffled white slip that peeked from underneath and a ruffled white blouse that fit snugly across her midriff and breasts but billowed into full, flounced elbow-length sleeves, she was undoubtedly beautiful.

Unaware that he was being observed, Stuart stopped on the steps and watched her for a moment. When he finally came inside through the door at the end of the hall, he was smiling. When he saw Mary Louise and Josiah standing there, the smile slipped, faded and was replaced by an expression Josiah could only describe as guilt.

After a few still seconds, Stuart turned and walked away. Her face pale, her lips pursed, Mary Louise left, too, going in the opposite direction. Josiah remained where he was, watching Annabeth. Wondering.

Why should his uncle feel guilty about having gone for a walk and a talk with Annabeth? Sooner or later everyone in the valley was going to end up talking to her. She had been sure of it from the beginning, and Josiah was starting to agree. She was that sincere, that interested, that charming. No one would be able to tell her no.

So if merely walking and talking with her wasn't cause for guilt, what would be? The reason, maybe, he had gone outside with her? The things he'd said when they had talked?

Feeling uneasy and disliking it, he went out through the door Stuart had used. Annabeth was standing at an ancient hickory, one of the few that had survived the logging that had gone on here years ago, her arm pressed to the bark, her face hidden in the crook of her elbow, and she was counting loudly to fifty.

Hide-and-seek. He hadn't played that game in years. From his place on the porch, he could see the hiding places of three of the younger children. He knew instinctively that Annabeth wouldn't "find" them until last. When she finished counting, she raised her head and called, "Ready or not, here I come!" Then, spying him, she gave him a grin and a wink before setting off to locate the hidden children.

He had been right. She found the older kids first and let the little ones think they had outwitted her. Then, excusing herself, she came to the porch, standing close to him, so close that he could smell the autumn scent in her hair and could hear her uneven breathing. Catching a couple of the older boys before they made it to base had left her out of breath.

He had had the pleasure of leaving her out of breath a few times himself.

"You never grew up, did you?" he asked, gazing down into her gorgeous brown eyes.

"Only in the ways that count." She brushed a wayward strand of hair back, then solemnly asked, "Are you okay?"

He nodded.

"The kids don't bother you?"

Briefly he let his gaze slide past her to the children, playing among themselves again. Most of them were too old to remind him of Kylie, although there was one, three, maybe four years old, a tomboy in a pinafore... "No," he replied, only partly lying. Then, with a sigh, he continued. "I wonder where she is today, if she's playing with kids like this, if they're having a big dinner at home or if they've gone to a restaurant instead. I wonder about every holiday. What kind of cake she has for her birthday. What kind of gifts she gets for Christmas. What kind of costume she chooses for Halloween. If she's afraid of the fireworks on the Fourth of July." Softly, barely whispering, he added, "I wonder if there's some other man that she gives a card to on Father's Day, some other man that she calls Daddy."

Annabeth laid her hand on his chest above his heart. "Someday you'll see her again, Josiah. I know you will."

He tried to force a smile, but it wouldn't come. Laying his hand over hers, he asked, "How do you know? One of your fairies tell you?"

"You just have to believe...but you can't, can you?" she asked sadly. "You don't have any more faith." Twisting her hand beneath his so that she could clasp it, she squeezed it tight. "I'll believe for you," she offered. "I'll put *my* faith in you."

"Nice sentiment," he murmured, bending to brush a kiss across her forehead. "You're sweet, Annie."

"Take me home, and I'll show you—"

"Hey, Annabeth, will you tell us a story?" one of the kids called from behind her.

"Your public awaits you," Josiah said with a crooked smile, regretting the interruption. "Tell them a few stories, and then we'll go."

"I'll come inside and find you when we're through."

She automatically assumed he would retreat—that he wouldn't want to be close to the kids, that he wouldn't care to waste his time listening to her storytelling. On one point, she was right: he *didn't* want to get too close to the kids. It was one thing watching them play from a distance, but he certainly didn't want to get close enough to sort out voices and names. On the other, while he still didn't hold her storytelling in the highest esteem, he had learned that watching her do anything at all could never be a waste of time.

Two of the bigger boys carried an unpainted Adirondack chair to the side of the house, and Annabeth sat down. The kids gathered in a circle on the ground, except for the smallest, the little tomboy, who crawled onto her lap.

"Do you know what sound an owl makes?" Annabeth asked and got several credible hoots in response. "Does anyone know *why* the owl makes that sound?"

There were shaking heads around the group.

"Then I'll tell you. Once there was a baker who had two lovely daughters. They were twin sisters, but they were as different as night and day. One was sweet and kind and good, but the other was mean and hateful to everybody. One evening it was almost time for the bakery to close when a little old woman wearing a dirty old cloak and walking with a cane came inside. 'Could I have a bit of dough?' she asked the kind sister. 'Why, of course,' the sister said, and she pulled out a big chunk of bread dough. 'And can I bake it in your oven?' the old woman asked. 'Certainly,' said the sister, and she put the bread dough in the oven, and when it was done, she opened the door and stared in surprise. That bit of dough had risen and doubled to twice its size. She gave the warm bread to the old woman, who threw off her cape and stood straight and tall and beautiful, for, you see, she was really a fairy in disguise.''

Annabeth paused and glanced over her shoulder. Seeing Josiah still standing there, she gave him another of those devilish winks.

''The fairy touched the good sister with her cane and said, 'Because you are generous and kind, everything you do will always come out bigger and better.' And after that, every loaf of bread, every pie and every cake the kind sister baked always came out of the oven twice as large as when she put them in. A few weeks later, the same old woman came into the bakery again, and this time she found the mean sister working. She asked for a piece of bread dough, and the sister fussed and complained but gave her a little bit of dough. The old lady asked if she could bake it in the oven, and the mean sister said, 'Oh, if you insist.' So she put the dough in the oven, and when it was done, she found a nice big loaf of bread. 'Why, that's much too nice a loaf of bread to give an old woman like that,' the sister said to herself, so she put the loaf aside to keep for herself. She took an even tinier bit of dough and put it in the oven, and what do you think happened?''

''It got big again,'' one of the kids called out.

''That's right. The second loaf of bread was twice as big as the first one. And the mean sister said, 'Oh, that's much too nice a loaf of bread to give an old woman like that,' and she put the loaf aside to keep for herself. And this time she took an itsy-bitsy piece of dough no bigger than her thumbnail, and she put it in the oven, and it got bigger and bigger and bigger. When she opened the oven door, that bread had almost filled the oven, and it was golden and shiny and filled with raisins and nuts, and the sister said, 'No, no, that's much too nice a loaf of bread to give an old woman like that.' So she put the loaf aside for herself, and she went to the old woman. She was laughing so hard—she had a funny laugh, sort of a *hoo-hoo, hoo-hoo*—and she told the old woman, 'Your bread burned all up in the oven, *hoo-hoo.*'

"And the old woman knew she was lying, and she demanded, 'Is that all you have to say to me?' And the silly girl laughed even more. *'Hoo-hoo, hoo-hoo,* what do you want me to say?' So the old woman threw off her cape and stood straight and tall and beautiful, and she touched the mean sister with her cane and said, 'Because you are unkind and selfish, for the rest of your life, you shall say nothing else but *hoo-hoo.*' And the girl turned into an owl and flew out into the night. And that's why the owl always says *hoo-hoo.*"

There was no denying that she had talent, Josiah thought when she was finished. She'd done five different voices—one each for the daughters, the old woman, the fairy and the narration—and her own very nice imitation of an owl. It was kind of a pointless talent, but talent all the same.

She went on to another story, this one funny, and followed it with a scary one that he remembered from his own childhood. "Ain't nobody here but you and me," she repeated at the end of each passage, her voice low and hollow and spooky. How he wished that were true—*ain't nobody here but you and me.* Just watching her and listening to her voice, weaving in and out and around him, made him hot and hungry and hard. She could seduce him with no more than her voice.

"She's good, isn't she?"

Josiah glanced over his shoulder and found Tony standing in the doorway. His cousin hesitated, then came on out, closing the door behind him and standing nearby on the porch.

"Everyone's been glad to see you." Tony rested his hands on the porch rail, then slowly folded his fingers around it, gripping it tightly. "Some of the family thinks if *I* had stayed away for a while, you would have come back sooner."

Josiah turned his attention back to Annabeth. "They're wrong," he said flatly.

After a moment's silence, Tony remarked, "It must be different having a neighbor out there so close."

Was he supposed to agree with such an obvious statement? Josiah wondered. Was he supposed to stand here and make polite conversation with a man he really didn't give a damn about?

Once he *had* cared. Despite the two-year age difference, he and Tony had always been close, even as kids. Maybe it was because they'd been the only boys and had had numerous female cousins to torment. Maybe it was because Tony had always looked up to him—both literally and figuratively. It had been nice as a kid to have someone think you could walk on water. Or maybe it was because they had been so damn much alike.

Had been alike. As they grew up, though, there had developed some significant differences between them. Josiah never would have flirted with Tony's wife. He never would have had an affair with Tony's—or any other man's—wife. He never would have helped a woman sneak Tony's kid away from him.

Almost as if he had read Josiah's thoughts, Tony said quietly, "You like to put all the blame on me, don't you? If I hadn't been there when Caroline needed someone, she would still be depending on you. If I hadn't agreed to help her leave, she would still be living with you. But you're wrong, Josiah. She wasn't happy here. She wasn't going to stay here. If I hadn't agreed to drive her to Little Rock, she would have called her parents. She would have left you, anyway."

Slowly, stiffly, Josiah turned toward him. "So that makes it all right? Caroline 'needed' someone, and so it was okay for you to have an affair with her? She wasn't happy here, so it was all right for you to help her—to *try* to help her—take my baby away without telling me?"

He had never been sure about the affair, had long suspected but never known for absolute sure. Now, looking at the pained expression on his cousin's face, he knew.

He had told Annabeth just yesterday that he didn't care if Caroline had been unfaithful. So why was there an empty sort of feeling growing inside him now? He had suspected it for years; why did knowing for a fact make a difference?

Maybe because it had been Tony. When she had gone looking for another man, for someone to give her what *he* couldn't, she had gone to his cousin. To his best friend all his life. And that best friend had been waiting, willing and ready. Ready to become her lover. Ready to betray their friendship. Ready to forget a lifetime of caring and loving in exchange for a few hours in bed with Caroline.

"Josiah, I'm sorry," Tony said miserably, "but she was leaving you, anyway. I didn't break up your marriage. All I did—"

"All you did was make it easier for her to go. All you did was help her arrange it so she could get away with Kylie." He gave his cousin a look of disgust. "Why? Why did you do it? She wasn't that great in bed. She wasn't that great out of bed. What did you get out of sleeping with my wife?"

Tony's answer came soft and laced with pain. "I loved her, Josiah. From the first time I met her when I visited you at school... I was going to leave the Corner, to move to Little Rock a few weeks after she got settled there. We were going to get..."

Get married. Josiah heard the words as clearly as if they'd been spoken aloud. A part of him wanted to laugh at the absurdity of it. After seeing what *his* marriage to Caroline had become, after learning firsthand how little marriage vows meant to her, Tony had been foolish enough to want to marry her himself.

But another part of him just hurt. He couldn't imagine the sort of love that would make him disregard the sanctity of marriage vows—his own or anyone else's. He couldn't imagine wanting any woman so badly that he didn't care who he hurt in his quest to possess her—not even Annabeth, and he could never want any woman more than he wanted her.

But if Tony was being truthful about his feelings for Caroline, then he'd fallen in love with her about the same time Josiah had. And apparently he had loved her better, for his love had lasted a lot longer than Josiah's had. Love could make people desperate, and desperation could make them do strange things.

Like betray their best friends.

Like sit in a dark room and look for the courage to end the pain by ending your life.

Annabeth had finished with the kids and was coming toward them now. He watched the gentle sway of her hips, watched the skirt where it was unbuttoned flip open on every other step to reveal the lacy slip underneath. She was smiling and bright and beautiful, and for the next eleven months—at least, and maybe a little longer—she was his. That knowledge brought him such a feeling of peace that, for a moment, he couldn't resent even Tony.

Annabeth stopped on the top step, and Josiah slid his arm around her waist, pulling her close, then turned his attention back to Tony. "So as a reward for helping her sneak Kylie away, you were supposed to join her in Little Rock and get married. Only she sneaked away from you, too." Drawing Annabeth along with him, he took a few steps toward the door, then paused and looked back. "You're a damn lucky man, Tony."

Saturday's mail brought letters for both of them. Annabeth was outside when the mailman left them, so she picked them up and went in search of Josiah, working somewhere around the barn. His letter bore a Fort Smith address—from his mother, she guessed, regretting that Kate Miller hadn't been able to attend the Thanksgiving celebration, that she hadn't had an opportunity to meet her—and hers were from Charleston, one from her mother and another from her youngest sister, Christie.

She found Josiah working on the pasture fence. When he saw her, he picked up his shirt, which was hanging on a nearby post, and came across the field to meet her at the corral fence. By the time he got there, she was balanced on the top rail and grinning down at him. "Don't get dressed on my account," she teased. "There's not much I like to look at more than a sweaty, half-naked man."

"I bet." Sliding his arms into the shirt, anyway, he left it unbuttoned as he accepted his letter from her. "What have you got there?"

"Letters from Mama and my sister. Christie's the baby— although ever since she turned ten, she's resented being called that. She's eighteen and in her first year of college and thinks she's all grown-up now."

"Didn't we all?" he asked dryly, opening the envelope and withdrawing several folded pages of lined stationery. "I was eighteen and in my first year of college when I met Caroline."

"Funny. That's when I met Don."

"At least you had the sense not to fall in love and get married."

"Oh, I fell in love, all right. He's the one who ran off with my cousin Cassie, remember?"

He gave her a long, solemn look. "He must have been a fool."

Smiling, she bent to kiss his forehead. "Thank you. Although you might change your mind if you ever saw my cousin Cassie."

He stepped closer between her parted legs and pressed a kiss to the curve of her breast through her shirt. "No," he disagreed softly, definitely. "I wouldn't."

Annabeth felt his hands fumbling with her buttons, felt the cool air touch her stomach and his mouth brush a moist kiss across her midriff. His touch made her stiffen and sigh, made her skin quiver and ripple, made her muscles tighten and her blood go hot.

Then he buttoned those few bottom buttons again, slid one arm around her hips for balance and turned his attention to his letter. As if he hadn't just melted her inside. As if he didn't know he'd just made her go completely, thoroughly weak.

Her laughter was tinged with a bit of frustration. "You're a wicked man, Josiah," she chided him as she tore open her sister's letter.

The first paragraph was filled with polite questions about her: "How do you like Arkansas? How is your work going? Have you met anyone interesting—and, no, A.B., I don't mean those ancient, ancient people you find so fascinating." The real purpose of the letter came in the next paragraph. Annabeth read it, then laughed aloud. "How typical. Listen to this. 'I need a favor, A.B. I've met the most wonderful man. He's gorgeous, has a body to die for, is very intelligent and mature and sweet. He has the greatest British accent, and I love him dearly, and he loves me, too. The problem is Mama and Daddy. They say he's too old. Too *old?* He's only twenty-six! Not even as old as you! They say that as long as I live in their house, I can't see him anymore. They're just being mean because he works with Daddy—he's teaching history at the college on some sort of exchange program. At the end of the school year, he's going back to England, and I'll just *die* if I can't be with him until then! Will you talk to them, A.B.? Please? You know they'll listen to you a lot more than me.'"

She sighed softly, but not without sympathy. "Thank heavens, I'm not eighteen anymore."

"Are you going to talk to them, A.B.?" Josiah asked, teasing her with her sister's nickname.

"And say what? That they'd better lock this child in the closet until next summer? That if they let her continue seeing the guy, he's liable to break her heart? Or that if they don't let her see him, when he goes home, she's liable to be on the first plane to England?"

"Well, whatever happens, look at it this way—you rarely find true love at eighteen."

She looked down at him, and an achy feeling started growing around her heart. "Don't I know it," she whispered. It had taken her thirty long years to find it—and it might take another thirty to convince *him* of it. But that was all right. She had the rest of her life. She would gladly spend it proving to him that she was here to stay.

After a long, still moment, she pulled her gaze away, returned Christie's letter to its envelope and opened her mother's. After an initial paragraph filled with polite questions, the same as Christie's, Lynette also got to the point.

"So you've met Stuart," she had written,

> and you know that he was married when I met him. Thank you, sweetheart, for writing that information in your last letter without being judgmental. As soon as you decided to go to Arkansas, I knew I should tell you, but . . . I suppose I didn't want you to think badly of me. Not only did I have a baby out of wedlock at a time when good girls simply didn't do that, but I did it with a married man. That's the largest part of the reason my parents were so scandalized.
>
> And I have no excuse for it. Stuart didn't lie to me. He didn't lead me on. I knew from the first time I met him that he was married, and I didn't care. He was so handsome, so charming—everything I had been looking for in a man. I was infatuated with him from the first, and I didn't care that another woman had a prior claim on him. I never considered his wife. I never considered the sins we were committing. I saw something I wanted, and selfishly I took it.
>
> I can't even be particularly sorry for the affair, because it brought me you, and I can't imagine my life without you.

Smiling, Annabeth skimmed the rest—greetings from her stepfather, bits of news about Bradley and Bonnie and a frustrated paragraph about Christie's misguided romance that ended with a request that Annabeth please talk some sense into her sister—then put the letters in her hip pocket.

How could she sit in judgment of her own mother? she wondered. What Lynette had done was wrong, no doubt, but people made mistakes. They shouldn't be punished the rest of their lives for them. Besides, as much as she valued fidelity and trust, how could she know that she would have behaved any differently? If Josiah had still been married to Caroline when they'd met, if he had been attracted to her in spite of his wife, would she have had the strength to turn away from him? Could she have given up the opportunity to be his lover simply because he belonged to another woman?

She hoped the answer was yes. She hoped she was that strong, that unyielding. But the simple fact was she didn't know. Feeling the way she did about him, she couldn't honestly say for sure that she would have kept her distance if Caroline had still been in the picture. So how could she blame her mother for not caring about Mary Louise?

"Good grief," Josiah muttered, looking down at his mother's letter.

"Something wrong?"

"How long have you been here?"

She counted mentally. "Four and a half weeks."

" 'I hear you've rented the mill to that historian the state has sent in. I hear that she's pretty, too, and has charmed just about everyone she's met and that she's a school teacher from South Carolina who's never been married.' " He glanced up. "I didn't know you're a teacher."

"My degree's in education, but I've never actually taught."

"How is it my mother is more than a hundred miles away and has never met you and knows something about you that I don't?"

Laughing, she climbed down from the rails so that she was standing snugly between the fence and his body. "You asked me where I went to school. You never asked me what my major was."

"Is there anything else I need to know?" he asked, moving closer and sliding his arms around her waist.

"I graduated with a 3.8 average."

"I already knew you were smart." He bent to kiss her ear, making her shiver.

"I used to work as a guide at one of the plantations outside Charleston, where I dressed in long, flowing gowns with yards of crinoline underneath and played the quintessential Southern belle."

"I would have liked seeing you in long, flowing gowns with yards of crinoline underneath ... just so I could have the pleasure of taking them off." His mouth was on her throat now, leaving tiny little marks that faded as he moved toward the pulse throbbing visibly at the base. "Any other secrets?"

Her voice had gone husky and soft. "I was never quite sure what all the fuss about sex was until I met you."

He lifted her, wordlessly guiding her legs around his hips, bracing her carefully against the fence and slowly, sexily, sensuously, rubbing his arousal against her. "This isn't sex, Annie," he disagreed, his own voice thick and raspy. "This is wonder. Creation. Life."

Wrapping her arms around his neck, she leaned forward to kiss him, pushing closer to him, feeling his heat through her jeans, burning with her own heat. "This is *impossible* with our clothes on. Care for a roll in the hay?"

He laughed. "It would make you itch in places you can't scratch."

"Darlin', I've already got an itch," she whispered, catching her breath when he stimulated it more with the erotic thrust of his hips. "Put me down, and I'll race you to the mill."

"The house is closer."

Annabeth leaned back and looked at him. He had never asked her into his house, had never let her go farther than the front porch. She had thought he might never invite her into his bedroom. She had assumed it was a matter of trust—that as much as he had opened his life to her, the house was still his sanctuary, his private place where no one could bother him.

And now he had offered to take her there.

Hugging him tightly so that he couldn't see the dampness in her eyes, she murmured, "In that case, sweetheart, you can just carry me."

Chapter 9

The second week of December brought snow. Josiah paused in his work to watch it fall and wondered how deep it would get and how long it would stay.

He wondered what Annabeth would think of it.

No doubt she would be delighted by it this time, and the next time and maybe even the time after that. The valley was beautiful under a blanket of snow, and it brought out a sense of winter wonderland that no one could resist. But the longer the snow stuck, the quicker the wonder disappeared and the more intensely the cabin fever set in. At least a few times every winter, they became virtually isolated out here, unable to go anywhere or see anyone. It had driven Caroline nuts, and she had threatened to take him with her.

How would it affect Annabeth?

More importantly, how would it affect her tentative talk about staying in the valley beyond the one year she had allotted herself?

After mentioning it that one time before Thanksgiving, she hadn't brought the subject up again. Because it had just been idle talk? An impulsive suggestion she'd given no thought? Or because he had been so markedly unenthusiastic?

He had every right to be doubtful, he reminded himself. Caroline had come to the valley with much more of a commitment than Annabeth, had come intending to spend the rest of her life here. She had lasted ten years, but how many of those years had she been unhappy? He didn't know. Looking back, he couldn't recall exactly when the trouble had begun. It seemed as if one day he had just suddenly realized that somewhere along the way, their marriage had fallen apart.

But wasn't it wrong to judge Annabeth by Caroline's standards? As he'd pointed out to his aunt on Thanksgiving, other than surface similarities, they were nothing alike. But they were both from the city. They were both accustomed to an entirely different kind of life. Annabeth found the valley and everything about it charming now—but so had Caroline in the beginning. How about in five years, after five harsh winters and five hot summers? After five years of country living, five years without city comforts, without convenient medical care or shopping, five years away from her family and her home?

And if she lasted five years, a snide voice taunted, what would he demand of her then? Another five years? Ten? How long would she have to stay in the valley to convince him to trust her? How long would she have to live in the mill, a part of his life in every way but the one that counted—as his wife—before he could believe in her? How long would she have to commit herself to him before he could make the same commitment to her?

It shamed him that he didn't know.

It shamed him even more that he needed proof. He needed her to prove to him that she wasn't like Caroline, that she wasn't going to leave him.

The snow was falling heavier as he finished his work and made one last check on the stock before heading toward the mill. Lights were shining from every window, and thin blue smoke rose from the stovepipe. It would be warm and cozy inside, smelling of cinnamon and cloves and whatever she was fixing for dinner, and it would seem more like home than his house across the road ever had, because Annabeth would be waiting for him. She would be happy to see him.

Before going inside, he moved a sizable stack of logs from the woodshed to the shelter of the front porch. The snow might be gone by morning, or it might be three feet deep... in which case, all they could do was stay inside and keep warm until it started melting. He'd never found himself wishing for a blizzard, but Annabeth did have some intriguing ways of keeping warm.

He stamped the snow off his boots and brushed it from his coat and his woolen cap before going inside. He didn't knock anymore—she had teased him about the formality when they were, for all practical purposes, living together. Although he usually showered and shaved at the house, he spent the rest of his time over here. She had made a home for him over here. There was even a framed photograph of Kylie upstairs on the loft wall.

Annabeth, in a yellow sweater, black leggings and fuzzy yellow socks, was on her way to the kitchen when he stepped inside. She slowed long enough to kiss him and tug his cap off, then went on to stir a pot of chili on the hot plate. It was such a perfectly homey scene: the wife fixing dinner for her husband, who was just home from work. After they ate, they would share cleanup chores, spend a quiet evening talking, then go to bed to make love before falling asleep.

There was only one problem: she wasn't his wife, and he didn't know if he could ever be anyone's husband again.

He was certain he could never be anyone's daddy again.

"You smell good," she said, coming back to slide her arms around his waist as he pulled his coat off. "Like snow."

"Snow doesn't have a smell."

"Of course it does. It smells fresh and clean and cold."

"Cold, huh?" He tossed his coat, and it landed crookedly on the stair rail. His gloves fell to the floor nearby. "You want to feel cold?" Inching her sweater up bit by bit, he threatened to place both hands, cold as ice, on her warm skin, but she wriggled away from him with a laugh.

"I have a couple of mugs of hot cocoa over here. Warm your hands on one of them . . . *then* you can put them wherever you want."

He followed her to the sofa and accepted one of the mugs. The cocoa was rich and creamy and went a long way toward warming him, both inside and out. Looking at Annabeth finished the job. "Reading Emmalee's journal again?" he asked, glancing at the book on the makeshift coffee table.

She nodded.

"You feel connected to her, don't you?"

A little slower, a little more reluctant, she nodded again. "There's something about her. . . ."

"You see yourself in her."

She gave him a sharp, startled look. "Why do you say that?"

"You're a lot like her—strong, determined, optimistic." Seeing her satisfied smile start, he dryly added, "Hardheaded."

"To deal with a farm boy like you, I've had to be all of the above and then some," she retorted, poking him in the stomach with her foot, laughing when he caught and tickled it. "Emmalee and I also both came from the city, and we both love kids."

Mention of the city brought Josiah's earlier grim thoughts back too clearly and made him shift uncomfortably. "But Emmalee came to the valley with the intention of dying here," he pointed out.

Annabeth drew her foot back, then gave him a long, uncustomarily serious look. "And I, Josiah, came with the intention of *living* here."

She returned to the kitchen to dish up their dinner, calling to him as she did to wash up. But for a long time, he sat where he was, staring into the flames that flickered in the open stove doors. Maybe he should press the issue. Maybe he should try to discourage her. Maybe he should warn her that she could talk about staying all she wanted, that she could stay as long as she wanted, but it wouldn't change things between them. He couldn't offer her more than this: being lovers. He couldn't do more than care about her, couldn't marry her or have children with her or plan a future with her. He couldn't come to rely too desperately on her.

He could lose another lover.

But he couldn't lose another wife.

"Josiah?" She carried two plates, each holding a bowl of chili, to the sofa, then returned for glasses of tea, silverware, napkins and crackers.

It was a gentle prod, but enough to get him moving. He left the sofa and washed his hands in the small bathroom with its cold water, then joined her again.

"What do you do about Christmas?" she asked as she crumbled a handful of crackers atop her chili.

"Usually nothing. Last year Mom couldn't come home, so I drove over to Fort Smith to see her. This year she's bringing my grandmother and coming here." That news had been in her last letter, the same one in which she'd mentioned Annabeth. His grandmother would stay with the Dothans, but his mother was planning to stay in her old house. He needn't worry about her being underfoot, she had written. She was sure she could find plenty of work to keep herself busy.

That meant his house would finally get the cleaning it deserved. It also meant eating his mother's cooking again instead of Annabeth's. And sleeping in his own bed instead of Annabeth's. It meant stealing whatever sweet moments they could in place of lazy, long hours together.

Provided, he realized with a start, that Annabeth was even here. "You're not going home for Christmas, are you?" he asked so abruptly that she laughed.

"Of course not. Holidays are a part of my work. I know how they're celebrated in Charleston. I want to see how they're honored here."

"Good. Then you can have Christmas dinner with my family." And please, he silently requested, let it be held at Aunt Yvette's or Uncle Bobby's. Of course, Aunt Mary Louise would be there no matter where the dinner was held, but he'd come away from Thanksgiving dinner with the distinct impression that she didn't want to play hostess to Annabeth in her home again.

His aunt was wrong about her. She had no more interest in Stuart than in any of the others she'd met. She wasn't that kind of woman. She *couldn't* be.

"I know you haven't done anything special the last few years for Christmas," Annabeth said softly. "But tell me what you would do this year if Kylie were here. If you were celebrating with your daughter, how would you do it?"

His first impulse was to refuse, to tell her that it was too painful to think about Kylie and Christmas together. It did hurt—that was no lie—but not as badly as before. Not as desperately. Not as hopelessly.

"I had only one Christmas with her, when she was a day short of two months old. She didn't care about it one way or the other."

"But now she's four," Annabeth gently reminded him. "She's old enough to know about Santa Claus and the reindeer, old enough to know about Jesus being born in a manger. She's old enough to be excited and wide-eyed with wonder."

He sighed softly. "For starters, I guess I would take down the decorations from the attic and put up a tree. When Mom moved, she left all her ornaments here. Some of them date back to the early days of my grandparents' marriage."

"What else?"

Finishing his dinner, he pushed the empty dishes aside. "Go shopping, of course, and visit Santa Claus. And instead of the usual bedtime stories, she would probably want to hear Christmas stories."

"Was that your job—reading her bedtime stories?" she asked, leaning on one arm to watch him.

"No," he replied softly. "That was my pleasure."

He fell silent then, gazing into the fire once more. Lord, how he wished this wasn't just idle talk, that Kylie *could* be here this Christmas. She would love Annabeth, and he had to believe that somewhere—deep in her heart, if not in her mind—she would remember him. She would know how deeply he loved her. He would have the best time a man could ever long for: Christmas, with his very own angels.

He looked pensive, Annabeth thought, though in a good sort of way. She knew talking about Kylie hurt, but better that he endure a little pain now than keep his little girl buried under a mountain of heartache. She believed all the way down in her soul that someday Kylie would come back. Annabeth didn't know when or how, but someday she would come looking for her father, the way Annabeth had come looking for Stuart. She just hoped Kylie didn't wait as long as she had, because she would certainly get a much warmer welcome than Annabeth had gotten.

And whether it took five years, ten or fifty, Annabeth would be here waiting when she came.

"Why don't you rest?" she suggested, carrying the dishes into the kitchen. "I'll clean up." She filled a teakettle with water and put it on top of the Franklin to heat, then scraped leftovers from their bowls into Emerson's. Naturally, though, Josiah insisted on helping her with the few dishes before he settled again on the sofa.

He looked comfortable there, but she had other things in mind before she joined him. After putting another kettle of water on the stove, along with a saucepan, she dragged the metal bathtub over near the Franklin and began filling it with buckets of water from the bathroom. Josiah watched her with an interested smile. She had grown fond of the old-fashioned tub, of soaking in warm, sudsy water while an open fire crackled and popped a few feet away. Even when he offered her use of his bathroom with a full tub and a shower, she had refused, although when it got hot next summer, when bathing was strictly a necessity rather than a pleasure, she would probably take him up on it.

It took two pans of steaming water to warm the creek water to a comfortable temperature. While she waited for that, she went upstairs, undressed and slipped on a robe, then pinned her hair loosely on top of her head. When she came down again, Josiah was still watching, still wearing that strange little smile—and more. He was starting to get aroused.

"I always wondered," he said quietly, "why you preferred to bathe when I was gone. Now I know."

"Why?" She poured the water from the kettle into the tub, followed it with the pan, then pushed her sleeve up and swirled the water around. Next she got a washcloth, towel and soap from the bathroom, then, maneuvering carefully, she slipped out of her robe and into the tub without her modesty slipping one bit.

"Because you would never finish. We would never get anything done. We would never even make it upstairs to bed," he replied, his voice hoarse.

"Test your endurance, darlin'," she teased. "Show me how strong you are." She settled deeper into the tub, leaning against the comfortably sloped back. "That notebook underneath Emmalee's journal has some of my notes in it. Would you like to look them over?"

He reached for the notebook, flipped through the pages, then turned to the front again and started reading. The first pages were notes from her interview with Millicent Parks—Aunt Millie—the elderly midwife who had delivered Josiah, as well as so many others. With Stuart's Aunt Flo along to provide introductions, Annabeth had traveled up to Whistler's Rock, so named because of the sound the wind made coming through a long, narrow crevice in the sandstone ridge, to spend hours with a little doll of an old lady.

What would it be like to have your baby delivered by a midwife? she wondered. To know that your child's life wasn't in the hands of a board-certified obstetrician, that you weren't giving birth in a state-of-the-art hospital where nothing could go wrong? Maybe one day she would find out, since most babies in the valley, according to Aunt Millie, were still being attended by a midwife. Of course, this one was a registered nurse who had received her midwife training at a medical school—but she was still a midwife. Still not a doctor.

Simplifying the question further, she wondered what it was like to have a baby, period—in any fashion, in any place. How would it feel to know there was a life growing inside her—another daughter, or maybe this time a son, for Josiah? And how would *he* feel? Would he ever love a child with her as much as he loved Kylie?

Would he ever love *her?*

She slid her hands over her stomach, indecently flat, and wondered. Wished. Wanted.

He continued turning pages, occasionally pausing to look at her. She pretended not to notice, pretended that his glance wasn't making her nipples grow hard, pretended that the water couldn't possibly be a degree or two warmer. She pretended she wasn't starting to ache inside.

After the notes on Aunt Millie's midwifery, there were directions, including sketches, for making lye soap. She intended to try it herself when she'd collected enough ashes from the wood stove. Hickory ashes were best, Aunt Millie had told her, but just about any kind would do, Aunt Flo had added. Annabeth had asked Josiah what kind of wood she was burning, and he had told her a mix of hickory and oak. They ought to do just fine.

Tilting her head back onto a pillow she'd made with a towel folded over the high back of the tub, she sighed softly, contentedly. Then, seeing something she'd never noticed before, she asked, "Why is there a hook in the ceiling?"

Josiah glanced up, following her gaze to the rusted hook. "There should be four of them," he replied.

She searched for and found the other three, forming a rough rectangle, about twice as long as it was wide. "Were they used in the sawmill?"

"Nope."

"Then for what?"

He closed her notebook, got up from the sofa and slowly approached her. With perfect innocence, he said, "I don't know. Personally, I think my grandparents were into wicked games. You know—bondage, torment, intense pleasure, but never pain."

"Josiah!" She flicked a tiny spray of water at him, then asked again, "What are they for?"

He stood in front of the stove and began rolling up his sleeves. He was wearing a flannel shirt this evening, in red and black and gold. She knew—suspected—expected—what he was going to do, but still she shivered. *Intense pleasure*.

Kneeling beside the tub, he picked up the washcloth from where she'd hung it and took the soap from the metal dish. As he soaped the cloth, he said conversationally, "You can create some powerful feelings in someone who is totally vulnerable."

"Tied up," she said hoarsely.

"Or unable to get away. Or absolutely naked."

"While you're still clothed, of course."

"Of course." With a gentle smile, he pulled her hands from where they clasped around her knees and placed each one on the small, flat arms of the tub, then nudged her legs apart.

When he placed the cloth right between her breasts, then started washing her, she stopped breathing, stopped thinking. The lather made the rag glide across her skin in a sensuously smooth motion, while at the same time, the slightly rough texture of the cloth scraped across her breasts, across her nipples, and stimulated every nerve ending it came in contact with.

He drew the cloth in lazy circles across her breasts, her shoulders, her throat and her back. After rinsing it clean, he filled it with water, squeezed it over her skin and watched tiny rivulets of water race across her skin, leaving forked trails in the lather, did it over and over until every bit of soap was washed away.

Torment with intense pleasure. Annabeth closed her eyes, sighed and smiled. *Oh, my, yes.*

When his mouth closed around her nipple, she whimpered, settled lower in the tub and involuntarily moved her hips, seeking relief in the ebb and flow of the warm water. She slid her fingers into his hair, pulling him closer, filling his mouth, gasping when he bit her and darn near crying when he sucked harder. This might be enough, she thought helplessly. The sensations were so sweet, so powerful. Her muscles were twitching, her body throbbing deep inside, her skin rippling. She was ready, pleading, trembling....

And he stopped, pulling away, smiling at her wordless protest. He took her hand and guided it between his legs, folding her fingers around his arousal, sliding them along the length, up and down again. "It's hard to tell who's closer," he murmured.

When she tried to unfasten his jeans, he pushed her hand away, lathered the washcloth again and lifted her onto her knees. "Test your endurance, darlin'," he whispered, leaving the barest of kisses on her breast. "Show me how strong you are."

He bathed her belly, her bottom, her thighs. Finally, nudging her arms up over his shoulders for support and discarding the cloth in favor of his soapy hands, he parted her legs and touched her where she needed him most. The soap made his fingers slick, and they rubbed her everywhere, stroking, feeding, tormenting. They settled at last on that small bit of swollen flesh—hard caresses, slow at first until she whimpered, then faster, rougher, sweeter, until she cried, until relief exploded through her and left her trembling, shuddering, mindlessly clinging.

She couldn't think, couldn't lift her head from his shoulder, couldn't control the spasmodic clenching of her muscles. She had no desire to move, no desire to release his hand, trapped in such intimate contact with her body, had no desire to do anything at all but stay like this forever. *Forever.* When Josiah slowly pushed her away, she protested, but the warmth of the water as he lowered her into the tub silenced that. He rinsed the soap away with gentle

Sweet Annie's Pass

touches, washed her clean, then once more lifted her, wrapped a towel around her and carried her upstairs.

"Wonderful," she whispered from the softness of her bed, managing a goofy smile even if she couldn't do anything else, even if her body did refuse to obey any and all other commands. "It might take me forever to recuperate from that."

His voice came from somewhere up above her, along with the sound of clothing falling away. "Oh, I'm not through with you yet, sweet Annie," he teased, and then he was on the bed with her, touching her, stroking her, kissing between her thighs. The last thing she heard before the need started again, before the torment started again, was his soft, satisfied, amused voice.

"Oh, Annie—those hooks?"

The hooks. Yes, for wicked games.

Not quite. "They're for quilt frames." He laughed softly. "For quilting bees."

The snow lasted less than two days; by Wednesday afternoon, the last of it was gone and it was a bright, mid-fifties day. Annabeth had driven into town for lunch with Miss Hilda. When the old lady returned to the library afterward, Annabeth headed impulsively for the bank. Wednesday was the day they closed early. Maybe, if he didn't have any plans, Stuart would give her that tour of the valley he had offered.

He and the two tellers were just coming out the door when she arrived. Both women greeted her with polite smiles, called goodbye to their boss and went on their way. Annabeth waited expectantly for him to speak.

She had seen him only once since Thanksgiving—an unplanned meeting in the grocery store where she had gone to restock. He had looked at her cart, had remarked that that sure seemed like a lot of food for a skinny young girl like her, but he hadn't pursued the matter. Did he suspect that her relationship with Josiah had gone past the interested stage to the practically living-together stage? Did he not want to face that fact because he was too polite, because it was none of his business or because he was concerned for his nephew?

Or had he, she'd wondered wistfully, been feeling maybe a slight bit of fatherly discomfort when it came to her sleeping arrangements? Her stepfather had displayed that same sort of discomfort back when she was in college, when she had overheard a discussion between him and her mother about her newly acquired habit of staying out all night with her boyfriend, had heard Frank say exasperatedly, "I *know* she's sleeping with him, Lynette. I just don't *want* to know it."

But, no, Stuart hadn't been fatherly; he had just been uncomfortable. As he was now.

"I wasn't expecting you today."

"It's hard to call ahead when you don't have a telephone." She shoved her hands into her pockets. "Are you busy?"

"I was just heading home. What did you want?"

"That tour you promised. Hitting all the Dothan family hot spots in the valley."

He stood there for a moment, giving a distracted greeting to someone—one of Josiah's cousins, she thought—who passed. Sensing his reluctance, she reached out and touched his hand. "Forget it. I just thought this might be a good time. Why don't you find some time that's convenient and let me know?"

"No, today's fine. I don't have anything planned, and Mary Louise isn't home. She drove over to Eureka Springs to do some Christmas shopping in the crafts stores there. What would you like to see first?"

Annabeth didn't need to consider it. She already knew what she wanted most to see. "The family cemetery."

He gave her an odd look, then shrugged. "You're a morbid child, aren't you? But then, you do seem to have a fondness in your stories for ghosts and goblins."

"Cemeteries are more for the living than the dead," she remarked as they started down the street. "The older ones in Charleston are tourist attractions. They're peaceful and beautiful, and the old epitaphs contain so much more than names and dates. And I remember a cemetery in Virginia that has a picnic area right among the graves.''

The cemetery was a few blocks off the highway, past the school and a park with a baseball diamond and a single, crooked basketball hoop. The place needed some maintenance, Annabeth thought as she entered through the arched gate. The wrought-iron fence was rusted, the black paint flaked off, and there were weeds around most of the graves.

''You probably know that most families used to have their own private graveyards,'' Stuart said as they followed a brick path overgrown with weeds. ''Henry Dothan didn't hold with that notion. He was bound and determined to turn the settlement here into a real, honest-to-God town, and every town, of course, needed a graveyard. When he bought this land and proposed to use it for that purpose, I'm sure he had no idea his son Jeffrey would be the first one laid to rest here.''

The graves he led her to were at the back. First he showed her Jeffrey's grave, the carving on the small white-marble tombstone barely legible. On one side was Henry's, on the other another child's grave—the baby girl who had died at birth. Resting beside her was Emmalee. She had died more than ninety years ago at the age of seventy, outliving her husband by only six months. She had given birth to six children and had seen two of them die, had loved twenty-one grandchildren and seven great-grandchildren. Annabeth had no doubt she had died a happy woman. She had lived her life surrounded by the people she loved and had died with the unwavering belief she would be reunited in death with those who were already gone.

Stuart showed her the graves of the relatives who linked them to Emmalee: Matthew, his son Stephen and Stephen's son Herbert—Stuart's father, Annabeth's grandfather. He had died shortly after her seventeenth birthday. ''Did he ever know he had a grandchild?'' she asked softly.

"No. He was furious about—about my affair with Lynette. If he'd known there'd been a baby involved..."

"He knew?" she asked, somehow startled. She had assumed their affair had been a furtive thing, a secretive sneaking-around. "Who else knew?"

"Too many. It almost ended my marriage." They started walking back toward the cemetery gate. "I thought I was being so clever, so careful, but you know how small the Corner is. You can't keep secrets long. My father heard the rumors and warned me to put a stop to them or *he* would." He gave her a rueful smile. "He would have, too. He was a mean old man. Given the chance, he would have marched your mother out of here and had her thrown in jail if she returned."

"For what?" Annabeth asked indignantly.

"For getting on the wrong side of Herbert Dothan. I think you might have been able to stand up to him, but your mother couldn't have. She was too delicate. Too weak."

"So you were going to quit seeing her before you found out she was pregnant because of your father." Maybe Lynette wasn't the only one, she thought unkindly, who had been weak.

"Because of him, and because of Mary Louise. Believe it or not, Annabeth, I loved my wife. I didn't want to hurt her."

"You told Mama you loved her, too," she softly reminded him.

"I did. For a time. She was different. Exciting. She'd been places, done things. She had lived an entirely different life from anything I knew." He gave her a sidelong glance. "I imagine I felt the same things for her that Josiah feels for you."

Annabeth stopped walking and waited until he turned to face her. "You're wrong, Stuart. You were attracted to Mama *because* she was different, *because* she had lived an entirely different life. Josiah's attracted to me *in spite of* our differences."

After a long, searching look, he turned again, and they continued walking toward the main road. "What are your plans for Christmas?"

"I'm staying here."

"Won't your family miss you?"

"I certainly hope so."

"The town used to put up the tallest tree they could find in the yard of the Baptist church every year for Christmas and decorate it with lights and a giant gold star. It was a big event. Everyone from all over the valley came for the lighting and to sing carols. There were bonfires, hot chocolate and treats for the kids and mulled cider for the adults.

"When I was a kid, people came in cars and wagons, on horseback and on foot. A lot of people back then couldn't afford trees or parties or presents, so the tree lighting was their celebration. Then on Christmas Day, we all went to church before dinner. The services were always solemn for such a joyous occasion. I always came out determined to be a better person the next year." He smiled wryly. "Of course, that resolve lasted only a day or two. Then I was back to being a typical rowdy boy."

"When did they stop the tree lighting?"

"Back in the sixties. There wasn't enough money to continue, and interest in it had fallen off. People get involved with their own families, their own celebrations. Our worlds get smaller every year. When Mary Louise and I were first married, it was an unwritten rule that all grown kids had to have dinner with their parents every Sunday, and all holiday meals were taken with one set of parents or the other. Now it's not at all unusual for parents to live only a few miles from their children and see them only once every month or two."

At the highway, he gestured for her to turn toward the bank, then went on. "You don't know enough about the family to notice, but at Thanksgiving, not a single one of Martin's or Bobby's kids showed up. They're starting their own traditions in their own homes." His tone made it clear what he thought of that. "And look at you—a thousand miles from home not only for Thanksgiving, but also Christmas.''

"The rest of my family will be there," she protested. "They'll hardly miss me."

"Don't deceive yourself, Annabeth. A mother can have twenty of her twenty-one children home for a holiday and still find plenty of room in her heart to miss that twenty-first child." He pulled his keys from his pocket and unlocked the passenger door of the Bronco. "We'll need to drive to see the rest of the places."

Annabeth climbed in and fastened her seat belt. When he was seated opposite her, she continued the conversation. "Of course they'll miss me, but they understand. Mama left her family in Alabama when she married Daddy and moved to South Carolina. She understands that things change, that people can't always stay in one place. She's known for a long time that I probably wouldn't settle in Charleston, that my time there, my time at home with them, is going to be reduced to occasional visits, just as her time with her family back in Alabama is only twice-a-year visits."

He had backed out of the parking space and was waiting to turn onto the road. Seeing no traffic, she looked up to find him watching her, a strange look on his face. "What?" she asked, seeing a question in his eyes that he was obviously reluctant to ask.

"You call her husband Daddy?"

Annabeth felt a shivery unease inside, something vaguely akin to guilt. But she had no reason to feel guilty. *She* wasn't the one who had abandoned *him*. She wasn't the one who had turned her back, who had decided he had no place in her life. "Frank is the only father I've ever known," she said softly. "Of course I call him Daddy."

"Of course." He turned left, following the road out of town and in the direction of Aunt Flo's, but instead of climbing one of the mountains, they stayed on the valley floor. "I don't know why it sounded strange. I certainly haven't been a father to you." He smiled tautly. "It's odd, though. It's one thing to know you have a child out there somewhere. It's another entirely to hear that child—even all grown-up now—call another man Daddy."

Annabeth acknowledged that with a nod. What had Josiah said on Thanksgiving? *I wonder if there's some other man that she gives a card to on Father's Day, some other man that she calls Daddy.* It would break his heart if he heard Kylie do that.

But there was one major difference. Given the chance, Josiah would have fought the devil himself to keep his daughter with him. He hadn't given her up willingly.

Stuart had.

"What did you do today?" Josiah asked as he finished washing the dishes from their dinner. He took the towel Annabeth offered and dried his hands, then returned it so she could finish the drying.

"I had lunch with Miss Hilda, went to the cemetery and drove around the valley." She placed the plates on the shelf, then added the silverware to the glass alongside. "Not an exciting day, but I got some work done. I learned some interesting information." She gave him a grin with that last bit, making him wonder what information, assuring him she would share it when she was ready.

Finishing with the dishes, she hung the towel on a nail, then took a cake from the refrigerator. She had borrowed his kitchen this morning to bake it, had asked his favorite kind of cake, his favorite frosting. Coconut, he'd told her, and that was what she'd baked. Caroline had hated coconut. Even for his birthday, she had always baked chocolate cakes with chocolate frosting, even though *he* hated chocolate cake.

He stopped her before she cut the cake. "I'm not hungry yet."

"Are you sure?" At his nod, she put the knife down and returned the plate to the refrigerator. Then she took his hand and drew him across the room toward the couch. "Sit down, Josiah," she invited. "I'm going to tell you a story."

There was a mischievous look in her eyes, and she wore a devilish smile that said he was in no small amount of trouble with her. He knew immediately what she had discovered—Sweet Annie; that was her interesting information—but he let her drag him along, sit him down on the sofa and begin her story.

She pulled the twig chair close and sat facing him, knee to knee. "Dutchman's Valley is a truly enclosed valley, ringed completely by mountains, with the only access coming through a pass at the eastern end and another at the west end. The state built their highway through the west pass, but a hundred and fifty years ago, when settlement of the valley first started, people reached it through the east pass."

Through Sweet Annie's Pass. He had been right. She had promised that one day she would discover who Sweet Annie was—and she had. He wondered if it had been Miss Hilda who'd told her or if she'd dug up the information someplace else.

"Legend has it that Annie was an Easterner, a citified woman who came to the valley with her husband," she continued. "They homesteaded a piece of land just inside the pass, where settlers and trappers and explorers passed right by. Now, as fate would have it, Annie's husband died young and left her in the wilderness on her own. Being a friendly sort and finding mountain nights awfully lonely, Annie opened her home to these travelers, especially to the trappers and the explorers who weren't bringing their wives into the valley with them."

She emphasized that last part, the men traveling alone who had no women to worry about, no women to keep them warm, no women to get jealous of pretty Annie. Rising from the chair, she shifted to sit across Josiah's lap, one knee on each side, resting one hand on each shoulder, leaving no doubt at all exactly what kind of welcome the original Annie had offered, and she moved against him in a way that left no doubt at all that she would extend the same sort of wicked welcome to him when her story was finished.

"Annie made those trappers and explorers feel so welcome that it got mighty hard for a man to plan a trip anywhere within a hundred miles of the valley that didn't come right by that eastern pass," she said, her voice sultry hot and her smile infinitely teasing. "Men being men, of course they talked about Annie among themselves, and soon every man in the region knew that if he wanted a home-cooked meal and..." She paused, smiled, then chose her word delicately. "And...entertainment, Annie was the woman to see. Unfortunately, neighbors had moved in through the pass, and they didn't look too kindly on Annie's activities. They requested that she move on, and, being an agreeable woman, she did just that. She never came back to the valley again. But in honor of her...special talents, that eastern pass to this very day is still called Sweet Annie's Pass."

He was grinning when she finished, even though she wasn't, even though he knew it was dangerous, even though he knew there was more to come. It arrived with a playful blow struck square in his chest. "A whore?" she demanded. "Is that what you think of me, Josiah Miller? I remind you of a *whore?*"

"Sweet Annie wasn't a whore," he disagreed, wrapping his arms tight around her.

"She supported herself by having sex with men. What does that make her?"

"She was a beautiful, generous woman who brought a great deal of pleasure to the men in her life."

"To *every* one of them?" she asked with a scowl. "There must have been dozens."

"At least." He kissed the place at the base of her throat where her pulse was visible when she was aroused and hot and excited. "Maybe even hundreds. Men would travel days out of their way to sample Sweet Annie's treasures."

Freeing one hand, he began unbuttoning her blouse, seeking his own Annie's treasures, but she pushed him away, not ready to give in so easily. "And I remind you of her?"

Completely serious, he met her gaze. "You're as sweet as honey, and you bring me great, great pleasure. Looking at you, talking to you, hearing you laugh... Sharing your

meals, sharing your life... Touching you, making love with
you... Just knowing you, Annie, is the sweetest pleasure in
my life.''

He reached for her blouse again, but she stopped him
once more, this time clasping his hands between hers, raising them to her mouth for a kiss. ''I love you, Josiah,'' she
said. Not in a heated rush, not breathless with passion, but
quietly. Calmly. Intensely. *I love you.* As in permanently. As
in forever and ever, amen.

I love you.

Part of him cherished the words as the most precious gift,
second only to Kylie, he had ever received.

Part of him wished she had never said them. They were
having an affair here, not falling in love. When the time
came for her to go, as it inevitably would, it would be so
much easier if there'd been no talk of love, no hints of forever, no vows for him to doubt.

And part of him, some small, secret part hidden deep inside his soul, wanted to repeat them, wanted to respond with
''I love you, too, Annie.'' Part of him wanted to love her,
might already love her.

If only he knew she would stay.

If only he knew there *could* be a forever for them.

If only he didn't believe with all his heart that, like Caroline, like Kylie, she, too, would soon leave him.

He looked away guiltily, then cupped her face in his
palms. ''Annie...'' Annie what? he wondered, frustrated.
What could he say that she would want to hear? When a
woman said she loved you, you were supposed to recipro-
cate...but even if it wasn't true? Even if the mere words, the
mere believing, could destroy you?

Regretfully he lifted her aside, then stood up and walked
out the door. He came to a stop on the porch, leaning one
shoulder against the post, and stared into the moonlit night.

A moment later, Annabeth followed him out. She left the
door open so that a wedge of light spilled out on them, il-
luminating her face, so beautiful and sweet. He glanced
down at her, then miserably turned away. ''I'm sorry,'' he
muttered.

"For what?" she asked. "Being human? For wondering if I'm going to make promises and commitments and vows, then leave the way Caroline did?"

"I know you want—"

She stopped him. "I want a chance, Josiah. That's all."

A chance. It wouldn't be fair to let her believe she could have it. It would be downright cruel to let her think that if she stayed long enough, if she tried hard enough, one day he would love her, that one day he would marry her. "Annie, I can't . . ."

She stopped him again. "I'm not asking for anything you haven't already given, Josiah. This is enough."

Enough. The mere word made him ache inside. No marriage, no children, no love. No commitment, no respectability, no promises, no future. Just sweet sex and lazy hours together.

She was willing to settle for so little when she deserved so much more, but, God help him, he couldn't give it to her.

This was as good as it was going to get.

"You could do better with any other man," he pointed out.

She smiled gently. "I've been with a few other men, Josiah. I'd rather be with you."

"You need a husband. You need to have children."

That brought a flicker of pain to her eyes that he pretended not to see, even though he felt it, hot and sharp, around his heart. "I need *you.*"

Then, with a sudden shiver, she smiled again and the pain disappeared, and she took his arm, tugging him toward the door. "Come on, Josiah. Let's go back inside," she said softly. "We've talked enough."

Chapter 10

There was something to be said, Annabeth decided the next morning, for optimism. If she weren't a hopeful person by nature, the scene last night with Josiah might have broken her heart. There was something painful about telling a man you loved him, then watching him walk away like that. There was something particularly painful about that same man telling you he would never marry you, would never have babies with you—in effect, that he would never love you.

If she weren't so hopefully romantic, she would be curled up under the covers upstairs, crying her eyes out.

But she knew Josiah cared for her. He had said she brought him great pleasure. He had called her the sweetest pleasure in his life.

And she knew he trusted her, even if he didn't realize it.

She knew he needed her. Wonder, he'd called their love-making. And after losing Kylie, he had needed some wonder in his life.

Still, hopeful as she was, there was an uneasy little knot of pain in her stomach. There was the fear that, after last night, he would pull away from her in some misguided effort to protect her from himself. There was the worry that maybe she was wrong, that maybe he needed more than time, that maybe he needed more than she could ever give him.

What if she stayed five years and it didn't make a difference? What if after ten years, he still couldn't commit to her? She wanted to marry him, wanted to have a dozen babies with him, wanted to spend the rest of her life with him. What if she stayed and stayed and stayed and he never came to love her? What if she gave up her chances for any future—for any other marriage, for any other love, for ever having children—and he still never accepted her?

She shook off such thoughts. Faith, hope and wishful thinking had brought her this far; it would sustain her as long as was necessary. One day he would realize that he loved her. One day he would want her as his wife, not his lover. One day he would want to have a family with her.

She believed that.

She believed it with all her heart and all her soul.

A glance at the clock sent her scrambling from the couch. It was eleven-thirty. Josiah was due back any minute now for lunch. He had offered several times to get lunch at his own house, to have a sandwich or a can of soup there—exactly what they were having here today—instead of disturbing her work. But she liked taking a break, liked sitting down to eat with him. Besides, farm wives fed their husbands lunch, and while she was a long way from being a farm wife, she had hopes. Dreams. Fantasies.

She saw him coming across the road at the same time she noticed Mary Louise's truck pulling into the clearing. At first she was disappointed by the woman's presence; then she decided that, after last night, it might not be bad to have a third person around to smooth over any leftover awkwardness she and Josiah might have.

He opened the door, and Mary Louise marched into the room, her gaze sweeping around until it found Annabeth in the kitchen. There was a sudden chill in the room, Annabeth thought, slowly approaching, and it didn't come from the winter air outside. "Hello, Mary Louise. Josiah."

He didn't greet her with a kiss—because he was still uncomfortable about last night? she wondered wistfully. Or because his aunt was here and was obviously none too happy?

Mary Louise didn't waste any time coming to the point of her visit. Her hands on her hips, her cheeks a brilliant pink, she fixed her venomous gaze on Annabeth and flatly announced, "I want you to stay the hell away from my husband."

Annabeth stared at her, her lips slightly parted in dismay. "Excuse me?"

"Don't play innocent with me. I know you spent the afternoon with him yesterday while I was out of town. I know you arranged to meet him at the bank after it closed, that he took you to my house—to *my* house—on the pretext of helping you with your work."

The suggestion that she was involved with Stuart in that way would have been laughable if it weren't so ludicrous—and sick. "We didn't arrange to meet, Mary Louise," she said quietly. "And we were at your house maybe fifteen minutes while he changed clothes. We spent the afternoon driving around the valley. He showed me the cemetery, the original Dothan homestead, where Emmalee and Henry's kids settled, where everyone lives today. That's all."

Beside the open door, Josiah gave her an odd look. "You were with Stuart yesterday?"

"Yes. I told you—"

"No, you didn't. You said you had lunch with Miss Hilda, then you went to the cemetery and drove around the valley. You never mentioned Stuart."

She tried to remember their conversation from last night, but it wasn't clear in her mind. She had been preoccupied with the legend of Sweet Annie, had been planning how to best tell it, how to get the maximum teasing from it. "Well," she began apologetically, "it's no big deal—"

Mary Louise interrupted her. "No big deal—but you lied to him about it."

"I didn't lie—"

The woman interrupted again. "Funny. That's what Stuart said. He didn't *lie*—he just forgot to tell the truth. Just as he forgot to mention the other times he's seen you. You've gone to his office, he's taken you to lunch, he's come here to the mill—and it all just happened to slip his mind. If you've got nothing to hide, why the secrets? Why the lies?"

Annabeth's temper flared. She'd had enough of Mary Louise's suspicions and accusations. If the woman's husband had been unfaithful to her, that was their problem, not *hers*. She wasn't going to take the blame for it. "I don't have to explain myself to you, Mary Louise. If you—"

This time it was Josiah who interrupted. He did it not angrily, but quietly. Very quietly. "Then explain it to me, Annie."

She turned to stare at him. He was staring back, the look in his eyes as bleak as any she'd ever seen. As distrusting as any she'd ever seen. "What?" she whispered.

"You didn't forget to tell me that you had lunch with Miss Hilda. Why did you forget to mention that you spent the rest of the day with Stuart?"

"Because I had other things on my mind—you and Sweet Annie. Because who I spent the afternoon with wasn't important. He's part of my job."

"Part of your job and what else?"

The ache in her chest made it difficult to breathe, and the lump forming in her throat made swallowing nearly impossible. "Josiah, don't do this," she whispered. "I'm not like Caroline. Don't imply—"

"Imply what, Annabeth?" Mary Louise asked coldly. "That you're having an affair with my husband?"

She didn't look away from Josiah. She couldn't. But all she saw in his eyes was doubt. Suspicion. Distrust. He didn't believe her, because he didn't believe in her any more than he believed in fairies. But how could he *not* believe her?

Hadn't he learned anything about her in their weeks together? Didn't he have the slightest understanding what loving a man—what loving *him*—meant to her?

Such a short while ago she had been thinking blithely about her heart breaking. Now she knew it was. Nothing else could possibly hurt this badly.

"You are, aren't you? You won't even deny it." Mary Louise sounded perversely triumphant and sorrowful at the same time. "I knew it. I *knew!* He lies about seeing you. He's secretive about the time he spends with you. He refuses to talk about you with me, and he's acted so damned guilty ever since you came here. Josiah saw it himself on Thanksgiving, when Stuart came back after you two sneaked off to the creek together. What is it you think you're going to get, Annabeth? Surely you're not foolish enough to think he'll leave me for you. Money? Is that it?"

Annabeth's attention was still locked on Josiah. "Last night," she said, fighting the tears that thickened her voice, "I told you that I love you, and today you can believe that I'm..." She couldn't finish, couldn't say the rest of it: *that I'm having an affair with another man.*

She waited, prayed and pleaded for him to see the absurdity of this entire conversation, waited for him to say, No, Annie, I don't believe you could do that. Prayed for him to say, I'm sorry, Annie, for ever doubting you.

But he didn't. He looked at her—at the woman he'd made love with practically every night for the last three weeks, at the woman he'd kissed so gently and held so securely, at the woman he had called the sweetest pleasure in his life—and he quietly asked, "Are you?"

Blindly she reached for the stair rail, then sank down on one of the steps. Her legs wouldn't support her any longer. With those two flat, mistrustful words, he'd swept them right out from under her.

Oh, God, how could she have been so wrong about him? She had thought all he needed was time—time to see that she wasn't going to leave him the way Caroline did, time to see that she intended to stay here with him forever, time to realize that he did love her, that he trusted her and wanted and needed her.

But she had been terribly, miserably wrong. There wasn't enough time in the world to overcome this lack of faith. If he believed she could do this—could go to another man when she loved *him*—then he knew nothing about her. He cared nothing about her.

He truly never could love her.

Are you?

Josiah knew those two words were the biggest mistake he'd ever made. He saw it in her eyes, in the depth of the pain there, saw it in the anguish that shadowed her face, in the vulnerable, helpless way she'd sat down and sort of collapsed in on herself, and he felt it around his own heart. He had just lost—no, not lost—had just *destroyed* something very precious.

Something he might not be able to live without.

Moving from the door, he knelt on the bottom step. "Annie, I'm sorry. Please forgive me—"

"Don't be an idiot, Josiah!" Mary Louise broke in. "She's lying to you, making a fool of you just as Caroline did! There's something between her and Stuart. I've seen it! *You've* seen it! There's something going on!"

He reached for Annabeth's hands, finding them limp and cold, and gripped them tightly in his. "I'm sorry I asked," he said softly. "I'm sorry I doubted you. I know..." He paused, puzzling over those words.

I know... He *knew* Mary Louise was wrong, *knew* Annabeth wasn't having an affair with Stuart, knew it in his heart. He knew as surely as he breathed that she would never do that—not to him, not to herself. He knew because he trusted her as he hadn't trusted anyone since Caroline. He *trusted* her.

"You're wrong, Aunt Mary Louise. I know Annie wouldn't lie," he said quietly, and she abruptly met his gaze. Her brown eyes were still dark with hurt, but there was surprise there, too—surprise that he had finally found a little faith. It gave him the courage to almost smile, to almost hope.

Still holding her hands tightly, he faced his aunt. "That's enough. If you have questions about your husband, go to the bank and ask him, but leave Annie alone."

From the doorway came a calm, strong voice. "There's no need to go anywhere," Stuart said as he walked inside. "We can settle this here and now. When you left my office this morning, Mary Louise, I was too angry to think clearly. Finally I realized that you might come out here and try to cause trouble for Annabeth. I was right, wasn't I?"

Mary Louise's voice threatened to break under the weight of her anger. "So you came here to protect her."

"Yes, I suppose I did. It's an instinct long overdue, I'm afraid."

"Then you admit you're having an affair with her."

"No, Mary Louise, I'm admitting that there's something between us." He came to stand beside the stairs, touching Annabeth's shoulder through the spindles. "I think it's time I told the truth," he gently told her. "When I made you promise to keep our secret, I never imagined it would come to this. I never thought it would cost you so much."

Josiah felt a curious flutter of pain inside. *Our secret.* What sort of secret could she possibly share with Stuart? And, he selfishly wondered, how would it affect *them?*

It wouldn't. Whatever it was, he wouldn't let it affect them. He wouldn't let it come between them.

Turning away from Annabeth, Stuart said, "You're right, Mary Louise. There is something between us." Pausing, he glanced at Annabeth, then Josiah, then Mary Louise, and then he went on.

"Annabeth is my daughter."

His uncle Stuart was Annabeth's other father.

That was one Josiah hadn't considered. At least it helped explain her strong interest in the valley and its people. This was her family, her heritage. She belonged here as much as he did. She had a family history here almost as long as his own.

She *belonged* here.

With him.

All he could do now was hope he hadn't, like an idiot, driven her away.

Stuart and Mary Louise had gone, leaving the mill cold and still in their wake. Annabeth hadn't spoken, hadn't moved, hadn't done anything at all since Stuart had appeared in the doorway. Her hands were still in his, but only, he suspected, because she couldn't find the strength to pull them away.

He wondered what words he could say to make her understand why he had asked, to make her forgive him for being such a fool. She was so much better with words than he was, so much better at expressing her feelings. All he knew was how to suppress his.

He'd done a good job of that in the last three years, an even better job in the last few weeks. Just last night, he had insisted that he couldn't love Annabeth, not when he believed in his heart that she would leave him. He could care very deeply for her, could worry about her, could want and need her, could wake up each day only for the pleasure of spending it with her. He could make love with her and make a life with her and a home with her, but he could not love her.

But what was love if not caring, worrying, wanting and needing, making love and sharing and living? All these things he felt for her, these things he had allowed himself instead of love, were the best definition of love he could imagine. He had lied to her—worse, had lied to himself—about it.

He loved her.

And now that he could see it, now that he could say it, was it too late?

He was afraid to find out.

He was more afraid not to.

"Annie, I'm sorry," he said again.

"You're always sorry, Josiah," she whispered. "This time it's not enough."

"I was wrong to let Aunt Mary Louise influence me. It was just so easy to think..."

"That I would betray you?" Just the thought of it brought tears to her eyes. "Josiah, I *love* you... but you don't believe that, do you?" she asked sadly. "You don't believe I'm going to stay here, you don't believe I love you, you don't believe you can trust me. It doesn't matter if I stay here five years or fifty, you're never going to believe in me."

"You'd damn well better plan on staying at least fifty years, because when I die, Annie, I want you by my side. I want your face to be the last thing I see in this world."

A tear spilled over and coursed down her cheek. "And your obituary will say, 'Survived by the lover who lived across the road.'"

"No." He dried the tear, then softly said, "It will say, 'Survived by the wife who will live forever in his heart, and by all their children and their grandchildren, and their grandchildren's children.'"

Another tear broke free, followed by more. She pulled her hands away and covered her face. "Please don't, Josiah," she whispered brokenly. "You don't have to..."

"I'm trying... Annie, I'm trying to say that I love you."

That made her cry harder. "Why now?" she demanded. "Why not last night? Why not this morning? Why do you love me only now when you think you've ruined things between us?"

"Because being afraid can help a cowardly man find courage," he replied, drying her cheeks, brushing her hair back, gently forcing her to endure his touches even when she pushed his hands away. "And I am afraid, Annie. I'm afraid I've hurt you once too often, once too deeply. I'm afraid I've taken the light from your eyes. I'm afraid I've lost my best, last chance to know what happiness really is."

"I'm afraid you have, too," she whispered painfully, clasping his hands tightly in hers. Then, in a voice that broke his heart, she pleaded, "Please, Josiah . . . go away. I don't want to be with you anymore."

Watching Caroline drive away, taking his daughter away from him, had been the worst pain Josiah had believed a man could endure.

He had been wrong.

Living without Annabeth was.

It had been three days now since the scene in the mill. He had given her the only thing she'd wanted—his absence—for the rest of that day, but he had gone over that evening, wanting to make sure she was all right, needing to see her, aching to hold her. But, though her car was parked out front and the lights were on inside, though he heard Emerson's snuffles and whines, he'd gotten no response to his knocks. Annabeth had refused to open the door to him.

He had gone back Friday and again Saturday. Last night, frustrated and frightened by the knowledge of what his life without her would be, he had gotten angry and had shouted into the cold, still night. "I know you love me, Annie," he had said, "and I know I hurt you. But you were willing to give me a chance before. Why can't you give it to me now? Give me a chance, and I'll prove to you . . ."

Prove that he could love her, and love her well. Prove that he could trust her, that he could put his heart and his life and his future in her hands. Prove that he could be the kind of man—the kind of lover, the kind of husband—she deserved.

But she hadn't been in the mood to give him a chance last night. If she'd heard him, she had given no sign of it. But today she would find it easier to give in than to get rid of him. Today, when she returned from wherever she had gone, she would find him waiting, and she would have to listen, because he wasn't going home again until she went with him.

He had brought a rocker from his own porch and settled in it now beside her door. To pass the time he'd also brought a chunk of wood and his grandfather's old knife, well used and nicely sharpened. Whittling, for his grandfather, had been a craft, a creative process of transforming a bit of wood into a piece of art. Whittling, for Josiah, learned at the old man's knee, was a seldom-used method of dealing with frustration, generally resulting in the transformation of a piece of good wood into a pile of shavings and chips.

He didn't know yet what he was going to say to Annabeth, and he considered it as he began work on the wood. He didn't know what arguments to use. He couldn't try to convince her that she would be getting any great prize in him. Marriage to a farmer in his situation was nothing to get excited about. He came with debts and sorrows. He couldn't give her anything special—not even a honeymoon or a pretty diamond ring.

All he could do was love her.

And he'd given her good reason to doubt his love would be enough.

Maybe he should just throw himself at her mercy. Plead for whatever kindness she might give him. As sweet and generous as she was, there was no doubt she would feel sorry for him. No doubt that eventually she would begin to trust him again.

But he couldn't wait for eventually.

He needed her *now*.

He was making headway on the block of wood—had reduced its size by half and started to form a crude figure—when he heard the chug of her little Bug. She pulled into the clearing, got out and slammed the door twice before it caught, then just stood there and watched him.

She looked sad and surly, none too happy to find him waiting here. Did she miss him at all? he wondered, knowing in his heart that she did, but not whether she missed him enough—enough to take him back, enough to forgive him, enough to give him another chance.

Enough. Only a few nights ago she had been willing to settle for enough. *I'm not asking for anything you haven't already given, Josiah. This is enough.* He wasn't as generous as she was. He wanted that and more. He wanted everything.

Slowly she moved away from the car and came as close as the hitching rail. "I didn't know you liked to carve," she said flatly, warily.

"Only when I'm too frustrated to do anything else but not frustrated enough to be dangerous with a knife."

"What do you want?"

Studying the piece of wood, he gave a rough shape to one side, then began duplicating it on the other before looking at her again. "Isn't that obvious, Annie?" he gently chided her. "I want *you*."

"You miss your Sweet Annie?" she asked sarcastically, her voice thick and unsteady. "The home-cooked meals, the entertainment, the easy sex?"

"Do you think that's all I want from you?" he asked. Then, after a heavy pause, he continued. "Or was that all you were offering?"

She didn't answer, but she had the grace to duck her head and blush.

"Go inside and bring that chair out here, Annie," he commanded.

"Why?"

"I'm going to tell you a story."

Embarrassment gave way to suspicion. "You don't like stories."

"No," he agreed, then gently added, "but you do. Get the chair, Annie, please."

After a moment's hesitation, Annabeth unlocked the door and obeyed. She left her purse on the sofa and carried the twig chair out, setting it a safe distance from him. Naturally, he just moved the rocker closer until they were knee to knee, the way they had been when she'd told him the legend of Sweet Annie.

For a moment he continued carving, saying nothing to her. She watched his hands and the easy, sure way they manipulated the wood and the knife. Such strong hands, and so capable. They could split wood, build a shed or repair a piece of machinery as easily and efficiently as they could carve this figure, scratch Emerson's belly or caress her. They were wonderful hands, big and tanned, scarred and callused and gentle.

She missed them—missed *all* of him. How many times in the last few days had she been tempted to forget everything and go to him? After all, he *was* sorry. He *had* come to believe her before Stuart provided the proof. He *did* have memories of Caroline and her infidelity to deal with.

And she *was* so terribly lonely without him.

But she had needed more than an apology. She had needed time for healing. She had needed to believe, and for those first few days, she hadn't had any faith to place in him.

But her faith was returning. Last night he had stood outside and shouted, "I know you love me, Annie. Give me a chance, and I'll prove to you..." All the things he could prove and all the wonderful ways he could prove them had darn near sent her racing to the door.

But she had wanted more.

Finally, his hands still working the knife, he glanced up at her. He was solemn, his eyes dark and sincere. He was at his sweetest when he was serious, she thought, about ready to accept his apology—certain that was what his "story" would be—before he even made it.

But he was ready, his words chosen, and so she sat back and listened.

"There was a man, once, who lived all alone on a farm. Everyone he had ever cared about was gone. His father had died, and his mother had moved away. His wife had divorced him, and she'd taken his little girl away so he couldn't see her. All he had left was his farm, and he had even lost a big piece of that when he couldn't pay a bank loan."

"Stuart foreclosed on his own nephew?" she asked in dismay.

"No, it was a bank outside the valley. Hush now, and don't interrupt again."

Suppressing a smile, she sat obediently quiet.

"The man was alone and lonely, and he thought he would be that way for the rest of his life. One day, on his daughter's birthday, he decided he didn't want to live that way anymore. He decided . . ." His voice faltered. "He decided he didn't want to live at all. He had a bottle of whiskey and a bottle of pills, and he sat in his empty kitchen for a long time, and he thought about all the pain he'd lived with since his wife took his daughter away."

Annabeth heard all that pain in his voice and felt it in her heart. She had known when they'd met that he was haunted by sorrows, but she'd had no idea how deeply. That a man as strong as Josiah could be driven to even think about ending his life amazed her. It touched her.

"But," he continued with a hopeful sort of sigh, "after sitting there awhile, the man decided that the next day or the next week would be just as good a time to die. The next day, a woman came to see him, a beautiful woman with golden hair and a face like an angel and a smile that brightened the man's soul. She had come to live across the road from the man, and she wanted to be his friend. She made him smile again, made him laugh. She made him want to live again.

"She changed his life. She gave him love and tenderness and hope." His voice grew soft, his expression distant. "He had forgotten how it felt to hope. But she couldn't teach him how to not be afraid. No matter what she did, no matter what she said, he was always afraid of losing her. He was afraid of being alone again. He was afraid to trust her, afraid to have faith in her.

"One day she needed his trust, but he was afraid to give it to her. Finally he did, and he discovered everything that the fear in his heart had been hiding—that he loved her. That he did trust her. That he needed her to stay with him forever. But he might have been too late."

After a moment's silence, with tears in her eyes, Annabeth gently urged him to go on, but he shook his head. "I can't finish."

"Why not?"

"I don't know the end. It's up to you. I love you, Annie, and I want to marry you. I want to have children with you. I can't offer you much more than a home and food on the table, all the babies you can cuddle and all the love you could ever need. I can't promise an easy life, but I'll share it with you. I'll be beside you through it all. I'll love you through it all."

Before she could say anything, before she could throw herself into his arms and kiss him and promise him anything and everything, he brushed off his finished carving and offered it to her. She turned the tall, slender piece of wood in her hands, noting the crudely carved long legs with tiny slippers, the flowing hair, the short outfit and the wings—yes, very definitely wings—protruding from the figure's back, and she laughed with delight. This man, who didn't believe in the fanciful nonsense that filled her stories, had carved her a fairy.

Smiling through her tears, she pulled the knife from his hand and laid it on the ground, then moved to sit on his lap, wrapping her arms around his neck, giving him a sweet, gentle kiss.

He brushed his fingers through her hair, then softly, wistfully asked, "How does our story end, Annie?"

"The only way a love story can," she replied.

And they would live happily ever after.

Epilogue

It was a hot summer day, not bad for working in the fields but better for a lazy walk in the woods or wading in Dancing Creek. It was definitely better, Josiah thought, for spending with his wife and son, no matter what they did.

Stopping on the back porch, he removed his boots. Wearing mud-caked boots into the house was a habit he'd gotten into when he lived alone. It was one Annabeth had quickly broken him of. Not on *her* kitchen floor, she had insisted. It was tough enough to keep clean with Johnny crawling around, and she wasn't having his father add to the mess.

He was reaching for the screen door when he heard her soft voice around the front. She tried to find time each pretty afternoon to take Johnny outside, insisting it made him sleepier at nap time and gave her the energy to work on her book. Once the history of Dutchman's Valley had been finished, she had immediately started something new, something she was intimately familiar with these days: a love story. She hadn't finished the book yet, hadn't sold it, but Josiah had no doubt she would. There was nothing, he'd discovered in the eighteen months they'd been married, that his wife couldn't do. She amazed him.

She knocked him off his feet.

She gave his life meaning.

He cut through the house to the front porch, pausing for a moment in front of the screen door. The tape deck was in the open living room window, a cassette of country music playing, and on the porch outside, Annabeth was dancing Johnny around in slow circles, making him laugh and coo. He loved to dance, loved to sway in time to the music, to twirl around and around. Annabeth insisted it was because of all that dancing they'd done at the autumn festival last November, only a month before he was born. Josiah figured the kid just liked being close to her.

God knew, *he* liked it.

He had turned thirty-six last month, but he felt brand-new, spiritually at least. Annabeth's coming to the valley had brought him new life. Last season, and so far this one, had been the best the Miller farm had ever seen. They weren't out of debt, but they were making headway. He still worked hard, but he had part-time help from one of his uncle Bobby's kids, and Annabeth pitched in whenever necessary. He could take time off from work without feeling guilty, could spend a few lazy hours with his wife and son. He could face the future with pleasure and with hope.

Life was almost perfect. With the exception of Kylie—nearly six years old now, still missing and still very much missed—his life couldn't possibly get any better.

Annabeth saw him through the screen and extended her hand, welcoming him to join her and Johnny in their dance. He went outside and twirled them around, ending in a snug embrace. "Daddy," his little boy greeted him, patting his face with an open palm and melting Josiah's heart. He had thought he could never love a child again, could never risk losing another one the way he had lost Kylie, but he had been wrong. This little stinker, nine months old and already walking and talking, was one of the great treasures—and one of the great joys—of his life.

"You're just in time to give Johnny a kiss before I put him down for a nap."

Leaning against the porch rail, Josiah glanced down at the baby nestled between them. "Have you informed him yet that he's about to be put down for a nap?" he asked dryly. The child was a shining example of *bright-eyed and bushy-tailed*.

"Oh, he'll go right to sleep. How long can you stay?"

"Long enough to tuck his mama into bed," he replied with a grin.

"Maybe even long enough to take a shower first?" With a teasing grin, Annabeth wrinkled her nose. "You do get sweaty, Farmer Miller."

"Hard work, sweet Annie. It'll do it every time." He kissed her forehead, then scooted her back. "I'll take a shower and you put Johnny to bed, and I'll meet you in the bedroom."

He had opened the screen door when the sound of a car engine became audible. She glanced at him, then turned toward the road to watch. They had company out here on a regular basis—Miss Hilda, Stuart, Tony and other friends and family from town—but rarely in the middle of a weekday.

The car slowed and turned into the driveway, clearing the worst of the ruts and stopping behind her Bug. It was an expensive model, deep burgundy, and surely had all the extras. For a moment she coveted it, but not because it was so much nicer than Josiah's old truck or her own car. Heavens, a car like that could buy Josiah a new tractor. It could buy back those two hundred acres of land he'd lost a few years ago. It could start a nice little college fund for Johnny or pay off a few of their debts.

For a moment the driver just sat there; then she shut off the engine and got out. Annabeth heard Josiah mutter, and she caught her own breath. Only Johnny, trying to twist a button from her blouse, seemed uninterested in the newcomer.

It was Caroline.

And coming around the car to stand beside her, sweet and beautiful and looking like a little doll, was Kylie.

Josiah's daughter had come home.

After dinner that evening, Josiah was standing in the living-room door, watching Kylie flip through a bright cloth book with Johnny, when Annabeth slipped up behind him and put her arms around him. "Are you all right?" she whispered.

"I'm better than all right, Annie. Do you know how long I've waited for this?"

"Yes. I do."

He tugged her around so he could hold her close. "You always believed it would happen, even when I couldn't. You said you would believe for me."

"I'm an optimist at heart."

He shook his head, still somewhat in awe of the beautiful little girl his daughter had grown into. "In spite of your faith, I never really believed. . . ."

"Love makes people do funny things."

He settled Annabeth snug against him and watched Kylie and Johnny play. Yes, love could work wonders. He was a prime example of that, and apparently so was Caroline. She had fallen in love, she'd said, with a man who had a daughter from an earlier marriage, a man who never got to see the daughter because of problems with his ex-wife. Seeing his heartache and sharing his pain had made her realize how unfair she had been to Josiah. She wanted to make up for that, she had explained, wanted Kylie to spend as much time as possible with her father.

It wasn't a perfect arrangement. Caroline and the man she was going to marry lived in Baton Rouge, too far for regular visits, but they would work something out, she had promised. Weekends, holidays and summers—he would have as much time with Kylie as they could manage. He would see his little girl. He would be a part of her life, and she would fill the empty space in their lives.

They would be a family, and somehow, he was sure, Annabeth was responsible. She had brought such joy to his life, had brought laughter and sunshine and warmth and such incredible faith. Somehow, he had no doubt, her faith had stretched as far as Louisiana and had brought Kylie home to them.

"Daddy," she called, balancing Johnny between her legs, gently tugging away the book he was determined to eat. "Will you come and read us a story?"

He pulled Annabeth into the room with him, and they settled on the couch, Johnny on her lap, Kylie on his. He wasn't familiar with the book Kylie gave him to read. He didn't know the story or how it ended, but he knew how *their* story—his and Annabeth's, Kylie and Johnny's—would end.

They would all live happily ever after.

His sweet Annie had made him a believer.

* * * * *

HE'S AN

AMERICAN HERO

A cop, a fire fighter or even just a fearless drifter who gets the job done when ordinary men have given up. And you'll find one American Hero every month only in Intimate Moments—created by some of your favorite authors. This summer, Silhouette has lined up some of the hottest American heroes you'll ever find:

July: HELL ON WHEELS by Naomi Horton—Truck driver Shay McKittrick heads down a long, bumpy road when he discovers a scared stowaway in his rig....

August: DRAGONSLAYER by Emilie Richards—In a dangerous part of town, a man finds himself fighting a street gang—and his feelings for a beautiful woman....

September: ONE LAST CHANCE by Justine Davis—A tough-as-nails cop walks a fine line between devotion to duty and devotion to the only woman who could heal his broken heart....

AMERICAN HEROES: Men who give all they've got for their country, their work—the women they love.

IMHERO5

Silhouette Books
is proud to present
our best authors,
their best books...
and the best in
your reading pleasure!

Throughout 1993, look for exciting
books by these top names in
contemporary romance:

DIANA PALMER—
Fire and Ice in June

ELIZABETH LOWELL—
Fever in July

CATHERINE COULTER—
Afterglow in August

LINDA HOWARD—
Come Lie With Me in September

When it comes to passion,
we wrote the book.

BOBT2

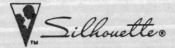

Premiere

Silhouette Books has done it again!

Opening night in October has never been as exciting! Come watch as the curtain rises and romance flourishes when the stars of tomorrow make their debuts today!

Revel in Jodi O'Donnell's STILL SWEET ON HIM—
Silhouette Romance #969
...as Callie Farrell's renovation of the family homestead leads her straight into the arms of teenage crush Drew Barnett!

Tingle with Carol Devine's BEAUTY AND THE BEASTMASTER—
Silhouette Desire #816
...as legal eagle Amanda Tarkington is carried off by wrestler Bram Masterson!

Thrill to Elyn Day's A BED OF ROSES—
Silhouette Special Edition #846
...as Dana Whitaker's body and soul are healed by sexy physical therapist Michael Gordon!

Believe when Kylie Brant's McLAIN'S LAW—
Silhouette Intimate Moments #528
...takes you into detective Connor McLain's life as he falls for psychic—and suspect—Michele Easton!

Catch the classics of tomorrow—*premiering* today—
only from ❦ *Silhouette*

**Relive the romance...
Harlequin and Silhouette
are proud to present**

by Request

A program of collections of three complete novels by the most
requested authors with the most requested themes. Be sure to
look for one volume each month with three complete novels by
top name authors.

In June: **NINE MONTHS** Penny Jordan
Stella Cameron
Janice Kaiser

**Three women pregnant and alone. But a lot can
happen in nine months!**

In July: **DADDY'S HOME** Kristin James
Naomi Horton
Mary Lynn Baxter

**Daddy's Home... and his presence is long
overdue!**

In August: **FORGOTTEN PAST** Barbara Kaye
Pamela Browning
Nancy Martin

**Do you dare to create a future if you've forgotten
the past?**

Available at your favorite retail outlet.

HARLEQUIN   Silhouette

REQ-G

MEN MADE IN AMERICA

Fifty red-blooded, white-hot, true-blue hunks from every State in the Union!

Beginning in May, look for MEN MADE IN AMERICA! Written by some of our most popular authors, these stories featuré fifty of the strongest, sexiest men, each from a different state in the union!

Two titles available every other month at your favorite retail outlet.

In September, look for:

DECEPTIONS by Annette Broadrick (California)
STORMWALKER by Dallas Schulze (Colorado)

In November, look for:

STRAIGHT FROM THE HEART by Barbara Delinsky
(Connecticut)
AUTHOR'S CHOICE by Elizabeth August (Delaware)

You won't be able to resist MEN MADE IN AMERICA!

If you've been looking for something a little bit different and a little bit spooky, let Silhouette Books take you on a journey to the dark side of love with

Every month, Silhouette will bring you two romantic, spine-tingling Shadows novels, written by some of your favorite authors, such as *New York Times* bestselling author Heather Graham Pozzessere, Anne Stuart, Helen R. Myers and Rachel Lee—to name just a few.

In July, look for:
HEART OF THE BEAST by Carla Cassidy
DARK ENCHANTMENT by Jane Toombs

In August, look for:
A SILENCE OF DREAMS by Barbara Faith
THE SEVENTH NIGHT by Amanda Stevens

In September, look for:
FOOTSTEPS IN THE NIGHT by Lee Karr
WHAT WAITS BELOW by Jane Toombs

*Come into the world of Shadows and prepare
to tremble with fear—and passion....*

SHAD3